KARMA UNDER FIRE

KARMA
UNDER FIRE
A NOVEL

LOVE
HUDSON-MAGGIO

SWEET AUBURN
PUBLISHING

Library of Congress Cataloging-in-Publication Data is on file.

ISBN 979-8-8868-0685-4 (paperback)

ISBN 979-8-8852-5366-6 (eBook)

Printed in the United States of America

23 24 25 26 27 SAP 5 4 3 2 1

This book is dedicated to all the little girls and boys who dared to dream big. The kind-hearted librarians who introduced me to the world of books. For every English teacher and editor who red-lined my work and encouraged me to finish my book. A heartfelt thank you to my loving family, friends, and editors. Thank you for sharing your time with me.

HARLOW

THE PEW WAS HARD, THE SANCTUARY WAS HOT, AND AUNT IZZY smelled of mothballs and "medicinal" wine. When I tried to slide away, she pulled me closer. She held my hand, a show of affection, but it was a move intended to keep me in my place, to stop me from racing down the aisle to the front of the church and yelling at Daddy to wake up.

May in Atlanta, when lemon-scented magnolias wave from stately trees, the promise of summer stands just around the corner, and mosquitoes lurk in the early evening ready to pounce on the ankles and necks of anyone foolish enough not to keep moving. Daddy and I were supposed to go fishing outside of Raleigh. There was the Father-Daughter Dance at school in September.

We had plans.

And now, what was left of him, his "earthly shell" as Aunt Izzy said, lay in a box at the front of the Ebenezer Baptist Church.

"Where's the other part of him?" I had asked.

"Heaven," Aunt Izzy said.

"Is that near Savannah?" I asked. That would be fun. Daddy and I could go to the beach and look for shells. We could catch blue crabs, boil them in a pot on the sand, eat our fill, and sleep on a porch listening to the waves. But why would Daddy go to Savannah without me?

Aunt Izzy was crying again. I took a deep breath as she enfolded me in her heavy arms. She needed a hug, one I would provide despite my irritation about what she made me wear.

"Child, you can't be wearin' no dungarees to the church. And wash with this."

She had shoved a bottle of cream-colored slimy stuff into my hand. Now I looked like a daffodil in a ridiculous yellow print dress, and I reeked of coconuts. A satin bow about the size of the Georgia State Capitol stabbed me in the back every time I tried to slump into the pew. The lace collar chaffed my neck.

My irritation subsided a little when I looked at Aunt Izzy. Tears rolled in a steady stream from her big brown eyes. I hugged her again. This time I stayed in place. She radiated warmth and affection, something I would not find much, not with Daddy gone.

Three days after Sophia left, Izzy had shown up at our back door, suitcase in one hand, a hatbox in the other. "I got to look good for the Lord on Sunday," she said. Izzy never asked if she could stay. She simply moved in and took over.

She taught me how to ride a bike. She shooed away the monsters that lurked under my bed. She made biscuits that threatened to float off the plate and fried chicken in ways no Kentucky Colonel ever dreamed.

Daddy told me I was too young to remember the good times with him and Sophia, the artist formerly known as my mother. My memories were disconnected puzzle pieces: a picnic or two, an argument because Daddy came home late from work, a big Christmas tree, Sophia throwing back glass after glass of wine while Daddy tried to make her smile.

On the rare occasions Sophia put me to bed, she would peck me on the head and say, "I promise it will be okay."

Sophia was not good at keeping promises.

I missed her hugs and her scent, how her hair brushed my face when she kissed my neck. And I hated myself for missing any of it because she had left me—gone somewhere to another life. I asked when she was coming back; Daddy and Izzy never gave much of an answer. One day, I quit asking.

I leaned into the aisle and looked to the front of the church. I could see the side of the wooden box. My father was in there "in eternal repose," whatever that meant. I started to cry.

"It's okay, sweetie." Izzy's voice stroked my ears in a kind whisper. "You cry it on out. It's fine."

"Why is the box closed?" I asked.

Izzy patted my knee, not in an "it's okay" sort of way, but more like a warning.

"Better this way," she said.

Pastor John stood in the pulpit and looked out over Daddy's casket to a sea of brown faces. He said words—a lot of them. The choir sang. "It's all right, it's all right. Jesus is comin', and it's all right."

But I didn't believe any of it. When Pastor John announced it was time to pay our respects, Mrs. Guthrie, our neighbor, launched into an award-worthy performance. She didn't like Daddy. She didn't like anyone, and no one liked her. But she could flail and weep and keen with the very best. The outer limits of her expansive mourning hat bobbed up and down like an inner tube in the surf, and she said "Jesus" so many times, and in such rapid succession, it all sounded like one word. As her legs gave way in a practiced "collapse," I giggled at the sight of her ham hock calves, but a sharp poke in the side cut me off. Izzy glared at me.

After the ushers fanned Mrs. Guthrie into submission, Izzy leaned in. "Harlow, are you ready to say goodbye to your Daddy."

It sounded like a question. It wasn't. Izzy was already hoisting me off my backside and moving me into the aisle. I fingered the necklace hanging across the yoke of my dress. The pendant felt odd. I never wore it outside the house.

People are funny. They either think kids are deaf or stupid. I'd never been to a funeral, but I knew about them. I knew the casket was always open, always. But I could hear the people behind me.

"Terrible thing."

"Who found him?"

"Does the little girl know?"

"I didn't know he owned a gun."

And, of course, the "Christian" comments.

"I hope the Good Lord will forgive him."

There wasn't anything to see. I stared at a shiny, cheap wooden coffin. I knew the difference between oak and maple. This was pine, more likely pressboard made up to look like it.

The grain didn't look right. There was no mirror finish like on the dining room table. I just stared at a tan slab at my eye level while Izzy bowed her head.

I imagined Daddy lying in the box. I could see his smooth, almost feminine complexion, high cheekbones, and straight dark hair. I imagined the big hands and the long, refined fingers, the pencil moustache. And I remembered the smell. Lilac Vegetal, always Clubman brand, and baby powder. After his shower, Daddy's excessive talcum habit made the bathroom look like it had been hit with a snowstorm. Daddy used to let me "ice skate" on the powder. Sophia "put a stop to this foolishness" the day I bumped my head after an unsuccessful double Axel. After that, Daddy always cleaned up the floor before I was allowed to come in.

I saw his face in my memory. I heard voices, loud, strident. Daddy and Sophia were downstairs. I leaned through the spindles of the upstairs landing and strained to catch Daddy shouting words I knew but did not understand . . . *affair* . . . *whore* . . . *money* . . . then the worst phrase of all, the one destined to shape my every move for the rest of my life: "Get out!"

Whoever was in the coffin smelled like lighter fluid, and I had a brief vision of a burst of flame from a barbeque grill, my father's killer smile, and his traditional proclamation, "The Grill Master is in the house!" I touched the box. It was warm, but I shivered and remembered how Daddy used to hold me in his arms when I returned inside after playing in a rare Georgia snowfall. I looked over my shoulder at sympathetic faces. I heard more than one "poor child."

I stood to the side and watched Izzy put a black cloth on the coffin. The veil with a white cross, obviously etched out with chalk.

"What's with the drape?" I asked.

"The wife or mother usually puts it on the casket to preserve the soul of the dead. Your father's parents are gone to Glory, so the task fell to me."

"Why didn't Sophia help?" I could see the statuesque woman at the other end of the pew. The veil on her tiny but very fashionable hat obscured her face.

Aunt Izzy stiffened. "She's on the row as a courtesy," she said. "But she's no longer part of this family."

Leaving the church, Izzy slipped the necklace over my head and put it in her purse. The patent leather Mary Janes pinched my feet on the long walk to the cemetery. We lined up in front of a large, engraved headstone with Daddy's name on it. They put the box into a hole in the ground and shoveled in piles of dirt. Pastor John said some more things, then people I'd never seen before pulled me to their heaving chests or patted me on the head. It was hard to hear what any of them said over the sound of my own sobs.

No one spoke on the drive back to Aunt Izzy's. I was still trying to figure out how to see Daddy in Heaven when we walked inside, and I smelled allspice berries, fresh ginger, and brown sugar. I set sail into the kitchen and came out with a drumstick of roasted jerk chicken.

I knew she'd come to the house—she needed to put on a show. She'd probably bring another gift, just like the ones she hauled in when she visited for Christmas. Something frilly, something girly, something unsuitable for tree climbing.

"Don't ignore your mother," Daddy always said. "She came a long way to see you, so be nice."

Well, he could make me be polite, but no one could make me like her. He didn't even try to get Aunt Izzy to be nice. I heard her talking to him.

I heard how she talked to Daddy. "She thinks she's a big shot and likes to boss people around."

Aunt Izzy came across the den. I knew what she wanted. I tried to avoid eye contact. Maybe she wouldn't see me.

"Harlow, she wants to see you."

"I'm good," I said.

"It was not a request, sweetie. You need to go into the study and see her."

I wiped the sleeve of my dress across my mouth. Sophia gave me the dress. I hoped the chicken would leave a stain. I stood and moved toward the study. Aunt Izzy's voice filtered over my shoulder.

"Remember, child, call her *Mother*. She says it hurts her when you use her first name."

I knocked on the sliding door.

"Come in, Harlow."

I pushed back the heavy door, stepped in, and dragged the door back closed, a considerable wrestling match for a nine-year-old.

The woman in the wingback chair sat ramrod straight. Her skin stretched flawlessly over high cheekbones. Her most startling feature, crystal blue eyes, scrutinized me like an art expert trying to spot a counterfeit Monet.

"Take a seat, child," she said.

I moved to the chair opposite hers, took a seat, raised my head, and said, "Hello, Sophia."

CHAPTER 1

TEJ

"Mmm. That's nice." Rati moaned as my hand moved up her side. I counted. One . . . two . . . three more pins left on the fold.

I whispered, "Hold still and stop wiggling." Her warm skin smelled of jasmine. A swath of amethyst-colored silk fabric floated to the floor. One more pin. My tongue slid to the hollow of her neck.

"You know your way around a sari," she said. Her breath came in halting gasps. "We would never . . . get . . . away . . . with this . . . in India."

I pulled her closer. Her lips parted as she encouraged my kiss. "Good thing we are thousands of miles away," I said. "Less talk, more of this."

I ground my lower body into hers. She moaned and responded.

I can't get that last stupid pin.

"Is it true they wanted you to marry Parvati?" she asked. "Girish wasn't their first choice?"

I acknowledged her question about the newlyweds with a grunt as I buried my head into the valley between her generous breasts. I looked up to gauge her reaction. Rati, a vibrant and lush woman with inky black lashes and almond-shaped eyes, let her head roll to the side. She pushed her chest closer. I noticed her slightly crooked nose, her overly-large pores, minor flaws I was more than willing to overlook now.

Why does a woman in the throes of passion want to talk about a bride? Does she know my parents asked me about marrying Parvati?

I pushed the remaining cloth to the ground. Rati, my childhood crush, lay on the couch. She was panting now, short gasps of pleasure, ebbing over closer to "the Promised Land." The only impediments to the fulfillment of my carnal dreams were a scanty lace bra and a pair of French cut panties, both red.

"Do you care where we are right now?" I asked. "Or are you more interested in what we are doing?"

Rati in Hindi meant "pleasure, desire, sexual delight." Rati was also the Hindu goddess of love. Always symbolized on horseback. Riding, yes. I could imagine her saddling me with her long legs wrapped around my waist. I could hear her shrieks of ecstasy. I could visualize her hair spread across—

"I can't blame them. You are the most eligible bachelor here."

The voice in my head screamed, *Woman, quit talking and focus. I've wanted you since I was fifteen. Kindly shut up before you ruin every fantasy I've ever had.*

I had chosen my prey well. Rati was a safe, soft target.

Fifty-year-old, divorced women were hardly marriageable by traditional, well-heeled Indian family standards. Her expiration date had long since passed, and she held no silly, romantic ideas of endless love and blissful togetherness. We both knew what she was asking when she invited me for a "walk" around the gardens.

But, my God, the woman talks all the time.

I kissed her again, partially out of lust, mostly because her soliloquy on marriage was killing the mood. Besides, I was not risking my reputation for chit chat.

I should not have been there. I hated weddings in general, but I despised Hindu weddings. The elaborate rituals reminded me of my continually shirked obligations as a son. But the Indian community in Atlanta was small, so my presence was expected.

Mysore silk pillows slipped to the thick rug as I positioned Rati. The Singhs had spared no expense with this wedding. The lavishly decorated tent, the perfect place for my intended debauchery, stood as testimony to the expenditures Indian parents endured to marry off a child.

Rati made fast work of my open-necked sherwani, moving past the long jacket, and lifting my kurta. Her warm, soft hands slid toward my silk pajama pants and tugged at the waistband.

Happy to be rid of my wedding attire, the uniform of all well-groomed, well-bred Indian gentlemen, I felt a twinge of guilt. Rati was a one-time, no follow-up deal. I would not be sending gushing texts tomorrow. But Rati and I were seeking the same thing. Relief, not a relationship.

"Yes, right there," she said. I massaged her inner thigh and moved up her leg to the warm spot that had brought us here. Years of manners and tradition momentarily overwhelmed my lust. I disentangled from her long enough to attend to the six yards of discarded silk. A woman's sari, draping fabric, and the traditional gift of Indian females for centuries, represented her culture, history, and the way she lived her life. I was a cad, but not a clod. I would not ignore centuries of heritage for a quick, meaningless romp.

She giggled as she watched me lay the discarded garment on a nearby chair. "I hope you know how to get me back together," she said.

"If your primary concern right now is getting dressed, I need to do a better job," I said as I slid my face across her belly.

"Oh . . . oh . . . oh my." She threw her head back and unleashed a feral moan.

"Don't worry . . . you'll be pinned, pleated, and tucked back together in no time. Just enjoy."

And shut the hell up.

She was cresting for the third time when we heard the voice.

"Rati? Where are you?"

Her face blanched. "Oh, God!"

"Shh," I said as I licked her ear. "We are fine. Don't make any noise. It will be more intense."

The voice was closer. "Rati?"

"Who's that?" I asked, my voice a whispering croak.

"My fiancé."

She was in mid-climax when I stood, my passion deflated by

the word *fiancé*.

Bloody hell. When did this happen? Isn't she too old?

"Come back," she said. "He will go away." She reached for me, her experienced hands like silk.

"Are you insane?" I said. "We have to get out of here. We cannot have a scene."

"Rati!"

The guy sounded like a child lost in the mall. I almost felt sorry for him. Almost.

"Stand up." She obeyed. With grudging lust in her eyes, she slid on her panties and began to fasten her brassiere. Neither of us moved. Thirty seconds—fifty—more than a minute.

"He's gone," she said. Her cheek brushed my stomach. "We can keep going."

I was beginning to throb again. In another half minute, I would be incapable of any rational decision.

"No," I said.

I placed my hands under her arms and lifted her to her feet. "Get dressed, and let's get out of here."

"Are you afraid?" she asked. "Is the great Tej Mayur worried about karma?"

I was already dressed and moving to drape her sari over her bare shoulder. "No, it's just not easy to stay, *ah*, in the moment when some bloke is crying about fifteen feet away."

"Well," she said, "it was a nice distraction to get out of my system before I do my duty and wed. Too bad you didn't get as much out of it." Her hands grazed the front of my pants. "But, it's never too late."

Two thoughts raced through my mind simultaneously. *Why are you getting married again, old woman?* And, *Tej, you will never get this chance again.*

I shook off the latter consideration and pinned her sari in place.

"I won't be getting married any time soon," I said.

"Really?" Her expression was one of genuine surprise. "You're practically royalty, Tej. I'm sure fifty women would claw my eyes out to have the opportunity I just enjoyed." She saw me tense. "Don't worry, love. I'll never tell."

"Well," I said. "I'm not sure marriage is in the cards for me—or in the stars—or whatever I am supposed to consult."

"You don't think you can outrun your fate, do you? None of us can."

"Watch me, sweetheart," I said and planted a perfunctory kiss on her cheek before I darted out of the tent. The darkening skies covered my retreat. But I could not escape the notice of a young sari draper who was seated at the far side of the garden, finishing her dinner.

"There is a woman in the purple tent over there who needs a few discreet adjustments," I said.

She averted her eyes and slipped the one hundred-dollar bill I gave her into her pocket. "You were never here," she said.

CHAPTER 2

HARLOW

"Can I get a little help here?"

I was struggling and it was getting ridiculous. When Legacy hired me nine months ago, they knew I had no experience. "We will teach you the Legacy culture" was the Gospel according to Arlene Nettleman, founder, owner, and Grand High Poohbah of the hottest coding company in the hottest city in the New South, Atlanta, Georgia.

Though she was always a little vague about her educational background, Arlene had built a stunning reputation throughout the Southeast by hiring a phalanx of brilliant technicians capable of everything from devising inventive apps to hacking into the Pentagon. (Ezra claimed he had—once—when he was high. But everyone knew Ezra, though gifted, was always trying to impress people without success).

Arlene never raised her voice; she didn't have to. Whenever her head popped out of her office, a glacial freeze enveloped the office. Funeral homes were noisier. Her low growl always carried a veiled threat. To ignore her was to court professional disaster.

"Would someone go help Harlow?" It was not a request.

Ezra plopped his ever-expanding ass on the edge of my desk. "What's up, kid?" he asked.

Ezra Simonton, part-time stoner, MIT dropout, and perhaps the most brilliant person I'd ever met.

"Ezra, you really should go easy on the onions, especially when you have a tuna melt," I said.

He popped a handful of Tic Tacs in his mouth and blew at me. "Better?"

"Onion *and* wintergreen," I said. "Captivating."

"You gonna insult me, or do you want my help?"

I pointed to my screen. "I'm stuck," I said. "I can't figure out what's going on?"

"Who's this for?" he asked. "It doesn't matter, 'cause I see the problem. Just curious."

"Judy's House of Cosmetics," I said. "I thought I was going to be working on interesting stuff. I do the same old crap every week."

"Let me guess," he said. "Arlene told you the work would be challenging, exciting, and culture-shifting."

"Word for fuckin' word," I said.

"Well, you gotta crawl before you can walk," he said. "And you're going to keep falling on your lovely ass if you make the same syntax mistake you've got in line six."

I glared at the screen. "First of all," I said, "that's workplace harassment. Second, damn it, why didn't I see it?

Third, thank you for the help."

He nodded.

"And fourth," I said, "thanks for the compliment. I'm kinda proud of my ass."

Someone called his name from across the room. He burst into his patented cackle, a combination of a laugh and an Oogah horn. I looked up to see a Frisbee sail through the air with Pickles, the office dog, in hot pursuit. For all of Arlene's stick-up-the-ass personality, she knew what it took to run an office full of computer geeks.

I stood to stretch at the exact moment one of the long-time guys lifted his clenched fists over his head. His announcement bounced off the walls. "Another record, my friends. I own Donkey Kong!"

I bet he doesn't own a dress shirt.

My phone rang.

"Hi, Lita," I said, "I thought you were in India."

My best friend's sparkling voice came through so loudly I yanked the phone away from my ear. "Hi, Lo. I am. How're things in the States?"

I made an *eek, eek, eek* warning sound, then said, "This is the emergency idiot system. You may be halfway around the world, ma'am, but there is no need to shout. *Eek, eek, eek.* This is a recording."

"You are such a nerd," she said. "Sorry. It's just so noisy here all the time. I never know when I'm screaming. When you get here, you'll see."

"Can't wait," I said.

"I've got your flight info right here. We'll be there to meet you."

"You and your fiancé?" I asked. "That'll be great. What's he like?"

Lita laughed. "Girlfriend, I have no idea. I don't even know his name yet. I'll learn all that after you get here. I need you next to me at the Big Reveal just in case he's an Uggo, and I need you to cover my escape—or to kill me."

She could not see me roll my eyes. "That is so effed up," I said. "You're still getting married, right?"

"Yep," she said, "and you will be here for every party."

"I'm taking two weeks. What am I supposed to do after the wedding?"

"It's India, Lo. Explore the Land of Mystery."

I felt my pulse quicken. "Well, Daddy always promised to take me. You know that," I said.

"Yes, you told me. It's really cool," Lita said. "Your pop came from the West Indies, but his people were from here, I know."

I paused. This was a little awkward. "Ah, Lita," I said, "I don't think I can do a lot of touring and stuff. You know, I haven't been here very long, and I got special permission to stay a little—"

"Harlow Kennedy!" Lita's voice was sharp and sassy. "My father will die if you try to pay for anything while you are here. You will have a driver at your disposal, and Daddy will cover everything. You're our honored guest. You just come and have a good time. After all, I'll be on my honeymoon, and with any luck, I'll be having the time of my life."

We both laughed. "I hope he knocks your socks off, honey," I said.

"May all the gods look upon your request with favor," she said.

"I've never heard you so excited," I said. "You're not afraid?"

"Terrified," she said, "but I trust the system. I know the matchmaker has selected someone from our station—wealthy and young. We might not love each other at the beginning, but . . ."

She trailed off.

"But you can live on lust for a few years, right?" I said.

"Good point."

There was silence for a moment. She was either smiling or wiping away tears, but Lita's voice betrayed no emotion.

"Hey, babe," I said, "who's coming with you to meet me?"

"It'll be me and my driver."

"Ooooooo, Madame le Bigshot her own self," I said.

"Shut up," she said. "It's how we do things here. Besides, when you see the traffic, you will understand. The people in Atlanta drive like nuns compared to the loonies here."

I saw Arlene scowling at me from her window. Her "that's not a business call" radar was working overtime.

"Hey," I said, "I gotta run. Did you need anything?"

"No," Lita said. "Just wanted to make sure you are squared away. The travel agent got the ticket for you, right?"

"Yes, but you shouldn't have put me in first class."

"Shut up," she said. "You're my best friend. Okay, I know you gotta scoot, busy queen of industry and all."

"More like scullery maid to the stars," I said.

"Kisses," she said. She hung up before I could reply.

I put down the phone and returned to my screen without looking over at Arlene's office.

CHAPTER 3

HARLOW

I FINALLY LOOKED UP AN HOUR LATER. MY EYES WERE KILLING me. My readers needed cleaning. And Ezra was back.

"How's it going, kid?"

I banged my head against my desk. "I suck at this."

"Yeah," Ezra said, "but we knew that when we hired you."

"Seriously, Ez," I said, "have you ever seen anyone worse than me?"

"Well,"—he ran a hand over his thinning hair—"my Uncle Zac can't figure out why his TV remote won't turn his computer on."

I smacked him on the shoulder. "That's mean, even for you."

He peered over my shoulder. "Sequencing problem—there," he said.

"I know. I was just testing you."

"Whatever makes you feel good about yourself."

I snuck a glance at Arlene's office. The light was off. The

Wicked Witch was not back from lunch or was gone for the day. It was hard to tell.

"Want to see something?" I asked.

Ezra pulled back. "Is this some sort of reverse sexual harassment deal?"

"Shut up," I said. "But you can't tell anyone. You swear?"

He crisscrossed his chest with his index finger. I opened my desk drawer and extracted a small velveteen bag.

"Hold out your hand," I said.

When he did, I tipped the bag and dropped a ring fashioned from multicolored strands of wire. A trio of stones shimmered in the light.

"Beautiful," Ezra said. "Who gave it to you?"

"I made it," I said. "It's my hobby. Well, truthfully, I hope it will be my job one day."

"You make rings?" he asked.

I rolled my eyes. "I craft custom jewelry. At least, I want to. What you have there is supposed to be a silver and opal ring. It's a mock-up made with wire and a few shiny rocks I picked up in a store and polished."

"Why didn't you use the real thing?" Ezra was holding up the ring and admiring it.

"Cost," I said. "Right now, I can't afford a lot of materials. If I make a mistake, it would be bad—so bad. Before I go out on a limb and buy high-quality stuff, I have to get the design just right and perfect my techniques."

"This is really nice," he said. "Where'd you learn how—"

I interrupted. "Daddy. My father was a jeweler and designer. He had a very loyal clientele. My Aunt Izzy told me his business was getting ready to take off, but he died."

I faked a cough, so I could bend over and wipe away an unexpected tear. *Damn, I still can't talk about Daddy without choking up.*

I could see Daddy hunched over his workbench, magnifiers over his eyes, some tool in his fingers. He handled precious metals and gemstones with a surgeon's touch. I was his "test model." He would hold a ring on my undersized finger or loop a dazzling bauble around my neck.

"What do you think, Princess?"

I stared at my bejeweled reflection in the mirror next to his bench.

"It's wonderful, Daddy. Can I keep it?"

"You know better," he always said, and I did. I also knew what was coming next. "But if my designs get hot, you can have more jewelry than the Queen of England herself."

But I never did.

His designs were barely warm when he "flung himself into Jesus' waiting arms." That's how Izzy put it. I knew something bad had happened. After all, they had never opened the casket at the funeral.

Ezra's voice brought me back. "Earth to Harlow."

"What?"

"Really, lady, you wonder why you have trouble with code. You can't focus on anything for more than about thirty seconds."

"Sorry," I said. "What did you ask me? I'm all ears. Fully present."

"I wanted to know what happened to your father's stuff.

He must have had finished pieces when he died or unused stones or something."

I could see Daddy's workspace in my mind as clearly as I could see Ezra's stubble-coated face. Two weeks after the day of the pinching Mary Janes, I dragged myself down the stairs to his shop.

I turned on the light and gasped. The only thing there was an abandoned workbench and a solitary jeweler's loupe.

CHAPTER 4

TEJ

DINESH STUCK HIS HEAD INTO MY OFFICE, CONCERN STRETCHED across his weathered face. "Heard something fall," he said. "Everything okay, boss?"

"All good. Just knocked over a few books," I said.

"You know, I could straighten all this up in an afternoon if you'd like," he said.

"Not necessary," I said. Every hour in the restaurant business brought some new crisis. I liked order. I wanted precision, but the pace was taking its toll, and my office was beginning to look like a hoarder's paradise.

Dinesh nodded. He held on to the old ways, never questioning authority but always knowing much more than he ever said.

"Have you heard from the Burham Agency regarding the publicity for the frozen food line?" I asked. "What do you have for me?"

He stepped into the room. I had tacitly given permission

by asking him a question. He fished a pad from his back pocket and referred to his notes. "Richard Burham promised to send the final plans for your review this evening."

I beckoned to a chair. Dinesh sat, flipped through a few pages, and cleared his throat. "Sir, there are a few items on the shipping logs we need to discuss. It appears the new logistics company ran into a bit of a problem and misplaced an order destined for Los Angeles."

"How far off were they? San Diego?"

"A little worse, sir. The shipment arrived in Kansas City."

I thumped the desk with my fist. "Send me a list of replacements. I'm spending too much money for stuff like this to happen. Get things ironed out and—"

Dinesh finished my sentence. "—and get a new logistics company. Consider it done. Reynash is helping track things down, and I have Legal scheduled for a meeting tomorrow to review our options. Given the foul-up, I imagine we can get out of the thirty-day notice of termination clause."

I nodded. "Good work."

He did not acknowledge my appreciation. His job was to anticipate my thoughts and make things happen. At least, that's how he saw things. Like I said, old school.

"Sir. Here is tonight's menu for your approval."

I glanced through the food selections.

"Good. Instruct the kitchen to add sandesh to the dessert offering. We sold out last week."

"A cheese, cardamom and saffron sweet, what's not to like?" Dinesh said.

I looked at the next page. "These are the final numbers

for tonight's reservations?"

"Yes, sir. We are expecting a much larger crowd tonight. The front desk says we are up five percent from last weekend,"

"Good, when will the reservation app be ready?"

"Not sure, sir. We have a meeting with the designers coming up."

"What do you think?"

"With respect, sir, you know what I think. It's Arlene Nettleman's group."

"So, it's pay, delay, pay, delay, pay, pay, repeat."

"Yes, sir. I've never liked her, sir."

My ears picked up. Dinesh seldom gave opinions. I learned to listen when he did.

"Suggestions?" I asked.

"They've had plenty of time," Dinesh said.

"Okay, talk to Bishal. Put a drop-dead date on the calendar, then do what needs to be done."

"Yes, sir."

"Are we all set for the morning staff prep meeting? We've got a lot to cover."

"Yes, sir. Everything is ready. Can I get you something to drink? The usual?"

"Excellent. A cup of masala chai." The creamy concoction of Darjeeling tea, cinnamon, nutmeg, ginger, and cardamom always soothed my nerves. The froth, the fragrance. There was nothing like it. In a few days, I would be able to savor a variety of chai selections on the streets of Delhi.

"Thank you, Dinesh."

"Yes, sir, of course." He stood to leave and turned around. "Sir . . . um . . ."

"Spit it out," I said.

Dinesh flushed and straightened. "Sir, your day is busy. I thought maybe we should cancel the VIP dinner, just this week, to give you more time—"

"Absolutely not. No need. We'll get it all done."

"As you wish," he said.

A small smile tickled the edge of Dinesh's mouth. He nodded and left the room. He knew I wouldn't cancel the VIP dinner, but he wanted me to remember how on top of stuff he was.

Two years before, I'd selected Dinesh as my assistant. I'd wanted someone of Indian descent, someone young who understood the progressive cooking style I used to craft my Bombay Baby brand. I needed an assistant who understood the intricacies of regional Indian cooking, the perfect blend of spices to create the dazzling range of flavors, concoctions that had to be mixed, toasted, and pounded into mortar with precision.

But I also needed someone who understood the ways of my native country. I'd decided to become a chef when I was eight. I used to sneak away from my governess and wander through the streets to watch women squatting by wooden boards. They kneaded their families' bread with persistent dedication. Proper Indian cooking requires little in the way of utensils but proves very time-consuming. I was fascinated by the commitment and labor involved in every morsel of bread, in every chopped ingredient. I wanted to mirror the same devotion in my kitchen, and I needed an assistant who felt the same way.

Dinesh had exceeded my expectations while shattering my preconceptions. At sixty, he was at least thirty-five years older than me, I'd imagine. He was from Goa, the southwestern part of India. He and his wife moved to Atlanta to be with their son and daughter-in-law. In his golden years, Dinesh got the chance to pursue his dream of working in an innovative restaurant with high-quality food. We traded expertise: my love of new cuisine with European and Caribbean influences, and his knowledge of the traditional Indian cooking style.

On my way to the kitchen, I almost tripped over my bike. I rode it to work every morning by way of the Sweet Auburn Market on Auburn Avenue, where I picked out my spices. I used my senses, honed through the experiences of my life in India, to select allspice, nutmeg, scotch bonnet, and black cardamom. The aroma of roasted cumin seeds slid through the air.

The kitchen was already a study in controlled chaos when I stepped in for the morning meeting. My staff went about their tasks with the precision of a SEAL team on a mission. Every move reflected the excellence I so painstakingly built. Since opening Bombay Baby, my restaurant on Atlanta's historic Auburn Avenue, the team had increased to thirty employees. But even with the extra hands, I felt I needed to be in the restaurant every day. Someone always needed something only I could do or had a question only I could answer.

Being away for two weeks was going to be a challenge. Well, at least for me. The kitchen staff might dance around and sing, "Ding dong, the witch is dead."

I looked around the kitchen at the beginnings of the food preparation for the night's menu. A tower of diced green mangos stood high on the chopping block, ready for use in the fruit punch and curried dishes. Other items were being readied for packing and shipping.

"Where is the aloo bonda? Were they left out? Where are the vegetable samosas?"

I looked around to see a row of workers shaping the chapati flour for rotis. The finely milled, stone-ground whole durum wheat flour was superior to other whole wheat flours found in the US. It was worth the expense to ensure our rotis were light and nutritious.

"We're going to have a full house tonight, people," I said. "The spreads in *Saveur* and *Food and Wine* are bringing 'em in by the busload."

A lot was going on. I expected my staff to handle the food shipments with the same grace they exhibited in the kitchen. It had not been a great week. The first shipments of the new line of frozen foods had gone out and landed in Kansas. Opening impressions were not looking positive.

Reynash handled shipping. He knew I expected perfection. Right now, he looked helpless. I caught his eye and shook my head, mouthing, "Not good."

I banged on a pot with a wooden spoon until the kitchen quieted. "Do you guys know what '*Atithi devo bhava*' means?

No one spoke.

Then, a small voice floated in from the back. "It means that our guest is the embodiment of God."

Jenny, the accountant.

"Thank you, Jenny." I waited for my words to sink in. "At least one of you understands the concept at the heart of the Bombay Baby brand. It's an Indian tradition: hospitality, giving your guests your very best, every time, no exceptions. We're not just a place serving food; we are providing an experience, a chance to reconnect with family and friends, to relax, to relieve the stress of the day. You got it?"

Earnest faces bobbed up and down. "Good, then let's get to work," I said.

I listened to the chorus of "Yes, sir." The noise resumed as if someone had flipped a switch. I turned to leave.

"I got some great footage, Mr. Mayur. That was a rousing speech."

Ugh, Richie!

I turned to face the photographer. "You played well for the camera with that bit about hospitality," he said. "A few edits, and this will go viral. This is a winner. I'll post tonight."

I tried to smile at the freckle-faced, agency-appointed social media dork. I was sure I looked constipated. I had forgotten we used the restaurant kitchen to film a series on my lifestyle blog.

"Thanks, Richie," I said.

"Mr. Mayur, can I join you? I need a little more—"

"Sorry," I said. "Headed for my office."

My office was the forbidden zone. No cameras. I fumed. *Rousing speech . . . go viral . . . the fool does not recognize the sacred nature of mealtime in India. That was not a speech. It is a way of life!*

CHAPTER 5

HARLOW

"You want me to what?"

The gala was in full swing. Sophia stood out in the crowd. I had no doubt she'd snooped around to discover everyone was wearing muted colors before she picked out her flaming red dress and cinched it with a wide gold belt. She looked like a botoxed rose in a room full of beige thorns.

A statuesque beauty who could still turn heads at "forty-nine," her thick black hair fell in long spirals across her olive shoulders. Diamond cuff and chandelier earrings diffused the light and cast little stars across her strong jawline and surgically perfected cheekbones.

"I don't mumble, Harlow," she said. "Addison Whitmore is the perfect match for you. He's taller than you, prettier than you, and richer than me. Besides, you have known him since you were knee-high to a grasshopper."

"That's the problem, Sophia," I said. "We dated, sort of,

for a while, but it always felt like I was with a cousin or something. No spark. No pizzazz."

Sophia snorted and pursed her lips. "Give up the Cinderella, Sleeping Beauty idea," she said. "True love and eternal happiness are a mirage, a marketing campaign. Marriage is like chess. It's all about strategy, positioning, and power."

I felt naked standing next to her in the black Chanel dress and Louboutins I'd permanently borrowed from Lita. My friend since high school, Lita was more of a sister to me. I spent a lot of my childhood at her house after Daddy died. Sophia had moved in a few days after the funeral; she was always entertaining the latest in a long string of gentlemen callers, unsuspecting flies drawn to her web of long legs, spectacular enhanced breasts, and easy morals.

How Sophia had managed a string of consecutive marriages without agreeing to a prenup baffled me, but I had to give her credit. Apparently, her pelvis could actualize any plan she devised. The day after every financially beneficial divorce, her phone was ringing with calls from men more than eager to find out if the reality of an encounter with Sophia matched the legend.

"Addison Whitmore? "I asked. "Are you kidding? I can think of—"

She didn't let me finish. She seldom let me finish. "You can't think of anyone," she said. "Your love life is a non-existent joke. Addison is exactly the sort of young man you need to set your eye on. He is handsome, well-groomed, and he comes from . . ."

I tuned her out. I knew the speech. Handsome, well-groomed, good stock, will make pretty babies, and—the most important thing—he had a fabulous trust fund. I hated it, but she had a point. The last time I had a date was . . . well, I wasn't sure. Did kissing Ezra under the mistletoe at the office Christmas party count?

"Wasn't he a fabulous lover, child? When was it he took you to his bed?"

"Sophia, honestly." I stared at her. "Want to say that a little louder? I don't think they could hear you over at Braves Stadium."

Sophia cackled, a cold-hearted, humorless eruption from the Lady in Red by Estee Lauder or Sherwin Williams. Whoever did her makeup must have used a trowel.

"If you really want to know, Sophia, he had the touch of a piano mover, the endurance of a gnat, and slobbered like a St. Bernard."

"Honey," Sophia said, "they're all like that. Let them have their fun. Say 'oh baby' a few times, then roll over, and go to sleep. Trust me, the money's worth it."

"Sophia," I said, "I am a strong, independent woman. I don't need a man to get through life."

"Strong? Independent?" The laugh again. "How do you figure?

"I am making my way through the Femtech world. I have a great job with Legacy. They hired me on my own merits. I'm writing app code for some very influential companies. And then there's my jewelry."

Sophia put her hands on her knees. For a moment, I

thought she might be sick. But when she looked up, I could see mirth smeared across her face. Her eyes glistened with tears as she tried to stop giggling.

"Darling," she said with an affected magnolia accent, "you have me to thank for that pissant job of yours." She read the shock on my face. "Did you think you did that on your own, that Arlene Nettleman was desperate enough to select a newbie programmer with no experience or online certification? Honey, I made calls, and I pulled strings. Arlene and I go way back. My second husband was her third—or fourth—I can't keep it straight. I never said anything because you were so very excited. And as for your home enterprise, despite what I thought about your father's, ah, artistic efforts, let's just say he'd be humiliated to have his name linked to your pathetic little trinkets."

My voice came out in a snarl before I realized what I was saying, "Shut up."

The giggle stopped. The wrinkle-free, two-hundred-thousand-collar face went cold. Her voice hissed like an enraged cobra. "Watch it, Missy. You just put one foot over the line. You do not want to cross all the way over because if you do, you will truly know what it's like to be on your own."

She straightened an imagined crinkle in her hair with a backhanded flip and moved within six inches of my face. A casual observer would see a mother leaning close to share something affectionate with a daughter. But I could see the menacing steel in her eyes.

"Stop making this hard on yourself, Harlow. You're barely making it on the allowance I send you every month. Defying me will only end badly for you."

She pivoted with the grace of a runway model and swished away. I watched as she turned and moved back into the crowd. She looked good for a woman of her age, but I noticed she'd put on a few pounds.

A little too much ham for the bag.

I was "this close" to calling my mother a bitch when I felt an arm slither around my waist. Pain began pinching me behind the left eye, a sure sign of an oncoming headache.

"Hello, Dollface!"

Addison unleashed his notoriously abrasive laugh, tossing his head back and to the side, flicking thick, curly hair away from his impossibly blue eyes.

"Still the worst Bogart impersonation I've ever heard," I said. "Hello, Addison. And please, watch the hands."

His palm had already begun migrating south and was just off my right hip. He returned it to my waist.

"A penny for your thoughts," Addison said. "Scratch that. How about a we get out of here and go to my apartment."

"What do you think I am?" I asked.

"Hey, babe," he said, "we established that a few months ago. Now, we're just negotiating."

Everyone within fifteen feet heard the slap. Most of them had the social grace not to turn and stare. Addison recovered nicely, rubbed his left cheek, and chuckled.

"Nice hook, babe," he said. "Very impressive."

I turned. Addison touched my arm very lightly. "Hey," he said, "sorry. That was an asshole thing to say."

"Ya think?"

"I was just horsing around. I've missed you," Addison said.

Now it was my turn to laugh. "That why you broke up with me in a text?"

OMG, Addison Whitmore is blushing.

"Yeah, about that," he said. "I might have been a little drunk. After I sent it, I was too embarrassed to call."

Even though I could feel my ears burning, it was impossible not to notice how well his Brioni tux hung on him. But the silk scarf was a little over the top. I guess he thought it matched his patent leather black and white shoes.

"Where are your top hat and cane?" I asked.

"Left the hat in the car. Always carry my cane with me if you know what I mean."

"Good God, you are gross," I said. But I laughed. I couldn't help it. Addison had never quite gotten out of the teenage boy humor stage. I bet he giggled whenever someone said *boob*. But we'd been playmates and off-and-on friends since nursery school. I was never very nice to him—well, except for the time we'd both gotten completely naked. In fact, I was probably rude to him most of the time, but it was the way I expressed the very platonic feelings I had for him. Addison was the old pair of shoes that didn't quite fit anymore, but the ones you could not bear to throw away."

Addison was talking. "I really have missed—"

"Stop," I said. "Please stop. Look, we've been friends or something for a long time. But this is never going anywhere. We hooked up once, mostly out of curiosity. Let's just say I don't think we should ever go in that direction again. Now, these shoes are a size too small, my feet are killing me, and

Sophia is being Sophia. So, I am outta here. Go find someone else to charm."

Addison looked hurt.

"It's okay, Addy," I said. "We can still be friends. Call me some time. We'll do Starbucks."

I saw him brighten.

"And only Starbucks," I said and walked away.

CHAPTER 6

TEJ

"You still here?" The world's most perfect teeth dazzled from my office doorway. "You've been holed up in here for four hours straight?"

I glanced at the clock. *Noon already.* I walked to the door to greet Bishal, second in command. Corporate genius, company assassin, and I would trust him with my life, money, and golf clubs—but not with a girlfriend if I had one.

"*Chachera bhai!*" he said and grabbed my shoulder in an iron grip. We were not related, but both our families came from Delhi. It was natural for him to greet me as "cousin." I liked Bishal. Had we lived in India, I think we would have been friends. He was my age, and I did not have to explain many of the traditions, at least the ones I chose to honor. I was the worse type of hypocrite.

He placed his satchel on the floor and began to unload his laptop and a pile of notebooks.

"Did you leave anything in your office?" I asked. "Show

me what you got."

"Wait until you see this!" He took a colorful sheet from the pile and unfolded it accordion style. I saw a series of rough sketches labeled as numbered scenes.

"The marketing video," I said.

"I've been working on a script for the commercial. It will run thirty seconds. Here,"—Bishal pointed—"are the screenshots, and here,"—more pointing—"is what you'll say."

"Will we get international pub on this? We've got to nail it on the launch of the frozen food line. Full coverage, the restaurant, the food, the tradition—"

"Don't forget the most important thing," he said. "We sell you. Tej Mayur, celebrity chef, owner-operator of the most popular Indian restaurant in Atlanta and the South's most eligible bachelor."

"That makes me want to gag, you know," I said. "I have no desire to be a celebrity anything."

Bishal raised a cautioning finger. "You think people buy other frozen and canned foods because the stuff tastes better than anything they can make at home? Absolutely not. I've seen the time you spend picking out a single pepper. More than anyone, you know that nothing beats fresh, nothing beats homemade. But people out there, the ones who are hurrying between three jobs and kids' soccer practice, are tired of the same old crap. The chicken sandwich in a bag, the pot pies. They want to eat what famous people eat. If you are not popular, it doesn't matter if your food is the best."

I opened my mouth to protest but realized he was right. "Okay," I said. "But can you keep that social media a-hole out of my face?"

"I will tell him to be as inconspicuous as Obama's photographer, Pete Souza."

"Who?" I asked.

"See what I mean," he said. "One of my jobs is to make you a household name—no, a legend. You're like India's Ryan Gosling. People love that beautiful face of yours. I'd kill for your looks."

"Don't be an *arse*. Show me more."

Bishal was doing what I was paying him to do, but he didn't understand. Nobody did. He understood marketing, not food. But I guess he had a point.

We were doing well—better than that—we were exploding. Bishal went over plans for the frozen food line.

"In eighteen months, we'll launch a test expansion in Charlotte," he said.

"Why North Carolina?" I asked.

"Young demographic in the Queen City. Lots of money, banks, NASCAR—"

I laughed. "You think the good ole boys are going to want biryani?"

"You are way behind, my friend," he said. "NASCAR is corporate now. MJ himself has just jumped in with his own racing team. It's not bootleggers and hillbillies anymore. It's a young, hip crowd, and they want excitement and something more than steak houses."

"Okay," I said.

Bishal knew his stuff. I had an idea that he'd brought to life. He handled the details, the staff, décor, restaurant logistics, and corporate image. Everything except the kitchen, my domain. Bombay Baby regularly had two hundred on the waiting list every week. This was what I wanted.

Bishal was still talking. "I think we need to do a TV ad. I'll round up some hot Desi babes to do the shoot. A smart man always finds a way to make work look like a good time."

We spent the next hour reviewing everything media related: emails, social platforms, mobile, native, and long-form video advertising to be distributed across North America and Canada. I loved his content strategy, the YouTube and Twitter video series. Customers always asked how some of the basic dishes could be made at home, and now they could learn from me right online.

"They can make the dish at home and test it against the frozen food, or supplement the meal. Make sense?"

"Bishal, you are doing a great job," I said.

"Thanks." He leaned back in his chair, crossing his arms across his protruding mid-section. He looked awful smug for a guy that could use some gym time. "So . . . you're going home. You leave in two days, right? Let me be the first to say congratulations."

"Huh?"

"Your upcoming nuptials, of course! Come on, man. You're headed home just before marriage season. Your maataji has you in the crosshairs. Oh, how the mighty fall. I hate to admit, I'm going to miss reading about your escapades on the gossip sites."

"Bugger off, mate. What are you going on about?"

The Indian community gossiped worse than older women

at a Baptist church social. My life was well chronicled. I continually endured meddling, marriage-minded Indian mummies, their vapid, status-seeking betis, and the unrelenting brutality of social media. Success carried privileges and liabilities. Women lying about my intentions were part of the latter. I enjoyed the pleasures accompanying my notoriety, but more than a few of the exploits reported on popular websites were with women I'd never met. If I'd slept off as many wild nights as claimed or with as many women, my business would have collapsed before I opened the door.

Bishal was a dog with a bone. "Your mummy is back on the warpath, huh? She's telling you that fun time in America is over, time to come back to India and do the right thing for the family, marry a good woman, have a truckload of babies, make her proud?"

I pushed away from my desk. "If you already know the speech, why are you asking about it?"

I should never have told him I was going home. I should have said Bermuda.

"Not what this trip is for," I said. "Ma has been ill. I'm checking in on her, making sure that she's all right."

"Well, I hope she's better," Bishal said. "And don't worry. If she sets something up, it won't be like the last time, I am sure things will work out."

Last time.

Haiya.

My mind tumbled in a swirl of pleasure and pain. I'd had no complaints about the bride selected for me. Haiya and I were from the same caste, region, and class. Checkmarks in every column. The elders and the astrologers all gave us their approval. My parents knew Haiya's family. I remembered her a little. I'd seen her one day when she was a young girl, and I was playing in the river with my cousins. She lifted the hem of her salwar kameez, dipped a foot into the stream, and splashed cold darts into our eyes. Then she ran away in a burst of giggles.

I liked it, a fiancée with spunk! A girl who went after what she wanted, a girl who could make life fun.

Wrong. Haiya was a she-devil. The incident by the water had been predictive, a warning.

"Tej," Bishal said, "you know that the matches are the way it's supposed to happen. For me. And you too."

I knew no such thing, so I changed the subject. "Thanks, man," I said. "You're doing great with all of this. Now I need to put out a few fires."

I bolted from the office, but Bishal's voice chased me as I fled down the hall.

"You can run, but you cannot hide. You are Tej Mayur. Someone will land you, and she will be spectacular!"

CHAPTER 7

TEJ

Music and laughter filled the dining room as people filtered in for their early dinner reservations. I walked toward the
hostess, a slender young woman in a sleek emerald halter dress.
Only models and aspiring actresses at the front. Not very PC, but
my restaurant, my standards.

She pressed the phone to her ear. "Bombay Baby," she said.
"Yes, you are confirmed in forty-five minutes, a party of six.
We look forward to seeing you at Bombay Baby."

Her voice was sultry but professional. A pencil pierced the
top of her braided bun. Perfection. She hung up the phone.

"How many openings do we have today, Naima?" I asked.
Candy-scented perfume tickled my nose. Her bare shoulder
looked inviting, but I had a strict "no playing with the help"
personal policy.

"We're totally booked through 9:30," she said. "I have taken
the liberty of adding a 10 p.m. seating."

"Good, nice initiative," I said. "Please notify the cleaning crew. We'll pay extra for the late hour."

"Yes, sir." She picked up the phone to dial.

Bishal had been right about social media. He'd promised me that folks would show if the site clicks morphed into conversions even if there were a lot of non-related things. It all sounded like nonsense, but I didn't need to understand. Bishal knew what he was doing, and we were golden.

I knew how to mesh innovative flavors with Indian culinary tradition. I could pay other people to tweet, blog, and bring in the crowds.

As soon as I walked into the kitchen, Dinesh appeared, smiling. "Lively night, boss."

I nodded, checked the plated dishes moving past on the serving cart, and called over to one of the chefs. "Make sure the mint chutney tin stays full. It's always the first one to get empty."

"Yes, sir."

"Keep the baskets full of naan. Don't limit it to two per table." I moved into the kitchen. Servers were loading appetizers into small metal dishes and banana leaf bowls. I wanted to create the mood of Mother India, ensuring each table featured a complimentary bowl of channa, a mixture of spiced, salted, and toasted peas and peanuts.

"Let's put some green coriander leaves on that yogurt garnish," I said. I added another kebob to a plated entrée. "Americans like things big."

Dinesh scowled but said nothing. He was an artist, creating beautiful plates of color and texture, but I had to remind him to make the serving sizes "homestyle" rather than "gourmet."

I turned to another of the chefs, a whirl of energy. "Benny, be careful with those knives. Not a hibachi grill."

"Sorry, sir."

"I expect more from you. You shouldn't be brandishing cutlery Samurai style."

Showing off for coworkers was a surefire way for someone to get hurt. He knew better.

"Yes, sir."

"Have you plated the macchi yet?"

"They're working on it now." He pointed at the kitchen staff.

"No worries, mate. Be careful and keep up the pace. We'll be packed all night, and I'll need you to pick up some slack while I pay some extra attention to a special table."

"A celebrity? Hang on while I call TMZ." He saw my immediate reaction. "Kidding, boss. Just kidding!" Benny knew we had strict rules about protecting the privacy of guests, some of whom were famous.

"Put your autograph book away," I said with a smile, but my intent was clear. "It's just an old chum. He proposed last week and wants to seal the deal over a romantic meal."

Benny smirked and flipped a knife in his hand. "Another player leaves the game. More lovely ladies for Benny, right? They won't catch this boy. I'll be the last man standing."

"Me too, mate. Me too."

✦

A couple of hours later, I approached Rajeev's window table, the best seat in the house. He stood and hugged me.

"Looking good, old boy," he said.

"Well, you haven't changed since boarding school," I said. "Did you sell your soul for eternal youth?"

He laughed and extended his open hand toward the attractive woman in the chair opposite his. "Buddy, this is Jenya. Darling, I present the owner of this fine establishment, known to the world as Tej Mayur. He and I went to boarding school together."

Jenya blushed and looked away. Rajeev had found a shy one, thin, and Gujarati from the looks of her. Everyone from my country could identify the features and mannerisms of a damsel from the western region of Gujarat, "The Jewel of Western India." I had fond memories of Gujarati women—big foodies, high energy, attractive, and ready to dance the Garba at the drop of a hat.

"Big news, mate. Congrats." I turned to his fiancée. "I'm so happy for you, both."

She looked away again.

"You too, chum," Rajeev said. "Look at you. Bombay Baby's everywhere. I saw your frozen food in the grocery the other day."

"Never a dull moment."

"How's the family?" he asked.

I had hoped to keep the focus on him and his intended, but I could not be rude to a friend and a customer.

"Ma's been under the weather, but now she's doing better," I said. "I'm getting ready to head home for a proper visit to make sure she's okay."

He raised a questioning brow. "Back to India. Now? At the

beginning of wedding season? That's like America's Black Friday, Christmas, and New Year's all rolled into one."

"Only worse," I said. "There are ravenous mummies and eager brides-to-be."

"True," he said. "Be careful, my old friend. You might beat me to the altar, after all."

"Does that mean you're off the market?" Jenya asked me. She pouted. When Rajeev looked away, she flashed me a smile, an unadulterated invitation.

Rajeev better keep an eye on this one.

Taylor approached in his server's outfit. "Here you are, sir." He presented a large dish of kulfi, a dense, creamy Indian ice cream. I could almost taste the pistachios, almond slivers, and crushed cardamom pods.

"I'm sorry," Rajeev said. "We didn't order this."

"On the house," I said, "with a hint of rose water and extra pistachios. I hear it's your fiancée's favorite." I pointed to the dessert, trying to avoid looking at her.

"It's almost too lovely to eat." Jenya kept her eyes on me as she inhaled the essence of rose water. She stared directly at me and licked her lips.

Rajeev, pay attention, mate. I'd seen that look before but never from a woman engaged to a chum.

"Thanks, my friend," he said, watching the food and not his girl. "This looks incredible."

"The pleasure is all mine. Enjoy. Let me know if I can do anything else to make your evening more enjoyable."

Did she wink at me? I needed to get away.

♦

Half an hour later, I stuck my head out of my office. "Coast is clear," I said.

Jenya buttoned her blouse as she walked down the hall. "That was some serious customer service," she said. "Best powder room break in history. You know, just a little something before I settle into the life of boring, marital bliss." She blew me a kiss. "Later, babe!"

♦

I trudged into the small, cozy dining room off the kitchen.

"You're late," said the tiny voice from the center of the room. I smiled at the dimpled, brown-skinned girl of eight looking at me with disapproving eyes.

"Dakota, where are your manners? Mr. Mayur is a very busy man. He doesn't have time to—"

I waved her mother's words away, looking down at my feisty little guest. "A thousand pardons," I said. "A true gentleman should never leave a lady waiting. Please accept my sincerest apologies." I finished with a deep-waisted bow.

She smiled, delighted with the ceremony, the display of chivalry, and being called a "lady." It was an accurate statement. Despite all her directness, Dakota was a kind, sweet little girl, and my friend.

"Fine. You're forgiven," she said, "but I started without you. I couldn't let this good food go to waste."

"Of course, wise choice." My tone reflected her seriousness, and I took my seat opposite her. Dakota was all business, no BS. I wished more women of my acquaintance possessed the same quality.

I looked around the table at the VIP guests. I started the

VIP Night three weeks after my Grand Opening. It had been an easy choice. Auburn Avenue, a once forgotten part of town, had become an eclectic food haven. The allure of a new renaissance of construction and the influx of business enterprise made it a prime site for my version of Little India.

Re-gentrification created casualties, though, victims like my guests, like Dakota and her mother. I was under no illusion that my monthly charitable dinner party would solve the city's problems. Rising rents, changing demographics, brown faces displaced by pale ones, marginalized families struggling to hold on to their piece of the American dream—none of those issues would disappear just because I dropped a plate of Butter Chicken in front of a school kid.

But I refused to ignore the city's population that was increasingly threatened with homelessness or with neighbors struggling to find work. The role of hero held little appeal to me, but it was hard to turn a blind eye to what was happening. Whenever I had a new driver, one wrong turn would land me on a street littered with debris, boarded up tenements, and a row of idle young men waiting for trouble. The scenes reminded me of India: poverty, hunger, the forgotten children.

I decided to do something. Every Thursday, Bombay Baby hosted a dinner party from 7–9 p.m. We invited five elementary school students, their siblings, and any adult who lived in the house. The setting was fancy but not stuffy. No one had to put on airs or go out and buy clothes they could not afford. Jeans and T-shirts were welcome. But I insisted that any male attendee take off his hat.

The staff rocked the VIP dinner every time with traditional

Indian food but toned down the "pop" a little for first-timers. I knew not everyone could handle Indian spices dialed up to eleven. At the end of every evening, we collected everyone's address. From then on, every Tuesday and Thursday, any family who had ever attended a VIP dinner could drop by the kitchen door at Bombay Baby from 6:00–8:00 p.m. and pick up a nutritious, three-course meal. Salad or appetizer, main course, and dessert. Watching the list grow every week filled my heart, and the business's ever-increasing profits offset the program's gradual build-up.

I had plans for something bigger: a community food service with healthy Indian dinners for the displaced and the poor. My finance team ran new numbers every month. As soon as we could carry the extra expense, I wanted to launch, but I did not want to set up an ambitious program only to watch it collapse under the weight of its own generosity.

There was one rule to VIP Night: no repeats. There was one exception to the one VIP Night rule: Dakota.

"Did you enjoy the samosas tonight?" I asked as I pointed to the half-eaten plump pastry of peas and potatoes on her plate.

"It was good, but not as yummy as the tandoori chicken," she replied. She was right. Smoked paprika, garam masala, ginger, and garlic hit all the right flavor notes. I smiled after my first bite.

"Dakota, enough!" Her mother gave her a stern glance and looked at me with apologetic eyes.

"I guess I better tell the crew to work a little harder." I winked at her as she took another vegetable samosa from the basket.

We continued our meal in comfortable silence. A few minutes later, I felt the gentle tug on my rolled-up sleeves. Dakota leaned in. I bent over to catch the whispered words.

"Mr. Tej, can I ask you a question?" She looked up at me, her expression serious. I nodded yes. "How do you find a husband?"

"Not sure. I never had to search for one," I said. I was going to laugh, but I realized she was not joking.

"Why do you ask?"

"Well, it's not for me. I'm only eight, you know." I nodded in agreement. "It's for my momma." She dropped her voice even lower. "She needs a husband real bad, and Ms. Grady, my teacher, said that in India, people find you a husband, and it's so easy, and you live happily ever after like in the fairy tales, but I don't believe in fairy tales. But if there was a way to find a husband and maybe get my mom . . ." Her voice trailed off.

Her teacher had painted a pretty picture indeed. Sure, some arranged marriages ended well. But my situation had ended quite differently. Still, Dakota didn't need to hear about my issues. She needed help.

"Yes," I said. "In India, there are matchmakers who help a man or woman find a partner. Sometimes other family members, like grandparents or aunts and uncles, help with introductions. But, Dakota, I think the American way of finding love is okay, too. Maybe we can help your mum find someone right here."

Dakota looked down and considered my answer.

"I don't know, Mr. Tej. I think those Indian matchmakers sound like a better plan."

She sat back in her seat to ponder. Dakota's father had died during his first week of deployment. His passing was buried deep in the *Atlanta Journal Constitution: Local soldier killed in Afghanistan.*

Dakota believed marriage would change her life, repair her fractured future. Maybe she was right, but there wasn't a damned thing I could do about it. The reality punched me in the gut. I was nobody's hero, and I was fine with that. Most days. I hated to rain on Dakota's parade, but I wasn't a matchmaker.-

CHAPTER 8

HARLOW

THE DOOR WAS WITHIN MY REACH WHEN I HEARD SOPHIA'S voice.

"Harlow."

So damn close.

"Yes?"

Even when no one was around, she strutted—one foot in front of the other—the catwalk stroll. Her aura shouted, "Sex!"

"I was too rough on you in our last conversation," she said. "I know you have your limitations, and I imagine you think I have not been the best mother."

What in the world gave you that impression?

"And?" I said.

"And I think I should do something to help you. Do you remember Geoffrey?"

"Your third—no—fourth—hell, your last husband?"

"Yes."

"The one with the oddly small nose?"

"Well, it was the only thing about him that was oddly small."

She winked. I tasted vomit.

"What about him?"

She leaned in as if to share the nuclear launch codes. "You would not know this, but our settlement was significant. Geoffrey had some, let's say, personal tastes he would rather not have out in the open."

"Oh my God, Sophia! You cannot protect a pedophile!"

She backed up a step, her hands stretched in front as if to ward off an attack. "Oh, Harlow, what must you think of me? I would never protect a monster. No, no, no, no. He just likes certain things done in a certain way with certain devices—"

I shrieked. "For the love of God, stop! I do not want to know. I *never* want to know. I never want to hear about you and the creepos you jump in bed with."

I thought I might have crossed all the way over the line this time, but Sophia grinned. "I know. I should be more aware of my daughter's sensitivities. You and I never discussed such things. In fact, I didn't know you were a virgin until Addison shared your encounter."

My head throbbed. An aneurysm could not be far away. I closed my eyes and began to count. I'd gotten to seven before Sophia spoke again.

"Again, my apologies. Let's move on."

"Let's," I said.

"I have a proposition," she said. "Something designed to put you well on your way to a happy and secure life."

"And to ease your conscience, no doubt."

She might have flinched, but she continued. "Let me ask you. Do you want to be married? You're not a lesbian, are you?"

"No," I said. "I mean, yes. I mean—damn, Sophia, ask me one question at a time. I am not lesbian, and I would like to get married."

"Thank you, sweet baby Jesus," she said. "I was beginning to worry. You dress a little masculine."

I shook my head. "Get on with it."

"Okay, you want to get married—*to a man*—and I want you to get married. I know for a fact that the Whitmore family is interested in you."

"They lookin' for a high yella?" I asked. "Let me guess, they want someone 'exotic,' but not anyone who might produce little black-as-coal babies."

"The Whitmores are very fine people. They are leaders in every civic organization—"

Now it was my turn to interrupt. "And it would not hurt little Master Addison's political ambitions one bit to look like he gives a crap about racial equality. Marrying a woman of color might allow him to skip the step of running for local office. He could jump right into the race for lieutenant governor, serve one or two terms, run for Senate, and then plop his finely tuned ass in a chair in the Oval Office. Little Addison, President of the United States by age forty-five."

"Well, it would be closer to forty-three, but who's counting," Sophia said. "Anyway, we have come up with a little plan for you and Addison—well, really just you because Addison, as you know, will never want for anything. You, on the other hand, have what I would politely call limited financial resources."

I tried to keep my face blank. "Go on."

"Cards on the table," Sophia said. "Addison Whitmore wants to marry you. More importantly, Judith and Wallington Whitmore want you to marry Addison. The three of us—we did not include Addison—have reached an agreement. I am putting in some, and they are kicking in a bit more. We want to give you a gift. Not you and Addison, just you. A gift you can use as you see fit. No trust, no strings. All yours. Something you can squirrel away for the future. You can indemnify yourself against any, ah, unforeseen occurrence."

"Like when Addison decides he wants to dump me for a younger woman with a tighter ass and bigger boobs."

"Don't be crude, Harlow, let's stay dispassionate and pragmatic. Anyway, the money would be yours, given to you on the day of your wedding immediately after the vows, before the reception if you like. So, what do you say?"

I took several long breaths to get my heart rate under control. The back of my head felt like it was going to explode. What had begun as a twinge behind my eye had morphed into the snarling beast of a full-grown migraine.

"Sophia," I said, "the offer is both disgusting and degrading. I might understand how your friends, Mr. and Mrs. Ofay America, the prototypical Cadillac liberals, could come up with a plan to buy a black girl for their politically ambitious son. After all, I am the right kind of AA. You know, not too black, not too militant. But your participation in pimping out your own daughter is contemptible. There's no amount of money in the world that would make me sell my dignity and my soul, especially not to a vacuous pretty boy like Addison Whitmore." I kept eye contact until the last second, then walked for the door. I was halfway out when I heard Sophia's last words.

"Five million dollars."

CHAPTER 9

TEJ

"YOU DO REALIZE YOU'RE HOSTING A PARTY RIGHT NOW? THERE are twenty people downstairs on the pool deck wondering where you are."

Miguel, my best mate, pointed outside. I looked. Yep, a party, now four dozen people and growing.

"I do know," I said.

"So, why are they out there having fun while you're in here looking at numbers like Ebenezer Scrooge?"

I gave him a wry smile and looked back at the spreadsheet. I'd been home from the restaurant less than an hour, and I still had a mound of work that required my attention. I wondered why my doorman let all those people out on the deck. Then again, tonight wasn't different from any of Miguel's other impromptu gatherings after the restaurant closed. Thirty minutes and a few text exchanges had conjured up a full-fledged fraternity party. It didn't take much to lure people to midtown. The promise of an open bar, free food, and pretty women always drew a crowd.

"I couldn't resist, man. Not everybody has Piedmont Park in their backyard." He pulled back the translucent white window sheers and stared at the twinkling park lights. "It's a hell of a lot easier to get lucky when your homeboy lives in one of the most exclusive places in Atlanta."

"It's cool, man, I get it. I'm used to hosting. I do it all day at work."

I didn't mind. A bunch of people conveyed a certain amount of comfort. No one from India minded a good crowd. The constant buzz of human activity—servants, parents, cousins, siblings, aunts, uncles, people you looked at and thought *Who are they?*—added to the tapestry of life.

By the looks of it, my guests were enjoying themselves. *I'm glad someone's having fun.*

Miguel hadn't left. "Hey, man, that's not for me out there. It's your going-away party. I want to send you off in style before you go do that Brahma-rama-lama-ding-dong thing."

"It's called *brahmachari*, asshole, and it's intended to help you focus and live on the path." I stared at the screen. I was adding up the numbers and making projections in my head.

"Are you really gonna do it?" Miguel asked. "You're headed to India, a place crawling with women who are hot for you, and you are not going to, ah, sample the goodies?"

I shut my laptop. "I'm not a monk, but I don't want to embarrass my parents with what would be considered inappropriate behavior."

"Speaking of your parents, did you ever get a straight answer out of your mother's doctor?" Miguel asked. He had the attention span of a gnat. "You said he was being dodgy."

"Baapa, my father, told me Dr. Khatri has taken up residence in our New Delhi home. Whenever I ask about her condition, all I hear is, 'Dr. Khatri is keeping a close eye on her,' or 'She is doing as well as can be expected.' What does any of that mean?"

"Damn, man, I'm sorry. I didn't realize it was that bad."

"Well, it took me a while, but I finally discovered Ma has a mild case of pneumonia and a major case of pain in my ass. She is going to be up my butt when I'm there."

"Well," Miguel said, "you could have picked a better time to go to India than in the middle of wedding season. Did you ever think that might send the wrong signal?"

"I know, I know," I said. "It's the only time that works for me. But I have been very clear. I am going to check on Mum, check out the food, and have a good time. Then, I am coming back to Atlanta."

"Your mummyji is as devious as ever. Love it! She's got you this time." Miguel began tearing up from the laughter.

"Bugger off," I said. "I'll be back in Atlanta before you even miss me."

"I've heard that bullshit before," Miguel said. "Remember Aarush? Left here on a Thursday. Came back ten days later with a wife. Within two years, he had a daughter and twin sons and was never seen again. He was teleported into the black hole of married life."

"Point taken," I said. "But it won't happen to me."

I didn't have time to trek halfway across the globe to play nursemaid, but I loved my ma more than life. I couldn't very well tell my family I was too busy to come for a visit, especially when I had been summoned.

The timing of the trip was purely coincidental, right? After the fiasco with Haiya, I was done with matchmakers. I drifted into memory . . .

◊

Ma's face had shriveled into a mask of pain tinged with something else.

"Why, my son? Why would Haiya not want to marry you? The astrologers told me it was in the stars. They said you two were a perfect match."

"It is complicated, Ma," I said. "Not everything is as it seems."

"What did you do? I know every young man sows wild oats. I have heard about your reputation. But did you embarrass her? Did you humiliate her with that nanny of a bridesmaid?"

"Bhavnah is not a goat, Ma, and I did nothing with her more than share a cup of tea," I said. Now I recognized the other thing. Her pain stood hand-in-hand with disappointment. I would rather lose my manhood than let my ma down. "Haiya simply told me she no longer wished to marry me."

There was more to the story, but I would never tell my ma.

◊

Miguel's voice brought me back.

"What?" I asked.

"Maybe it would be different this time," he said. "You know, the arranged marriage thing."

Miguel and I met on our first day at Goldman Sachs, a pair of diversity hires. We offset our grueling hours with legendary weekends: Tybee Island beach parties with newly minted swimsuit models, feel-good underground Stevie Wonder tribute celebrations and '80s retro karaoke dance parties. Miguel navigated the chaos with ease and took me along for the ride.

He had the tall, dark, and handsome thing down pat. Women by the score fell to his charm. I'd seen him melt the most cynical barriers. I watched and learned, determined to recreate myself in America. He taught me how to use the mysterious façade of India to its maximum advantage.

"Let's get out to the party," I said. "A twenty-minute break will probably do me good."

"Might be your last American party as a single man," he said. "You know, one final night of debauchery while you still can. Now, go out there and talk a little game." He spread his arms like a circus announcer. "Ladies and gentlemen, the man, the myth, the legend, Mr. Tag 'Em and Bag 'Em Mayur."

"You know my name is Tej, right?" I asked. "No one calls me Tag except you."

"How many others know how many women you've slept with?" Miguel asked.

"Good point," I said, then rested my hand on his shoulder. "Miguel, old friend, first, I am not getting married in India. Second, I appreciate the gesture, totally unnecessary, but very nice. Last, I am not getting married in India."

"Methinks thou dost protest too much," he said.

"I never should have introduced you to Shakespeare," I said.

The party was rocking outside, but we elected to relax in my great room. I stepped behind my bar and poured us each two fingers of Bunnahabhain 25. I stared at the rich amber liquid, then downed it in one swig.

"Geez, man," Miguel said. "That's the good stuff. Sure as hell isn't Three Roses."

"About seven hundred dollars a bottle, but what the hell," I said. "It's a party, right?"

"I hear you, man."

I headed to the Skytrak Sig12 golf simulator in the corner of the expansive room, snatched the driver out of my waiting bag, and ripped one right down the middle of the projection of East Lake Golf Course.

"Nice shot," Miguel said. "Too bad when we play for real, you bogey that hole every time."

"Fifty bucks says I make par now."

"You're on. You hit that drive about 280. You have 225 left."

I walked over to my bag, selected an 18° hybrid, and lashed at the ball on the mat. The ball smacked into the screen. The virtual image tracked my "shot" as it soared through the air and landed on the green about fifteen feet from the hole."

"Double or nothing on birdie?" I asked.

"Done," he said.

I lined up my putt and rotated my shoulders for my patented smooth putting stroke. Before I contacted the ball, Miguel asked, "Heard from Haiya recently?"

"Huh?" I hit the ball off the heel of my putter. It almost missed the screen. My virtual putt stopped woefully short of the hole.

"All square," Miguel said.

"You are a sorry son of a bitch," I said. "No gentleman talks in the middle of someone's putt."

Miguel laughed. "You are such an idiot."

"Why's that?"

"All this time, and you still think of me as a gentleman."

CHAPTER 10

TEJ

"Haiya reached out," I said. "Asked if we could meet up during my visit.

"Seriously? She's got balls. I'll give her that," Miguel said. He missed a three-footer for par.

"You may be the worst putter in history," I said. "You're down twenty dollars."

"We playing for money?" he asked.

"You know the rules," I said.

At the same time, we both said, "If we're playing anything, we're playing for something."

"Listen, mate," I said. "There's no way I go to Delhi and don't run into her."

"There are 18.4 million people there," he said.

"Yep, and about eighty-four thousand per square mile. They're packed in there like soup in a can. But we run in the same circles. If she's breathing, we will see each other. It's inevitable."

"No, brother," he said. "It's karma."

I hit my shot and stepped aside to give him a turn.

"So, what's your plan?" he asked. "How you gonna play it? Hug, kiss, fuck? After what she did, you ought to get her right to the edge, then walk away."

As if he was reading my mind.

"Don't get emotional. It'll screw you up. If you see that bitch, walk up to her like she's your best friend. Nobody's gonna remember that shit from two years ago. It's done, water under the damn bridge. Go in there and own it. You're the fucking man now. You are the Restaurant King. Let her know it."

"I win," I said. "That will be forty dollars, please."

"Put it on my tab," he said. "What is it now?"

"Somewhere between forty and a million," I said.

Things were back to normal, the tension gone.

"Shit! When did you get this one?" he asked.

He gestured to the back wall. Street art, pieces considered trash to a less discerning eye, covered the walls with a mix of graffiti-inspired creations. Miguel was pointing to the mismatched piece.

"The artist is Indian," I said. "S. H. Raza."

"That shit looks expensive," he said.

"The original is two million," I said, "but you and I both know I can't drop two mil for a painting."

There was a moment of silence. Then we both burst into laughter.

"That was a good one," Miguel said. "Okay, give it up. Where's the original? And does your baapa know?"

"Well, he thinks all the money he sends me on the sly is

going into the restaurant. He doesn't quite understand my need for a jet-set image. It's fine for him to own extravagant things, but he wants me to, I believe his words were, 'suffer a bit.'"

"He wasn't very interested in suffering when he asked you for financial advice when the rupee started spiraling downward."

"No, he wasn't, and he still isn't. With the investments I have acquired for him here—real estate ventures, hedge funds, blah-de-blah-blah, my baapa will still be one of the richest men in India two decades after he dies, if that ever happens."

"You still haven't fessed up about the painting. I know you own it. I can read it in your face. Where did you stash it?"

"I bought it as part of a consortium, several investors. The piece is in a temperature-controlled, high-security facility specializing in objects d'art," I said. "I can't have stuff like that hanging on my walls. Have you met our friends? Sable would get mad at a date, hurl a glass of merlot across the room, and smash it into the painting. Not good for Mr. Raza's color scheme."

"She'd do it, too," Miguel said. "She is one crazy—hey, speaking of crazy, Jeremy's been asking if you have dibs on the lovely and curvaceous Miss Kiara. Otherwise, he's going to make a move."

"Jeremy? He couldn't charm a woman with a how-to manual and a map."

Miguel shrugged. "Some women are into that, you know, awkwardness, the I've got no game game."

"Well," I said, "he's got no Kiara either." I threw back my

head in a hearty laugh at the skeptical look on his face.

"You care to wager, mate?" he asked. "If you're off the market, she'll snap up the next biggest bank account, and Jeremy's parents are loaded."

Images of Kiara floated into my mind: long, titian red hair, hourglass figure, full lips, and a wanton sexual appetite matching my own. She was daring, bold, willing to push the boundaries, never saying no. We enjoyed each other, fed off the other's wilder instincts. Miguel had no idea that Kiara and I had been "spending time" together.

I imagined Kiara's naked body, glistening with sweat, ready, willing, available. In my mind, her face gave way to Haiya's, sneering, her lips pulled back in a cynical snarl. "A cook? You want to be a cook."

Miguel snapped two fingers under my nose, bringing me back to reality. "Dude, you okay? Where did you just go? You need to party, that's an order. Let's take this fine Scotch and head downstairs to enjoy a few of your closest strangers."

"Yeah, you got it. Need to make a quick call. Give me five." I walked back to my desk.

"Okay," Miguel said. "I don't get the Kiara thing, though. She not up to your standards?"

I whirled as the blood pulsed through the veins in my neck. "What the fuck does that mean, my standards?" I asked.

Miguel extended both palms. "Easy, brother. She's smoking hot and all, like she was put together in some German lab. She's just not going to challenge anyone for a Nobel Prize. I meant it as a compliment. Slow your roll, dude."

I waved with the back of my hand. "Sorry, buddy. Just

business on the brain. I'll be down in a minute."

He hesitated at the door. "Mind if I ask you something that's been bugging me for a while?"

"I'm an open book," I said.

"Well, most people today name their kid whatever they want, usually something weird like Montana or Weathervane. Not your people."

"Your point?"

"What does your name mean, Tej Mayur?"

"If you tell anyone, I'll have you killed."

"My lips are sealed he said." He made the gesture of locking his mouth and tossing away an invisible key.

"It means Bright Peacock."

He waved and shut the door. I heard him laughing all the way to the elevator.

◊

I was under no illusion about Kiara. She hid her avarice under an avalanche of sexual ability, but I could see her true intentions. She paid too much attention to baubles and the trappings of wealth. When I told her I was part-owner of an original Raza and what it was worth, the idea of the wealth behind such a purchase made her wet enough to do me right next to the knock-off's frame.

She knew I wanted light, easy, and uncomplicated. I had told her so, word for word. And she claimed to agree. But I knew that under all her makeup, moaning, and maneuvers, she had marriage on the mind.

I scrolled through my cell, then pressed dial.

"Don, this is Tej." I looked at my clock. Ten p.m. "Sorry

for the late call."

"Good evening, Mr. Mayur." I heard him clear his throat. He'd been sleeping.

"Tell me about the Legacy Media meeting?"

All I wanted was the summary, but he gave me chapter and verse, a virtual reenactment. He explained the brilliant plans he had. He might as well have been reading my notes back to me. I listened for eight minutes.

"Don, enough. It's horse shit."

"Sir, I don't understand."

Yes, he does.

"You are paid to do one thing: a restaurant app. Do we have one?"

I heard a lot of words—a lot of excuses—a lot of *um, ah,* and *well.* He talked about some junior app developer and prototypes.

"So," I said, "she wants to revamp the eCommerce site to include commercial food delivery. She thinks we should revise the original design. How long will that take?"

"Sir, all due respect, I don't think we have time to make all the changes she wants with the app. I mean, adding in—"

"Damn it!" I didn't usually lose my temper, but incompetence always pushed my buttons. "Don, you have one job to do. If you can't get the developer to finish the work, fire her because if we don't get movement on this PDQ, I will fire you. Got it?"

His voice took on a mouse-like squeak. "Pretty damn quick, yes, sir."

There was a soft knock on my office door.

"Get it done, Don. Email your progress within twenty-four hours, or I'll have someone mail you your stuff. Got it?"

He was still mumbling apologies and "Sir, sir, sir" when I pushed the off button and turned to the door.

Kiara stood in the doorway, 5'8" of sexual advertisement. "Whatcha doing in here all by your lonesome?" She closed the distance with three seductive steps.

It wasn't hard to see her appeal. I could see her every attribute beneath the skintight dress. *That looks like body paint.*

She was exactly what I wanted in a romp. The wrong region of India, wrong caste, her skin tone a little too dark to suit my mother. She gave the black leather tufted Chesterfield sofa a meaningful glance and tossed the crimson and gold pillows to the floor before sitting.

"Maybe, we should stay up here," she said. "No one will miss us."

"I have a little more work to finish up." I turned toward my desk.

"You're leaving. This will be our last night for a while." She patted the space next to her.

"Our last night. Why so dramatic? I'll be back before you know it."

"Oh, I know you'll come back," she said, "but you might not have room for me anymore."

She was right. Even if Ma left me alone this trip, my fascination with Kiara and her custom-made body was fading. But right now, with my family half a world away, rising stress from work, and hellish memories of the past, what I needed was something mindless. Something to take my mind off everything. Something everyone in India would see as forbidden.

All of that was available to me just across the room. As I stood, Kiara peeled her dress over her head and reclined on the couch, naked and ready.

A knowing smile spread across her perfect face.

"I thought you might see things my way," she said. She guided me into her. "Bon voyage, lover."

CHAPTER 11

HARLOW

I DID NOT WANT THE BOMBAY BABY ASSIGNMENT, BUT NO ONE asked my opinion. The conversation had not been long.

"Harlow, my office." Arlene's intercom manners were non-existent.

I was standing in front of her within fifteen seconds.

"You've got a meeting in"—she looked at her Piaget—"forty-five minutes. It's with Bombay Baby. Ezra will catch you up."

"Isn't that Rupert's project?" I asked.

She glanced at her watch again—a prop–she knew the meeting was over. "Rupert's sick, some stomach thing. Gotta bolt."

Before I could follow her out, she called over her shoulder. "This could be big for us. Tej Mayur is the hottest thing in town right now. Do whatever you have to do. Get naked and dance the hula, but do not fuck this up."

Mr. Tej Mayur represented everything I despised in the

gilded upper classes of every society. His face was every-where—on billboards, on the sides of MARTA streetcars, and every imaginable social media platform. I was not impressed. I'd seen too many guys like him in Sophie's world: classically handsome, urbane, and smooth as fresh motor oil. They could charm the skin off a snake and the underwear off a virgin. Tej could move without effort in any arena. He was light-skinned enough to command respect in Atlanta's Black community and "exotic" enough to appeal to the crowd who summered at The Cloister.

Ezra shook his head during our three-minute debrief. I was scrolling through code so fast my head hurt. "This is a dog of an app," he said. "Rupert spent too much time on the bells and whistles and didn't build anything solid. Damn thing crashes about every third time."

"What do I do?" I asked. "I didn't have a damn thing to do with developing this, and now I have to defend it."

"Don't bullshit anyone. Tell the folks in that room that there are problems. Tell them you've just gotten on the project. Give them a legitimate time frame, then get back ASAP. We'll live here until we get it right. This is right up your alley with the India angle and all. Bombay Baby's hot right now, and they are making the most of their moment in the sun. Even if the restaurant fades, once they get their frozen food line cranked out, they could be as big as Bird's Eye."

"No shit?"

"No shit. Don't know if you've tried any Bombay Baby, but I got in on a sample tasting. Straight out of the microwave, and it was about the best Indian food I've ever had."

"So, how sick is Rupert?"

"What do you think? He's probably holed up in his apartment, firing up a doobie, playing *World of Warcraft*, and waiting for the dust to clear."

I slung my bag over my shoulder. "Send me the app link while I'm on the way. Maybe I'll get lucky during the demo, and it won't blow up. I don't have a lot of time to make a balanced recommendation of their application architecture. If they need to add any new interactive elements, it could take weeks."

"Don't worry about that," Ezra said. "Mr. Mayur's PR Team will provide direction. Listen and follow instructions. Say 'Yes, sir,' a lot. Don't try to innovate. Just give them what they ask for, nothing more. Remember, we are right up against the deadline we proposed at the beginning."

"Damn Rupert!" I said.

"Exactly," Ezra said. "Mayur expects the reservation app done first, but I think there is a push to get the updated lifestyle app and some other stuff in the market in the next month. Don't worry, it'll be fine."

Ezra chased me down the hall. "Hey, you're leaving tomorrow, right? Argentina or something."

"Close," I said. "It's my best friend's wedding, and it's in India. You only missed it by about ten thousand miles."

"But I know her name is Rita. Score one for me."

"Nice job," I said. "I'll tell *Lita* you almost remembered who she is."

"Have you met her fiancé?" Ezra asked.

"Hell, she hasn't even met him yet. It's one of those arranged things, old school. She comes from money, and her family wants to keep it that way. Her parents hired a matchmaker, big business in India. Lita's been there for about a week. You probably won't even see me before I leave." I hesitated. "Unless I have to come back here and clean out my desk."

Ezra winced. "Don't even joke about that. You're the only reason I don't kill myself. Everyone here's so so so gross."

I stepped into the elevator. Ezra yelled through the crack, "Good luck!" He blew me a kiss. I made a face, then laughed.

Fucking rich bastards. They have everything handed to them—money, cars, good genes, careers—and they handpick a spouse or a lover on the side from a bevy of women who are more than willing to put up with their vanity and infidelity just to be part of the action.

Sure, Mayur had a successful restaurant, but new places came and went in Atlanta like summer thunderstorms. They were big and loud for a while. When they were gone, everything seemed somehow fresher and less polluted. This year's Indian sensation would give way to next season's Thai thrill ride. And there would be another "genius" in the kitchen who probably knew as much about cooking as I did about astrophysics.

And who the hell names their kid Bright Peacock?

Thirty minutes later, I stepped out on the curb and smoothed out my skirt. On the way to the fortieth floor, I checked my makeup and hair in my reflection of the elevator doors.

"These guys will be putty in my hands," I said.

Boy, was I wrong.

CHAPTER 12

HARLOW

I was asleep fifteen minutes before wheels up from Toronto. Ambien is a beautiful thing. I probably shouldn't have topped it off with a half-glass of champagne, but I didn't care. I figured I'd awaken somewhere over the Atlantic. The "putty in my hands" meeting at Bombay Baby had gone sideways.

During the meeting a smelly cloud of Tom Ford's Fucking Fabulous had dominated the room.

"Harlow!" It was the source of the stench. Someone charged at me with an outstretched hand. All I could focus on was a mouthful of blinding white capped teeth that were at least one size too large.

Did this guy leave any hair product in the tube at home?

He wore a gold signet ring on the pinky of his right hand—David Yurman—and enough gold chains around his neck to resurrect a chapter of the Mr. T Fan Club.

He hugged me. I nearly passed out from the fumes.

"Arlene texted and said you would be with us. I'm Bishal,

head of the PR Team here at Bombay Baby."

"Good morning, Bishal," I said. "How are you today?"

"Good, all good. Just got some stuff to lay on you about the app. Been some hang-ups, right?"

"As you've been informed," I said, "I am sitting in for Rupert Rodriguez, the principal developer. He ate some bad oysters or something last night and is in no condition to be here today."

"But you were part of the team, right, baby girl?"

What's with the baby girl crap? I decided to suck it up. "Yes, I wrote several of the algorithms, but I was not—"

I didn't finish. The door opened. A ridiculously handsome man entered the room. Tall, about 6'3", athletic, elegant, tailored suit, tan Berluti Scritto loafers, no socks, and a silk shirt cut down to the middle of his hairless, mocha-colored chest. Jet black hair any woman would kill for was swept back into a ponytail. Stylish stubble graced his angular cheekbones and chin. He walked with a panther's grace. He looked like the love child of a young Brad Pitt and a mid-career Michael Jordan.

Well, here he was, in the flesh—the one *The Epicurean* called "a culinary mad genius of fusion experimentation." The quotation sounded dumber every time I thought about it. Everything I'd ever read about this strutting overdressed dingleberry was new age mumbo jumbo aimed at convincing people they would experience something cutting edge at a restaurant that eighteen months ago had been sliding "gourmet grilled cheese sandwiches" into paper sacks while trying not to laugh at the morons who were paying fifteen dollars apiece. Now, it was Bombay Baby. Seriously, how many ways can someone prepare curried chicken?

But I had to hand it to him. He thoroughly understood the contemporary hype machine. And he played his image to the max: the man with "bad-boy looks and a blue-blood pedigree."

Bishal gestured to the man. "Harlow Kennedy, this is Tej Mayur, founder, owner, and head chef at Bombay Baby."

"Hello," I said as I extended my hand.

"Hello," he said. "I have to go. Nice to meet you."

He nodded to Bishal and left.

As soon as the door shut, Bishal looked at me. "Ms. Kennedy, thank you so very much for your efforts. I am sorry to inform you that your services are no longer required by our firm."

Son of a bitch didn't even have the balls to say it to my face.

I didn't remember the ride back to the office. All I could concentrate on was the reality of the moment. Harlow Kennedy, the self-proclaimed rising star of Legacy Coding, had just been fired. Thirty minutes later, I staggered back into the office, told Arlene, and set an unofficial world record.

Fired twice in less than an hour.

When I sat down to load up my desk, I checked my bank account on my phone. Balance: $527.69. No, a tear had clouded my vision. I wiped my eye and rechecked. Still $527.69.

A voice brought me back to the present moment. "Well, hello, Sleepyhead."

I shook my head to clear it and then turned it to track the source of the rich baritone. *Maybe this flight will be okay after all.*

I stared at the stunning face, perfect teeth, and piercing brown eyes of a god with wavy black hair—Tej Mayur.

CHAPTER 13

TEJ

I KNEW WHO SHE WAS THE SECOND I SAW HER. I THOUGHT ABOUT asking the flight attendant if I could exchange my seat, but the cabin was full, and first-class travelers can be notoriously unco-operative. That juice was not worth the squeeze.

She was out for about half the trip. I took the champagne flute from her hand before it spilled. Seven hours is a long time to stare at someone—and probably a little creepy, but she was one of the most beautiful women I'd ever seen. Long legs, long hair, long natural eyelashes, an athletic figure, and high cheekbones.

The steward was next to me before I touched the call button. "Does your wife need a blanket, sir?"

"Yes, ah, no, ah . . . not my wife. Yes, a blanket, please."

The steward shot a glance at the slumbering figure. "You should be so lucky, my brother," he said. "Are you dating?"

"I don't know her," I said. An accurate recitation would

take too long. "But I plan on introducing myself before we land."

"If she ever wakes up," he said. He chuckled at his own joke. He returned in a minute later with supplies. He slipped a pillow behind her head with the deft touch of a concert pianist, then covered her with a plush blanket.

"Good luck," he said, and he was off to attend to someone else who was thinking about asking for assistance.

Jedi Mind Trick Airline Steward.

About mid-crossing, she stirred. She'd been tossing and turning, but this was different. This was pre-waking behavior.

She stretched, rolled her head, shook it a few times, then picked her head up and looked out the window.

Now or never.

"Well, hello, Sleepyhead."

CHAPTER 14

HARLOW

There was a moment when I thought about slapping him, nailing him with a palm right across that ridiculously beautiful face. Then it hit me.

Do I have morning breath?

I reached for my purse. He produced a box of cinnamon Altoids.

"Would you care for one?" he asked.

"Do I need one?"

Harlow, are you an idiot?

He laughed. "Just a little gesture. This is a little awkward, to say the least."

"You weren't here before . . ."

"Before you went off to La-La Land," he said. "I boarded a little late. The attendants were most kind to accommodate me."

Bet they wouldn't have held the door for me.

"Are you someone special?" I asked. "I mean, besides being the hottest restaurateur in the greater Atlanta area?"

You did not just say "hot." You are seriously stupid.

"Well," he said, "we are enjoying some success, but we have a long way to go. In truth, every day I am thankful we are still open. The competition is fierce, and the public's fancy can change like the wind."

The steward appeared. "Ma'am, you missed dinner. Would you care for something to eat?"

Dinner was a welcomed interruption. Tej slipped on a pair of noise-canceling headphones and listened to whatever pretentious self-help podcast I'm sure he routinely scanned while I picked my way through a meal in which I was not remotely interested. But the ice cream was good. When the steward cleared my tray, he winked at me.

"I thought you might like a little extra," he said.

"Good call," I said.

I looked at my watch. At least another four hours. I put my earbuds in and found my book.

CHAPTER 15

TEJ

I HAD HOPED SHE MIGHT TALK TO ME ONCE SHE FINISHED SPOON-ing ice cream into her mouth. I got a headache from side-eye watching her. She ate her dessert with a connoisseur's inten-tionality, savoring every nuance, moving the ever-melting concoction around in her mouth with delicate deliberation.

You are staring at a woman eating ice cream. Get a hold of yourself.

Once the dishes were gone, I'd hoped she might reengage in conversation. We needed to discuss "the recent unpleasant-ness." But she started listening to something.

She never even looked at me.

CHAPTER 16

HARLOW

WHAT KIND OF A CREEP WATCHES A WOMAN EAT ICE CREAM?

I considered going all Kim Basinger on him from *9 ½ Weeks*, sliding my tongue across my lips and such, just to make him squirm. But I decided just to eat my dessert, then listen to my book. I glanced at my Audible app.

Damn, only a little more than three hours left. I might have to talk to him before we land.

In my mind, I ran through the stuff in my suitcase. Packing was a little easier since Lita told me all my wedding gear was preselected. I would be fitted by a tailor upon my arrival. Still, I had to be careful. Lita reminded me to wear dresses, slacks, and long skirts with my arms and legs covered at all times. My suitcase was filled with appropriate linen shifts, wrap dresses, and scarves.

When my book ended, I returned my earbuds to their carrying case.

"Why are you going to India?"

Damn, this guy is watching my every move.

"A wedding," I said.

"Congratulations," he said. "Who's the lucky guy."

He said lucky . . . Jesus, Harlow, snap out of it.

I whirled in my seat. "You have a lot of fucking nerve, you know. Not very long ago, you fired me. Correction, your hired toady fired me because you didn't have the balls to do it yourself. After that—"

"Whoa," he said. He held up his palm like he was telling a car to stop at a preschool crossing. "I didn't fire you—Bombay Baby got rid of your company. My gripe is with Arlene Nettleman. She made a lot of promises she did not keep. I guarantee she knew what was going to happen when she sent you. If anyone lacks the, ah, balls—your word, not mine—it would be your boss."

"You mean my ex-boss," I said. I blinked three times in succession. *Damn it, Harlow, do not cry.* "She canned me before I had a chance to plop my fine ass back into my seat."

I could feel the pulse throbbing through my forehead. That damn vein is a surefire "tell" when I get mad. It sticks out, and everyone knows. I bit the inside of my lip. It was time to shut up. *Please don't let him say anything about my "fine ass" comment.*

Tej tilted toward me. *Oh, Jesus, Mary, and the other guy, he smells good.* "Ms. Kennedy—" He noticed my flinch. "Yes, I know your name—Harlow Kennedy. It is unjust that you were dismissed for Arlene's failures. When we return to the States,

I will be most pleased to make a few calls on your behalf. You need to know that as soon as Bishal came to my office and debriefed the meeting, I went out to find you, to explain. But you had already fled.

"I know when I'm not wanted," I said.

CHAPTER 17

TEJ

BUT YOU ARE.

I'd never wanted any woman more in my entire life. Her green eyes sparkled with ferocity. I could only imagine how they might blaze during passion. I thought about touching her cheek but realized it might be the bourbon I'd been sipping most of the flight.

"Ms. Kennedy—Harlow," I said, "I beg your forgiveness. While you were sleeping, I went over everything. I acted poorly—a lot of stress, some significant issues with logistics. Still, I should have been more professional, dealt with you directly, and generally, I should have been less of a dick. My beef was with your boss. I should have left you alone and terminated the contract through Arlene."

"Well, okay then," she said. "Maybe this will be the push I need to pursue my real passion."

"What's that?"

We talked about her jewelry making. She showed me a

piece—a mock-up, she called it.

"Like a taste testing," I said.

"Sort of," she said. "Only, I'm sure you don't use knock-off spices and the like."

"Only the best at Bombay Baby." I shut my eyes as soon as I said it and winced. When I cracked an eyelid, she was grinning.

"It's okay. I'm not made of glass."

No, my dear, you are made of precious stones and soft curls and the scent of spring.

"Tell me about the wedding," I said. "A close friend?"

"The best," she said. Her eyes lit with enthusiasm, and she spent the next twenty minutes talking about adolescent games, teenage secrets, crushes and heartaches, young adult folly, and a bond I could tell would never break.

She slapped herself playfully on the cheek. "Harlow, how you do go on," she said. "I must have bored you senseless."

"Not at all." Since I couldn't think of anything clever. I bailed out with a weak apology, "Again, please forgive me."

She looked at me for a long time. Her gaze softened. For a moment, I thought she might kiss me—no, I wanted her to kiss me. But she remained as far away as the seats would allow.

"Okay," she said. "But you said *dick*."

CHAPTER 18

HARLOW

AFTER I FINISHED BABBLING AND WE GOT PAST AN AWKWARD moment when I thought about kissing him on his full, inviting lips. I changed the subject.

"So, are you headed home to get married?" I asked.

"Oh no," he said. "I said it's wedding season, and I am going home. Those two things are mutually exclusive. My ma would love for me to accept an arrangement, but I've already had one of those bite me in the ass. Don't think I'll do that again."

His face darkened for a moment, a passing cloud, then it was gone. Whatever memory he'd just relived was painful.

"Miss Harlow," he said, "I'm not going to apologize again, but as a hospitable Indian, I would like to make you an offer."

"Not really interested in bussing tables at Bombay Baby." I instantly regretted my snappishness. Tej, however, played the gentleman.

"I would never think of insulting you in that manner," he said. "You told me you were scheduled to stay for a while after your friend's wedding. Would you do me the honor of allowing me to take you to dinner?"

My eyes widened. He noticed and began to backpedal.

"Not a date. Not at all. A rapprochement of sorts. Properly chaperoned, of course."

I could feel the smile in my ears. "Sure."

"And we can talk about your future and how I can help."

"Sure." *Are you trying to sound like an idiot?*

We had just finished exchanging phone numbers when the announcement came over the PA: "Ladies and gentlemen, we are beginning our approach into Indira Gandhi International Airport. Please return your seats and tray tables to their upright and locked positions and ensure that all your personal belongings are securely stored. Attendants will be coming along the aisles to pick up any items you may wish to discard."

Just before I put my bag away, I pulled up my bank app and checked my balance again. Arlene said Legacy would pay my severance immediately.

$3066. All the money I had in the world.

I'd committed to two years in my apartment, splurged on a lease for a BMW, and carried a healthy balance on my Visa card. I did some quick calculations in my head. All of Sophia's money went for extravagant things like food.

If I cut to the bare bones, I have enough money to last me exactly ... not very long at all.

The drone of the engines disappeared beneath the deluge of my mother's voice in my head. "Five million dollars."

Seriously, Harlow, how bad could it be? You get him off twice a week for a few months. He'll get bored and find a girl-friend. If he wins a few elections—correction—after his parents buy a few elections, you'll know how long you need to stay. You won't pay for anything during your imprisonment, and your money will earn interest. Ca-ching, ca-ching, ca-ching.

I jumped when the landing gear descended.

"Damn, gets me every time," I said. *Please, God, don't let me giggle.*

When Tej flashed his perfect smile, I felt a tingle. "Always sounds like the plane is coming apart."

I felt the familiar bump of a landing, and the plane taxied toward the gate.

CHAPTER 19

TEJ

I HESITATED AT THE CURB AND WATCHED HARLOW HUG A
friend and drive away in a Range Rover.

I was home in Delhi after two years away. The memories of
my last visit haunted me. Images of my ma's eyes swollen from
days of crying, my aunties camped out at the house praying
in Hindu, and my uncle shooing the photographers off our
property. My India had been a prison. When my family announced the engagement of their number-one son, a wedding
was expected. The United States could call off a presidential
inauguration with less fanfare than we could cancel such an
event.

And yet, we did. My parents had issued invitations. The
Prime Minister was coming. The venues had been reserved.
Exotic food had been flown in from around the world. The
finest chefs in India had sharpened their knives and reviewed
their most stellar recipes. Four different bands stood poised to
perform at the reception. The closing act was Parikrama.

Then, disaster. And questions.

Why did someone as lovely as Haiya walk away from the opportunity to marry into one of India's wealthiest families?

Was the girl sick?

Had she suffered a breakdown of some sort?

Had my family lost its money? There had been rumors, what with the devaluation of the rupee.

And, the biggest—the most pervasive—the one question still lingering in the back of everyone's mind: What did the young scoundrel do to cause such a scandal?

Addiction, perversion, abuse—all those subjects ricocheted back and forth like hyperactive ping pong balls. I was fine. I knew the truth. But the situation devastated my poor ma, a woman poised to enter the third stage of her life—matriarchy—the overseer of a brood of grandchildren and future heirs.

It had been two years, but India does not suffer from social Alzheimer's. The past is neither prologue nor history. The past lives in every breath, every whisper, every rumor. Delhi might have been the place of my birth and boyhood, but it was no longer home. It was the museum of my failure, an eternal monument to my disgrace.

My countrymen rushed through the crowded streets, hurrying as they had always hurried, and as they always would into perpetuity though no one ever bothered to explain the frantic activity. *Is it more important in India to be busy or to look busy?*

I could feel myself adapting to the beauty and ruin of my native land. The smell of curry mingled with the stench of death. Everything was different in this land of juxtapositions. Children with distended bellies waved at passing Mercedes limos and begged for coins. I reached into my Kiton sports jacket and dropped rupee notes into as many dirty paws as I could.

"Thank you, bless you," they said.

I ran my hand through my close-cropped hair. It felt weird without the ponytail, but I knew better than to show up at my home looking "unkempt," as Baapa would say. The socks—another acquiescence to my parents—made my shoes feel tight. No more open-necked silk shirts either. This one was pale blue, Sea Island cotton, custom tailored. I'd run my electric razor over my face as soon as the pilot announced our descent. And I'd replaced my flashy Audemars Piguet Royal Oak Offshore Self-winding Chronograph with a less ostentatious Tag Heuer Formula One. I saw no need to parade through the streets wearing a timepiece costing more than a million dollars. I would not see anyone from Atlanta on these grimy streets.

I felt like an imposter.

Two men hawked rickshaw rides. Poverty was stamped on their faces like a birthmark. They would never rise above their station. Indian society was as flexible as concrete. You were born into a caste, you lived in the caste, you died in the caste. Case closed.

I took in the landscape like I was watching a movie. This had been my life. Once upon a time, I wandered these streets, impersonating its denizens. They accepted me as their own. No one hassled me. I was never threatened. Now, somehow removed from my body, I saw children rushing at me like Buckhead kids racing for the country club pool on the first day of summer. I realized I threw away more food in one night than most of them ate in two months—or six. When I was a kid, I took in all the mystery, the smells, the allure of these magic streets. Now, all I saw was the squalor.

Had Delhi changed or had I?

"*Namaskar, Chote Malik, Sab app ki Intezaar kar rehe hai.* Namaste, you Master, they are expecting you at home. My name is Chirag. Your family dispatched me to fetch you to the house." Eighteen, deeply tanned face, thin and gangly, or was he hungry?. "May I take your bags, sir?"

He looked down as he was expected to do. I held my tongue. I wanted to shout, "Stand up straight, man. Look a person in the eye when you speak!" But that was not the way of Delhi. In Atlanta—at least new Atlanta, not the hoop-skirt-ed, throwback sections still desperately clinging to images of Rhett Butler and Mammy—we treated house staff with respect and paid them a living wage. I would not do business with any cleaning service that did not pay at least 50 percent above minimum wage and provide full medical and retirement benefits.

But here in India, my home, servants were taught their place, and very few aspired to rise. Though my parents treated the members of their staff with respect, the class lines never blurred. No one had ever called me by my first name, and only my nanny had ever summoned me with anything other than "Master."

"I've got 'em," I said. Chirag's eye bulged as I hoisted my

cases into the trunk of the BMW. I was neither surprised nor disappointed by my parents' absences. It was late, and age was beginning to win the race. I didn't like to think about the inevitable phone call I would get and the mournful trip I would make one day to put my parents to rest. But it would happen, and then I would be lord of the family estate and heir to the fabled family fortune.

It had always been the three of us, our cozy little family. Maata hadn't been successful in conceiving any other children. A series of miscarriages ruined the delicate system that resided inside her. She carried her "failures" like an anvil, a weighty shame for which she was constantly seeking to make amends. She poured every ounce of love in her tiny body into my baapa and me. We were the center around which she orbited like an adoring moon.

Now, after every sacrifice she had made—after the humiliation she had endured—I had returned. And if the subject of marriage arose, which was inevitable, I would once again smash the porcelain of her fragile dreams with the sledgehammer of my mammoth self-interest. It wouldn't be easy; it was never easy with Ma. I had thirty minutes to fortify myself before dealing with the onslaught. I would not surrender, but the fallout would be difficult and enduring.

"How is ma-ji? Has her health improved?" I asked.

"Sir, yes, sir. She is well. The doctor has gone home."

"Have there been visitors, other than family?"

I held my breath. *Please not a repeat of two years ago. No reporters, no paparazzi. Nothing else about Haiya. That is old news. Nothing to see here. Move along. Find someone else to torment.*

I was back. Would the publicity monster rise like a zombie and feast on us again?

"Sir, just the matchmaker and the astrologist."

"Ah," I said with a derisive chuckle, "so ma-ji is fine."

CHAPTER 20

HARLOW

I'D NEVER FELT MORE LIKE A COUNTRY BUMPKIN THAN WHEN I landed in the Delhi airport. A swarm of vendors charged at me, hawking everything from fruit to scarves.

I fled from them so quickly, I didn't pay attention to any sign. After a headlong rush of two hundred or so feet, I stood in the middle of a swirl of humanity surrounded by the stench of sweat mixed with curry. Completely lost, I tried to keep from crying and I failed.

I wiped the fog from my glasses, oriented myself, found a sign, and bumped my way through the crowd toward the baggage claim. No sooner did I reach for my case than a diminutive man put his hand on mine.

"Take your bag, Missy?" he asked.

"No!" My reaction was too strong. I realized I had shouted. "Thank you, I'm good," I said with less strain.

"You sure? I carry very fine, break nothing," he said.

"I'm sure." I turned to look for the exit.

From the airport window, I saw cabs racing by. They made the Daytona 500 look like a funeral procession. The vintage automobiles careened along apparently without concern for either pedestrians or lane markings.

Lita's face beamed. I almost wept. Her father stood behind her waving with enthusiastic affection. A uniformed driver took my bag, then opened the door of a black Range Rover.

My body was sinking into the seat when a rail-thin girl about six with sandy brown hair and penetrating amber eyes moved to within three inches of my face.

"Hi, my name is Nicole. You must he Harlow, but I know everyone calls you Lo. Can I call you Lo? Everyone calls me Nivi. You can call me Nivi because I think we're going to be friends. Was the flight long? Did you have fun? Is it true they give you alcohol on the plane?"

Lita laughed. "So much for introductions," she said. She placed a gentle hand on the girl's shoulder. "Down, girl. Give Lo a little time to breathe."

"Nice to meet you, Nivi," I said. "Yes, I think we are going to be good friends."

Nivi stuck her tongue out at Lita. "You know Lita shouldn't really be here. She's supposed to be in *puja*, in prayer, with the elders. Girls who are looking for husbands have to go to vigils during wedding season because they're desperate."

She dragged out the last two words in a taunt, then jumped when Lita's squeezed her knee. "Ow!"

"Brat," Lita said.

Both girls laughed at what was obviously a traditional routine. Lita looked at me.

"She's right," Lita said. "I should be there, but I got permission because I told them I had to meet you. The airport can be a bit much, as you see."

"I've seen calmer ant farms," I said.

I began to worry about after the wedding. What would I do? Lita and her dad had fended off the more aggressive vendors, some of whom grabbed potential customers by the arm. I saw a taxi driver snatch a bag from a new arrival and toss it into a car while the case owner screamed in protest. He had no choice but to dive in after his luggage. The driver peeled out while the back door was still open. Not exactly a Chamber of Commerce moment.

Left on my own, I might disappear into the maelstrom of humanity.

We fell into silence on the ride to the family's sprawling estate. I marveled at the sights along the way. They were a frantic mass of beeping horns, roaring motorbikes, and dilapidated rickshaws. The one time I rolled down the window, I quickly zipped it back into place after my nose was assaulted by a mixture of body odor and sewage. The traffic cycloned in tangled knots with no distinct car lanes and no heed to right of way. Cars darted in and out in suicidal maneuvers.

Adolescent beggars lined the streets, pressing their bleeding wounds against the car windows when we stopped at a traffic signal. The flies never stopped their assault on the festering sores. A dark-haired boy of six or seven and dressed in filthy rags smiled at me as if he knew a secret. I sent a silent prayer to whatever God could hear me that his life would somehow find inexplicable blessing.

I wiped a tear from my cheek.

"Lo, it's okay," Lita said, "it's India."

"I'm just tired," I said, but I intentionally shifted to put my back against the window.

Nivi leaned in again. "Did you see any cute guys on the plane?"

"Umm. I don't know."

"Nivi, please! Lo is tired from her trip. Don't badger her."

The youngster scowled. "Okay," She slumped in her seat.

I thought about my travel companion and felt a tingle. *Oh, good God, that's not right.*

"You okay?" Lalita said.

"What? Of course. I'm good."

"You moaned a little, Lo," she said. "Are you feeling poorly? Do you need us to pull over?"

I shook my head then turned back to the scenery. *I don't want to miss a second of this place.*

We passed phone booths, Internet cafes, and posters of Buddha, Hindu gods, and Bollywood stars. Cows mingled with hordes of people. *Why are the streets so crowded?*

Simple math. One-sixth of the world's population crammed into two percent of the inhabitable surface area.

There was no sense of order or logic.

It was sundown before we pulled up to the gated compound. I rolled down the window and caught the scent of jasmine. Candles in hundreds of small clay lamps lit the drive.

"They will burn all night," Lita said. "It's the beginning of Diwali, the festival of lights. It is a time to mark the triumph of goodness over evil and hope over despair."

India in a nutshell. Hope trying to stifle despair without much apparent success.

I noticed marble carvings of Hindu gods and goddesses.

"That's Shiva, the destroyer and Ganapati, the remover of obstacles, right?" I asked.

Lalita nodded.

"I could sure use their help," I said.

Servants moved through the gloriously flowered court-yard and hustled out of the grand house to grab my luggage, to whisk us inside. Bone-crushing fatigue pummeled me as I dragged up three flights of stairs to the guest room. A crimson and gold sari hung from the ceiling and cast a subdued re-laxed feeling over the large suite.

I dropped onto the bed. Fireworks lit to chase off evil spir-its in honor of Diwali spewed rivers of color across the sky outside my window. I felt the concussions more than I heard them. And I realized how alone I was with a friend, certainly, but thousands of miles from my home, unemployed, unat-tached, and in the strangest place I had ever visited.

I did not know the language.

I did not understand the customs.

I was not familiar with the history.

I fell asleep.

CHAPTER 21

TEJ

I WASN'T HAPPY ABOUT THE MATCHMAKER, BUT I WAS PLEASED to know Ma-ji felt well enough to begin meddling in my life once more.

"So, no one else, just the matchmaker and the astrologer?" I asked.

"Not yet, sir—" He stopped a little too quickly. Chirag came from old servant stock, but he was not old school. In my youth, a servant would never have made such a slip. They saw nothing, they heard nothing, and most importantly, they said nothing.

"Out with it," I said. *Odd, the patrician authoritarian tone came back so quickly.*

"I overheard talk of several requests from prominent families who are most interested in your arrival. I believe they would like to arrange a meeting."

"That didn't take long," I said.

"Pardon, sir." Chirag's brow had broken out in a sweat –

and not from the heat. "I have overstepped. I should never have said anything."

"That's fine, Chirag," I said. "No one will ever know anything about our conversation."

"Thank you, sir."

But it had not taken long, not for India where people still spoke of the British occupation as if it had happened last Wednesday. Two scant years ago, many a mummy sang a different tune. I was damaged goods. I would never find a suitable Indian mate. And they *certainly* would never allow a child of theirs to consider a marriage with someone like the rakish, obviously diabolical Tej Mayur.

But now, someone—several someones—wanted a meeting. And not to swap recipes for chicken marsala. I did not know whether to be pleased or disgusted.

"The communications lifted your maataji's spirits considerably," Chirag said. "Just the other day, one of the maids heard her singing—" He stopped again. Old customs die hard.

"Thank you, Chirag."

&

"I do not understand," I had said. "I thought you were all for this marriage."

Haiya's expression was haughty, not the same one she had displayed months earlier when she appeared before me as my fiancée for the first time. Then, she'd feigned a submissive demeanor. She'd spoken of her desire to serve me, to fulfill my every need, to satisfy my every desire, to make me a father of sons. Now, her face nearly cracked with cynicism.

"I thought you were going to inherit your baapa's estate,"

she said.

"I am—"

She continued her rant. "I thought you would live in your familial home in Delhi. I was to be mistress of the house. Now I find you want to move to America where people darker than the darkest untouchable roam the streets. They are elected to high office."

"America is a great land. We can be very happy there. I know—"

"You know *nothing*!" Her voice morphed into the screech of an angry hawk. "You know nothing of dreams! You know nothing of what I have endured! You know nothing about women!"

Arguing with an irrational person is hard. Arguing with an irrational, tradition-minded Indian woman is like trying to belly surf on razor blades.

"Please help me understand what I have done wrong."

Her nostrils flared. Her puffy eyes glistened. "You were going to be someone of note, a man of substance. We were going to be the toast of Delhi, the power couple of our generation. You have thrown it all away to become a common laborer, someone not worthy to take my coat much less to take me to bed."

I decided it was not the moment to mention I'd already accomplished the latter several times, with significant success. Instead, I went with the age-old male response. "What?"

"You are not going to oversee your baapa's oil and mineral holdings. You are not going to manage his banking interests. You are not going to watch over the expansion of his import-export business. No, you are going to do what only commoners do, the dirty people in the street with their little fires and their pathetic pots."

"Haiya, darling,"—I tried not to gag—"I intend to be a chef."

"Call it what you will," she said. "You are going to America to be a cook. And you will be going alone."

♦

Night had fallen by the time we arrived at Xanadu, the family summer home in South Delhi. A spotlight blazed into the sky as a greeting.

It's not a movie premiere, I thought.

We drove along the driveway toward the entrance of the stately white mansion. Our home was in West End Greens, the prestigious address we shared with some of New Delhi's most distinguished families. For a lot of reasons, I preferred Xanadu to our country estate, although it wasn't as opulent. It was closer to civilization with its proximity to the airport and shopping. My dad, a huge fan of Asian history, named the idyllic estate after the summer palace of the Mongolian general Kublai Khan, the grandson of Genghis Khan. The ten-acre manicured lawn, large water feature, and giant white pillars beckoned to me. I remembered a few unauthorized summer parties I'd thrown when my parents traveled abroad. One had left the lasting reminder of a small crescent-shaped scar on my left thigh from a game of beer pong gone awry.

When I caught sight of the imposing white doors for the first time, I realized how tired I was. I wanted to release the tension by relaxing in the marble shower and steam sauna in my room, then sink into the deep double-king bed. Tomorrow morning, I would take a few laps in the indoor pool and eat breakfast on the veranda.

My baapa's eyes lit up when I made my way past the doorman. Not even the most loving Indian parent would greet a child at the door, as it was not proper. "Welcome, beta, welcome," he said. We embraced in a long hug.

"Baapa, it's late. You didn't have to wait up."

"What kind of baapa does not greet his only son?" he asked. I remembered all the times he waited for me to return from my adventures, never to reprimand, only to ensure I was home safely and occasionally to compare my stories with the misadventures of his own youth.

I stood back to study him. Except for a little more salt than pepper in his beard and a vague tiredness in his eyes, he hadn't changed too much in the two years since I'd last seen him. Maybe a little frail, a little less steady on his feet. I squeezed his arm, thankful that he looked okay and silently vowing to visit more. "It's so good to see you, Baapa."

He nodded toward the table where one of the servants had left a pot of tea. Out of the shadows, a uniformed servant appeared to pour.

We sat. "So, how's Bombay Baby?" he asked.

I could see the pride in his eyes and hear the eagerness in his voice. He had always admired the Western World, the independent ways, the die-hard spirit. "You are doing a new thing, I hear. Frozen foods? That's it?"

It was good to be home. We sipped white Darjeeling tea. I closed my eyes and inhaled the delicate, nutty aroma and glanced around the room. The tablecloth was new with specks of gold filaments set off in a maze of patterns. But the delicate gold-spun teapot, with an etching of cobalt blue, was a family heirloom I had seen almost every morning of my youth.

"We are currently launching our line of frozen foods. In fact, we just shipped our first orders." I laughed. "Hopefully, all the packages are going in the right direction. I was checking on things during my flight."

His eyes twinkled as he joined in with my laughter. "We're proud of you, my son. Your mummy talks about you nonstop to anyone that will listen." He took a sip of tea. "I wish we had time tomorrow to go to the horse races."

I nodded. I missed the races with my baapa. "How's Ma? Still better, I hope?"

"She's stronger every day. It just takes longer to get over things when you get to be our age."

I'd feel better when I could see for myself, although I suspected she was tough as ever. Most likely, she was suffering more from my single status than from any pain or weakness. Still, the strain in her normally cheery voice when we talked on the phone bothered me. She'd spent her life worrying over others. It was my turn to worry over her.

"Rest up tonight, son." He stood, a dismissal. "Tomorrow, we will talk at length."

"Good night, Baapa."

"Good night, beta."

I got to the cascading staircase before he spoke again, and his words stabbed in my stomach.

"Tomorrow, we will talk about your wedding."

CHAPTER 22

HARLOW

I SAT UP. SOMEONE WAS IN THE ROOM.

A shadow. "Are you asleep?" A familiar voice.

"I'm awake, Lita," I said. "Sorry I crashed."

"No problem," she said. "I just wanted to sit with you, you know."

"One last time?" I asked.

She chuckled. "Something like that."

A crescent moon hung over the yard, a sickle of white in an ebony sky.

"It's all happening so fast," she said. "I don't even know who they are going to pick for me."

"You sure you want to go through with this?" I touched her shoulder. "If you want, we can jump on a plane. I'll hide you in Atlanta."

"You know I can't do that," she said. "This is my world, my parents' world. It's the way we do things."

"Do you ever think about *him*?" I asked.

"No," she said. "Why should I? He obviously moved on. I will too."

She didn't talk much about her first love, but she had not forgotten about it. I could tell his memory still stung.

"I'm going to miss you," I said. "Miss us. I'm not even sure what I'm supposed to do now. I mean, if you ever come back to the States, we can't exactly go out cruising the bars."

"No kidding. I'm going to be someone's wife. I hope whoever he is, he doesn't hate me too much."

"Or have a hairy back," I said.

We both cringed. "Eeeeeeeeew."

"Seriously. What's not to love? You are the complete package, honey. And probably my only real friend."

She pushed me back into the bed and tucked me in. "Rest," she said. "We have a busy day tomorrow. I need my bestie to be sharp when we go shopping with Daddy's money!"

I woke the next morning to the warmth of the sun beaming through the windows. The estate grounds were breathtaking, with lush green vegetation and bursting red and yellow marigolds. I was glad to be here for Diwali when India was its most joyous, purest self, when it honored the transcendent good in everyone. I tried to do that without much success.

Excitement trumped my jetlag as we piled into the back seat of the Range Rover. The driver spun onto the main road and floored it. He took every curve at full speed. I felt the back end fishtail twice.

"Is he trying to kill us?" I asked.

Lita laughed. "Honey, he's driving slow out of respect for

my honored guest."

The driver aimed the car into a tiny gap in traffic. No way could he make it. We cut back to our side of the road with five feet to spare. At the end of every curve, I was glad to be alive. All around us, other drivers moved as recklessly as ours.

Despite the imminent threat to my mortality, I loved everything. Even as I screamed in fear, my heart shrieked in delight, *Look, Daddy, I am in India!*

Men and women filled the streets in a moving, pulsing rainbow of purple, crimson, and tangerine. They carried baskets and bundles. They balanced boxes on their heads while vendors called to no one and everyone, all at the same time in excited voices.

India was rush hour downtown Atlanta on steroids. Shrill voices competed with beeping car horns and the clanging bells of bicycles and carts. The frenzy outside my window pumped adrenaline through my veins.

A man urinated in the street.

"Gross," I said.

"Happens all the time," Lita said. "But, gross, right?"

One by one, people stepped over sleeping bodies. *I hope they are asleep.* People played cards next to tables laden with trinkets for sale.

I pointed to a store sign. *We will clean out your ears.* "Seriously?" I laughed.

"Don't knock it 'til you've tried it," Lita said and cackled.

Lita's mother and other family members were already inside when we arrived at the dress shop. Two *mausiis*—aunties—and three-year-old cousin Gita joined in the fun of making the all-important trousseau choices.

The frantic activity of Diwali only fueled their joy. Shop-keepers bustled to prepare as customers seeking gifts and par-ty favors streamed in and out.

The store clerk greeted us.

"*Pranam, Aap ki Swagat hai.* I am Sima."

"What did she say?" I asked Lita.

"Greetings and welcome to our place."

New Delhi society was abuzz with the news of Lita's wed-ding. Her high-ranking Baljekar family commanded respect. Any mention of the impending event sped through the gos-sip circles. Surely, Lita's husband-to-be was another near-roy-al. There were whispers, but no one knew. Whoever he was, everyone knew he would be wealthy, educated, of high lin-eage, and fair-skinned.

Lita leaned over and whispered. "I know what you're think-ing."

"Really?"

"You think all this caste stuff is crap."

She was right, but the same obsession with coloring still showed up in some of the elite, well-established African American families in the States.

"It's not new to me," I said. "Just hard to believe it's so bla-tant here."

The oldest tests in the Black world: the paper bag test and the ruler test. To be "in," your skin needed to be lighter than a paper sandwich bag and your hair as straight as a ruler.

"It's an important trait in many castes," she said.

I knew too well. My mom had grown up during a time

when you could be accepted into the sacred inner circle only if you passed the paper bag or ruler test. Sophia was proud of her frothy light brown complexion.

I pushed the color wheel out of my head. "What is that delightful smell?"

"Would you like some malpuas?" Sima clapped her hands, and a girl in a bright yellow sari raced to the front. She extended a tray bearing the traditional banana-and-coconut dessert. Then she handed out cool, cucumber-scented towels.

"Thank you," I said.

Lita declined the treat but said, "I can't wait to try the karanji."

That's a surprise. Lita obsessed about her figure. She was always fearful of what she called "the maataji spread." Desserts made of ghee were not part of her usual fare.

I turned to eye the sea of rich and colorful fabrics set out for Lalita's perusal.

Shopping, my favorite pastime.

I picked up a sari in a luscious shade of ruby red. The finely woven silk slid easily through my fingers and settled into rich puddles of fabric onto my lap. I handed Lalita another sari from the collection, and she ran a gentle hand across the violet fabric, then one in green, then gold.

"Do you have a favorite, dear?" her mother asked. The pride in her eyes was obvious.

"They are all so beautiful. It makes it hard to choose. Don't you love the beading on this one?" She reached for a sari in seafoam green.

"And *this* color's great for you." I handed her a silky armful of vibrant peacock blue, a compliment to her complexion. How would she choose? Good news: Indian brides made multiple wardrobe changes on their wedding day. She could pick several.

She smiled at me and nodded. "I like it. Very nice." But instead of moving to the mirror to try the color against her skin, she watched her mother. My heart ached for Lita and for her dear Mama Darpita.

"Oh, here's one you have to try." Darpita handed her daughter an ivory *lehenga choli*. I'd seen Lalita wear lehenga cholis for events in Atlanta. The lower half of the two-part garment, lehenga, flowed from the waist to the floor and was four-to-five meters long. The choli blouse featured an intricate neckline in the current fashion. This lehenga was stunning with a silk pleated skirt embroidered in red and gold. I loved the antique design woven through the fabric. The cut of the lehenga was modern and sexy. It would leave Lalita's slender back and midriff bare.

"Okay. I'll try it on. Harlow, come with me."

"*Kya aap meri madat kur sakte hain*?" Lita called for help and signaled for assistance from the young attendant, who was waiting respectfully outside the dressing room.

Once inside, Lita undressed.

"How is Mama Darpita doing?" I asked. "Really?"

Lita smiled at my use of the affectionate name. "She has good and bad days. Removing the breast supposedly gave her a better chance at . . ." The words just stopped coming out.

I touched her arm. "And, how are you?"

Lita shook her head. She was going to be a gorgeous bride

in whatever sari she chose, but one without the facial sparkle a girl hoped to display on her wedding day. She was determined to go through with the wedding. I wanted to help, but I didn't know how.

"Hey, enough about me," she said. "Tell me about you. How's work? I know it must have been near impossible to get out of town. How did she-devil take it?" Lita picked up a sari. "She'd better back off. She doesn't want to lose her number one programming rock star." The luxurious folds of the eggplant-colored sari with thin gold trim already looked tailored. "Whaddaya think?"

"I hate you," I said. We dissolved in giggles. "But I don't have to worry about the she-devil anymore."

CHAPTER 23

TEJ

"WE WILL TALK ABOUT YOUR WEDDING" WERE THE FIRST WORDS I heard in my head when I awakened.

I'd rather have a colonoscopy, I thought. *Without anesthesia.*

But I was a son of India. My baapa deserved my respect.

On the other hand, I am a grown-ass man, and I deserve my freedom.

This was not going to be easy.

I knew the argument. I'd been allowed to pursue my dream, to build on my skill. But the time for chasing my pleasure was in the past. It had gone on long enough. Now, I needed a wife at my side, a companion. Someone to help me, someone to bear grandchildren.

Ah *grandchildren,* the magic word. Once a man had seen his first grandson, his work as a father was finished, his rest earned. He could spend the rest of his days living where he wanted, doing what he pleased, and getting closer to God.

I loved my baapa. I wished I could release him, tell him to go, travel, study, do *whatever he wished*. Why should he be denied a life of peace simply because I had not checked a box and installed a wife in my Atlanta condo on the other side of the globe?

I toweled off from the shower, dressed, and went downstairs with all the enthusiasm of a man approaching the guillotine. I was hugging Baapa when Ma entered.

She was on the mend, but her eyes looked tired, and she was aging faster than I wanted to accept. Her face was pale, her complexion more ashen than alabaster. She'd lost too much weight. Although professionally pinned by her dressers, her emerald sari showed her shrunken figure.

"My dear, beta." She offered her cheek, which I kissed. She smelled of cinnamon and gajra flowers, the delicate white jasmine flowered garlands that some Indian women used to adorn their hair. Her small frame seemed more fragile than usual. "How handsome you are. So like a Bollywood hero." She cradled my face in her hands. "Are you eating? You look thin, too thin."

My heart warmed at the enthusiasm in my ma's voice; she was happy to see me.

"You look well. Color in your cheeks," I said. "Have you been sunbathing on the veranda? What will the neighbors say—you in a bikini?"

"You scoundrel, for shame!" She lightly swatted at me with her small hands. I'd missed her more than I thought.

We sipped tea and ate breakfast in relative silence. Then Baapa said, "There are plans in place."

Ma's turn. "Isha has found a perfect bride. The girl is fair."

Which translated "light-skinned, not to be mistaken for a laborer or an American black."

"She is comely," Ma continued.

Which translated "full in the bosom, hips wide enough to birth a child but not elephantine."

"And soft-spoken. She's from the Lahiri family up north in Jammu. You two played together as children. I'm not sure if you recall. Of course, if you don't like her, you can help choose someone else. There are many interested families."

I felt like a horse at auction. *What am I? A bid for the prize stallion? He is sleek, fast, and has all his teeth. Better still, his organs function, and he'll knock your daughter up in record time.*

Perhaps she did not know, but Ma had just repeated the speech she gave right before they announced my disastrous engagement to the woman who thought Emeril Lagasse was someone who wore a paper hat at McDonald's.

"I know what you're thinking . . ." Ma was talking like a carnival barker trying to convince me to come inside the tent to see the hoochi-coochi show ". . . but you're wrong. She's university educated from the States. She studied bio-mechanical engineering. Graduated at the top of her class. You'll be a happy man, beta. Isha was very helpful."

For the price you paid her, I bet she was.

"Oh, and she plays the oboe."

"Isha plays the oboe?"

Baapa got the joke and blew a little tea out of his nose.

Ma remained clueless. "Why would we care if the matchmaker plays a musical instrument, dear? No, your intended plays, quite well, I am told. We worked very hard, and we are quite pleased, but you have the ultimate veto."

So, I can get any color or weight or style of bowling ball I want, even if I have absolutely no desire to have a bowling ball.

"Does this lovely side of mutton have a name?" I asked.

Baapa's voice was uncharacteristically harsh. "Beta, show respect, always. You have lost your manners in America!"

I bowed my head, genuinely ashamed. "I am sorry, Baapa," I said. And to Ma. "Please forgive me."

She did not care. I was not sure she noticed as excited as she was. Again, and this time with more courtesy, I asked, "What is this woman's name?"

Ma was about to answer when a servant entered. "Pardon me, mistress. You have a guest."

Ma sprang from her seat. "It must be the priest," she said. "He has determined the date. Hurry, hurry. Oh, this is so exciting, so very exciting."

He was a short, pudgy man dressed in the traditional garb of a Hindu priest. "The timing is perfect. Everything is set. We have a most auspicious date and time for the wedding," he said.

What is he talking about?

I had accompanied Ma out of propriety and politeness. Time to be more direct. "Excuse me, what is he talking about?"

Baapa's voice assaulted me from behind. "Your wedding, my son. Everything is arranged. I thought we had been very clear about your visit."

I fought for calm. "I came to visit Ma. Nothing more."

Baapa's face remained placid and his voice level. "Your presence here represents your assent to the proceedings. When you agreed to come visit, your ma began to make arrangements. If you did not intend to cooperate, you should not have come."

I must have looked like someone who stepped barefooted on a Lego. "Baapa," I said. "You told me that Ma was ill—"

"What I told you was she was stricken with an undiagnosed condition. As it turns out, she was mostly heartbroken. The fiasco with Haiya damaged our family's standing and reputation. It has been two years. Only now are some very old friends beginning to overlook *your* heinous breach of decorum. No one knows what you did to that young woman, the dalliance in which you engaged that led her to abandon a future with our family. But we are certain of one thing: you will not cause us such humiliation again. We have prepared another wedding, though on a slightly smaller scale. And this time, your duty as our son and heir is to see it through."

I opened my mouth. Nothing came out.

"Good," Ma said. "We are agreed. I do dislike disharmony. The priest has agreed with our date, and the astrologer has deemed that everything is in order." She stood and clapped her hands together.

"Oh *mere bete*, I am thrilled. On Saturday afternoon, you will be wed!"

CHAPTER 24

HARLOW

"Pretty!"

We turned to find Gita dancing around with Lita's discarded slip.

"What are you doing here?" Lita laughed and fluffed the little girl's curly hair.

"You could be a ninja, Gita," I said. "You came in like a secret assassin."

Gita screamed and ran out of the dressing room. "Mama, Harlow said ass!"

I bent over to pick up the teddy bear she'd forgotten. I rubbed its worn tummy, gazed at its crooked smile, and blinked back the tear of memory threatening to roll down my cheek. I'd had a bear, soft and brown, something I clutched tightly at night every time my father was gone on a trip. Joshua Bear kept me company. He knew all my secrets. And he told no one.

Joshua had been a gift from Daddy, the man I loved more

than anything, the man who would never see me walk down an aisle. Joshua Bear still sat on my bed. I'm sure a few of my dates—yes, they got to the bedroom, but nothing significant happened—thought it was a little creepy for a grown woman to have a stuffed toy, but it was all I had to remind me of Daddy.

Gita recovered from her horror and came back for her bear. She stayed after I promised not to say any more naughty words, and Lita gave her a vote on the final three saris. Armed with a beautiful trousseau, Lita left the shop and was one step closer to meeting the man of her dreams.

We went from shop to shop. Mama Darpita stopped from time to time. She needed a little rest, but when one of us offered to stay behind and help, she always waved us along.

"I'll catch up," she said.

The difference between that dear woman and Sophia.

Had Lita and I swapped places—if Sophia were in the enviable mother of the bride spot—how the emphasis would have changed. It would not be Harlow's day, not in the slightest. After a cursory glance at whatever I had selected, the entire gaggle of shoppers would have served as a command audience as Sophia modeled dress after dress, one design, then another.

We would have been forced to respond to the same questions for each outfit. "Does this color flatter my skin?" or "I think the cut makes my rear look a little big. What do you think?" or "Would it be too daring to lower the décolletage?"

It would never have occurred to Sophia not to show her breasts, even in a society whose distance from what she dominated in Georgia was more cultural than geographical. Women in India were expected to be glowing, not gaudy. Exotic, not exposed. Luxuriant, not loud. Radiant, not risqué. They might stand at the center of their husband's world, but they were never supposed to occupy the center of attention.

When Lita and I returned to her parents' home, we were exhausted but too elated to rest. An hour by the pool and three mimosas helped lower the adrenaline level. About 4:00 p.m., my dear friend hugged me, and we departed for our own rooms for a little nap time.

"It was a great day, Harlow," she said. "Thank you for being part of it. You're the best."

As I watched my best friend wobble to her room since she had not stopped after the third cocktail, I looked up at the ornately painted ceiling and spoke a quiet prayer.

"I hope one day I'll find a guy who thinks that."

CHAPTER 25

TEJ

"My son, do you remember living in London?"

I had not thought of London in a long time. It was always chilly and damp, and I was always happy.

"Were we poor then?" I asked.

Baapa chuckled. "Hardly. We were fine. Why do you ask?"

"Well, Ma cooked every meal herself. I helped, but we had no staff. I always assumed we were poor, like everyone else."

"What else do you remember, my son?"

"You were gone a lot. Ma always said you were studying. Whenever I was not with my friends, I helped Ma in the kitchen. She wouldn't let me handle the knives, but I stirred a lot. And I remember I washed a lot of vegetables. No matter what we cooked, whenever we finished, Ma always said it was 'parfait.'"

"You have a good memory," he said, "but some of your context is a little off."

"How's that?"

"Your ma had taken cooking classes. She loved it so much that we dismissed our cook. She wanted to handle everything herself, to perfect her skills. It is, no doubt, where you developed your love of cuisine. When she finally let you take part in more of the preparation, she said you handled a knife like you were born with one in your hand."

"We lived in a dingy little place, didn't we?"

"We lived in a luxury apartment with three baths and a magnificent kitchen," he said. "What was dingy was London. You are confusing the weather with our living circumstances."

"I just remember being cold all the time."

"Well," he said, "on average, it's about thirty degrees colder in London at all times than it is in Delhi, quite an adjustment for a youngster used to running barefoot and playing in the creeks."

"How long were we in London?"

"A little over three years," he said. "We got there when you were barely two and left before your sixth birthday."

"We came home because grandfather died, right?"

"Yes."

"And why didn't we return to London."

I'd never seen my father exhibit much emotion. For the most part, he was a stoic man, someone who kept his own counsel. He was affectionate in his own way, but his idea of doting on a child was a pat on the head and a word of encouragement. Now, his deep-set eyes reflected pain—no—remorse.

"We stayed to attend to the family's matters, your grand-father's multiple interests. You know I am the firstborn. My duty, first and always, was to the family. Whatever else I may have wanted or needed to do was put aside. It is our way, the way of India."

"What was it you wanted to do, Baapa?"

He was quiet for a long time, staring out the back window at the expansive gardens his father had paid to construct and the dozen or so laborers who attended them with skill and precision. When he turned back to me, a solitary tear migrated from the corner of his eye, trickled to his jaw, then fell to its death on the marble floor.

"We were in London for my education," he said. "I had completed medical college and my internship in India. I had been accepted into the Royal College of Surgeons for a fellowship. I had only three months left to complete my training when we returned to India."

"You are a doctor?" I asked.

"I was," he said. "I abandoned my license many, many years ago."

"Was that your dream?" I asked. "Your passion?"

He looked at me with doleful eyes. "Beta," he said, "regardless of what the younger generation says about passion and finding your destiny, the only thing that matters to a son of India is the duty to family. You have had your fun. You have proven your ability as a chef and a businessman. But now, your duty calls."

An energy sapping weight settled on my shoulders. I felt the fissure cracking my heart apart. I tried to hide my anguish, but Baapa must have seen it. He moved next to me with his aging arm around my waist and spoke in his typical reassuring manner.

"Do not despair, Beta. Love will find a way."

CHAPTER 26

HARLOW

"This is it, Lita," I said.

"I haven't been this nervous . . . well . . . ever," she said.

We were in Lita's room, now dressed and ready, both in saris and sandals. Lita looked radiant. I felt a little like a stuffed sausage and kept picking at areas of cloth I felt were clinging.

"Relax, Lo," Lita said. "You're just not used to it. Let the fabric settle. It'll find its flow."

"I would just be happy if it didn't settle into a river of cellulite. I feel so exposed in this."

"Girl, you have not worn anything so non-revealing since you were twelve years old. If you wore that in Atlanta, people would mistake you for a docent at some museum." She looked at the clock on her bedside table. "It's time," she said.

"You okay?" I asked.

"Will be, as long as you are there," she said. "It's not the guy of my dreams, but maybe this will turn out to be a dreamy guy."

"You know you haven't told me his name," I said.

"Didn't find it out until about an hour ago. I met him years ago when we were kids, long before we left for America."

"What's he like?"

"Well, I haven't seen him in, oh, ten years or so, but back in the day, he was pretty hot stuff. Good looking, smart, significantly good hair, and the single most important attribute in any guy."

I gasped. "Lita, that is not like you at all, you tramp!"

Lita hooted. "Oh Lord, Harlow, you should see your face. You think I have any interest in my soon-to-be-fiancé's physical attributes? You seen one, you seen 'em all. No, ole VC has the one thing every young girl wants more than a Georgia boy wants peanuts in his RC Cola."

"What's that?" I asked, genuinely confused.

"Money, babe. Word has it he is loaded with daddy's money."

"You said 'VC.' That all you know, his initials?"

Lita smirked. "Oh no, I have the full name, and I will only disclose it to those who pledge their undying fealty to me."

"I do so pledge, Milady."

"Will you honor my every wish, fulfill my every command, and drink copious amounts of alcohol with me if this guy turns out to be Jo-Jo, the Dog-Faced Boy?"

"Along with a sword upon which to impale yourself at the conclusion of this sordid and sad ballad," I said.

We fell over on the bed, giggling like schoolgirls. Lita grew suddenly serious.

"For real, Harlow, if this guy is Uggo McUgster, you're gonna have to help me escape."

"You do have a way with words. And you know you can always count on me."

"Thanks, you've always been a good friend."

"And I always will be." I paused for a second while Lita smoothed out her rumpled sari. "So, give it up, What's his name?"

She looked a little coy. "The name won't mean much to you because you ain't 'round from these here parts." She grinned at her Southern impersonation.

"C-plus," I said. "What's the name?"

"He is from a very prominent bunch. His father owns stuff everywhere. The family is very well thought of, highly regarded."

"You've mentioned that more than once. Name or I put a scratch on your red Jimmy Choos."

"Vikram Chatwal."

CHAPTER 27

TEJ

I STOOD OUTSIDE THE DOOR WHILE ISHA WENT IN TO ENSURE everyone was ready.

I heard her summons from the other side. "You may come in now."

I wore an emerald-green embellished sherwani with churidar and brunette-colored shoes.

Only one item remained. The introduction.

There were a dozen or so people in the room as I expected. A mother and a father were there, assorted aunts, sisters, hangers-on. But my attention went immediately to two young women standing in the center of the group. Both were dressed in traditional Indian attire. The one to my right was attractive. But the young lady to my left took my breath away.

Radiant in a shimmering sari, she stood with the elegance of a queen without projecting either haughtiness or arrogance. She was surrounded by natives, but she was clearly not

135

from India. And she seemed vaguely familiar.

I should be so lucky. I moved forward and extended my hand.

The woman stood. "Hello again, Tej," she said. "This is a surprise."

I immediately knew the voice from the airplane. "Harlow? I did not recognize you at first."

Her smile sparkled. "I look a little better with some sleep, a shower, and some nicer clothes." She twirled. "But I don't think you're here for me." She jerked her head to the side.

"My Lord," Isha said. "This is your bride. May I present Lalita Baljekar."

Isha indicated the shorter woman to my right. I took the woman's hand while trying not to be distracted by the original focus of my interest.

Harlow is stunning.

"Good afternoon," the young woman said. "My name is Lalita. My friends and family members call me Lita."

"Good afternoon, Lita," I said.

She looked at Harlow. "You two know each other?" Lita's voice carried the unmistakable note of feminine suspicion and jealousy.

"We met on the plane," Harlow said. "I woke up halfway across the Atlantic, and Tej was sitting next to me."

"Tej?" Lita whirled toward Isha. "I do not understand," she said. "When you told me I would marry Mr. Chatwal, I assumed you meant Vikram. I know you said Vikram. Who is this? As far as I know, there is no brother."

I'd never seen the grand maven of Indian matrimony

rattled. "But this is Vikram," she said. "I'm sure there is a perfectly reasonable explanation." She turned to me in confused horror as she envisioned her matchmaking empire crumbling around her. "Isn't there?"

I saw the panic in the matchmaker's eyes and smiled on the inside. *Even the great Isha has her breaking point.*

I decided not to milk the situation despite the strong temptation.

"Absolutely," I said. I looked at Lita. "And I apologize for the confusion. You see, when I went to America a little over two years ago, I decided to reinvent myself. My full name is Vikram Tej Mayur Chatwal. Everyone here in India knows me as Vikram or Vik, but everyone in Atlanta—my new home—knows me only as Tej Mayur, even my best friends. Just in case someone in the States knew of my father and his considerable business interests, I wanted to remain as anonymous and independent as possible. It was a harmless fabrication, a little business nom de plume."

Lita's lids narrowed, the slits of a cobra ready to strike. "And you two had never met before you flew over?"

I glanced at Harlow. Her eyes bulged in horror. I could tell she wanted to shake her head, but she was frozen in fear.

"No," I said. "We just shared some space in the air." In my peripheral vision, I saw Harlow's shoulder go limp in relief.

Isha let out a theatrical exhale. "Well, that was interesting and more than enough drama for one day. Let's give these two a little chance to get to know one another. Come, come, everyone out except for the chaperones. Scoot! Let's go."

Mother hen Isha shooed all the little chicks out of the

room, then turned before she exited. Her whisper was low and venomous. "You should have alerted me about the name. Brides and their families get very skittish, especially around the time of introductions. Did you see how Lita's mother recoiled? And she knows your parents very well. I will have to spend a considerable amount of time convincing her that you have nothing to hide. Are you telling me the truth?"

"There is nothing nefarious here, Isha, I assure you," I said. "I simply wanted to make it on my own. I did not mean to cause any consternation."

Isha's intense gaze shifted to a "happy picnic look" as she whirled back toward the others who were talking amongst themselves. She smiled and spoke in an animated voice. "Everyone have a good time."

When she closed the door, I looked at Lita. "Well, what else would you like to know about me?"

CHAPTER 28

HARLOW

I CLUTCHED A TEDDY BEAR AND DANCED AROUND THE ROOM, singing at the top of my lungs my favorite song from *My Fair Lady.*

"I could have danced all night . . . and still have begged for more."

I tripped on a casually discarded shoe and sprawled onto the floor. Fortunately, my huge stuffed partner broke my fall. Lita burst into laughter.

"That's not the first time Baloo has saved someone," she said. "Are you all right?"

"Nothing hurt but my pride," I said. "And Lord knows I have very little of that left anyway."

"Well," she said, "you might not be a great dancer, but at least you have a little of your dignity intact."

She turned toward the window and gazed into the darkness.

Her hand brushed her cheek. I stood, looked briefly at the little hole I'd torn in my jeans, then walked over and hugged Lita from behind.

"What's up, kid?" I asked. "You should be the one dancing around the room."

"And risk the chance you might knock one of my teeth out with your stunning moves? I don't think so," she said. "You know, a girl wants to look her best at her wedd—" She broke off, and tears streamed from her eyes.

"What the hell, Lita?" I asked. "I figured you'd be thrilled. You sounded so good when you called me a few days ago. I mean, this is how it's done over here, right?"

Lita walked to her nightstand and yanked out a handful of tissues. She wiped her eyes and sat on the bed. She wasn't sad, but nothing about her countenance radiated joy. Her shoulders slumped. Her jaw was tight. She looked . . . disappointed.

"Do you not think he is handsome?" I asked.

"Oh my God, are you kidding? He looks like a Greek god. Gorg, absolutely totes gorg," she said.

Confusion filled my expression. "Well, from everything you told me, his family is loaded. And from what I know about his restaurant in Atlanta, he's killing it in the States. You'll never want for anything."

"True," she said. "The Chatwals are one of the wealthiest families in the subcontinent. They are the closest thing we have to royalty. Marrying me into the Chatwal clan is, like they say, an upgrade for my entire family. Our status will skyrocket, and the effect will go on for generations. It's just not, ah, not the way I thought."

Her voice quavered. She twirled her hair, a sure sign she was upset. She was waiting for me to fix this, and there was no available solution.

"Did you imagine you'd fall head over heels in love with whoever walked through the door?" I asked. "You've talked to your folks. They had an arranged marriage. Didn't they say things like, 'It takes time,' and 'Love will grow,' and, you know, stuff?"

A small smile tried to crack the edges of Lita's mouth. It morphed into a soft smirk. "You know they did. And you would not believe how embarrassing it is to listen to your mother when she says, 'Give yourself to him in devotion and duty. Passion may grow.' I mean, that is spectacularly gross."

Echoes of Sophia licked at my brain. *Seriously, Harlow, how bad could it be? You get him off twice a week for a few months.*

"Yes, I would," I said. "But Tej—I mean, Vik seems like a really decent guy. And, as you mentioned, he is ridiculously hot."

Lita shrugged. "Well, if I didn't think it would kill my parents, you could have him."

I felt something—something strange. A twinge? A flutter? It was indistinct and vague, but something moved inside me, and it wasn't the curried chicken we'd had for dinner. I blinked hard and continued the discussion. "You want to back out?"

"It's not that," she said. "I agreed to an arranged marriage. It'll be a little weird at first. I mean, think about it, all those weddings you and I have gone to in Atlanta. Everyone standing up at parties and talking about 'Meeting my soulmate' and all that shit. Compared to them, this thing I'm doing seems a little sterile, a little clinical."

"I'm sure young Mr. Chatwal will be more than happy to do a little clinical exam," I said.

I dodged a box of Kleenex. "You're so nasty," Lita said.

"I know," I said, "but I made you smile."

The expression on her face looked more like someone trying to pass a kidney stone, but her eyes had brightened a little.

"That's better," I said.

CHAPTER 29

HARLOW

More than perhaps anyone else—except maybe for mothers—friends understand the value of presence. While an acquaintance will try to cheer you up with an endless string of stories or platitudes, a friend can sit for a long time without saying anything. The simple fact she is sitting in the same room brings the same comfort as the feel of a childhood blanket or the smell of Grandma's special homemade cookies, the ones she made only for you.

I wasn't sure how long we sat. Lita lay on the bed, head propped on three pillows, eyes closed, but I knew she wasn't asleep. I sat on the floor, legs crossed, and waited. However long it took, I was going to be there when my friend decided to talk.

Finally, "Harlow, how come you've never married?"

Somehow, I'd known the question was coming. Well, I suspected Lita would ask something about my life, anything to steer the conversation away from hers. Lita never moved her head; she never opened her eyes.

"And don't you dare lie to me and say no one ever asked you. I know about the guy who plays ball for the Hawks . . ."

"Too tall," I said. "And a little too, ah, experienced, if you get my drift."

"A walking advertisement for a penicillin injection?" she asked.

"Yep," I said.

"But he asked, right?"

"Three times," I said. "Each time right before he invited me to come to his apartment."

I heard a little snort—Lita's self-imposed wall of stoicism was developing cracks. "Then there was the lawyer dude."

"Already married to his work. Loved to talk about his eighty-hour weeks, how he was going to make partner in two years, and that he never had time for his real passion, chess."

"Oh, gag."

"Yep."

"And what's the name of that pompous a-hole? Armstead? Armitage?"

"Addison," I said. "Addison Whitmore."

"That's the one," she said. She sat up and moved her eyebrows up and down with great drama. "He's the one who 'made you a wo-man.'"

"If it had been in the back seat of his daddy's Chevy with some doo-wop music playing, it would have been a scene straight out of a bad Molly Ringwald movie."

"She didn't make any bad movies," Lita said.

"Good point," I said. I opened my mouth to speak, but she interrupted.

"Don't you dare start quoting movies even though 'It's really human of you to listen to all my bullshit.'"

I raised my middle finger. "So, you can quote *16 Candles*, and I can't?"

"Bridal prerogative," she said. After a moment, she asked again, "How come?"

"Well," I said, "since you asked, unless lightning strikes me dead here in the next few weeks, it looks like I'll be trudging down the aisle to hook up with that pompous a-hole."

Lita knew better than to get excited. She could read the lack of enthusiasm in my voice. "Give it up, Harlow."

I told her everything. When I finished my saga, she sat up straighter and assumed an imperious air.

"Well," she said, "I guess if you can only get a measly five million . . ." She couldn't finish with a straight face. Plus, I pounced onto the bed and began to tickle her without mercy.

"You are such a bitch," I said, but I was smiling.

"St–st–stop." She was beginning to beg. "I will pee myself, no lie."

I quit, and we lay on the bed giggling. I rolled over on my back. "I don't want to be like Sophia. She's spent her entire life marrying guys for money. She's been miserable. I mean, it's not like she's living on the street or anything. She's got more money than Carter's got little liver pills, but I don't think she's been in love with anyone ever."

"What about your father?"

A sharp pain hit me directly behind my right eye. I recognized what it was. Not a stroke or anything life threatening. It was my standard reaction to emotional stress, like a migraine encapsulated in a lightning bolt. I knew it would subside after a minute or two. I lay back and closed my eyes. That way, Lita would not see if I started to cry.

"Not sure about that," I said. "I was young when she left, and Daddy never talked about her."

"Ever?"

"Not once from the day Sophia left until the day he died."

"Why did she do it?" Lita asked. "Why did she keep getting married to men she obviously didn't love?"

The pain behind my eye slowly drifted away, replaced by a deep ache in my heart. "I don't know, Lita. I really do not know."

CHAPTER 30

TEJ/VIK

THE PARTY WAS RAGING BY THE TIME I ARRIVED. I SHOULD HAVE been more punctual. Future grooms usually met party guests at the door with all the "So nice of you to come," and "Has it really been so many years?" remarks everyone would expect. But I couldn't do it. I'd raged all the way to the mendhi celebration, where the bride is decorated with henna tattoos.

"They are best friends," I said.

My driver turned his head to hear what I said while trying to keep one eye on the road.

"Nothing, sorry," I said. I lowered my voice to a mutter. "I agreed to marry against my will and just to keep peace in the family and to fulfill my bloody duty, and it turns out my fiancé is best friends with a woman I know and like. How does that happen?"

I must have shouted again because the driver turned to look at me at the same time he swerved to avoid a man on a bike.

"Sir?"

"Just please keep your eyes on the road," I said."

"As you wish, sir," he said.

I heard voices in my head. "She's a beauty—Brahmin, well-educated, and she plays the oboe."

I don't care if she can sing all four parts of the hallelujah chorus backward in Spanish!

"She's not Harlow!"

"Pardon, sir. The name's Hussein."

"Thank you, Hussein." I rested a palm on the front head-rest. "Would you do me a favor?"

"Certainly, sir," Hussein said.

"Unless I tell you my pants are on fire, and I need to stop, would you please ignore everything I say until we get to the party? I'm having a bit of a moment back here."

"As you wish, sir. Would you like the privacy screen?"

Not sure why I had not thought of that. "If you would not be insulted, please."

"As you wish, sir."

The glass scrolled up, and I was alone with the voices in my head until we arrived at the party. Against all protocol, I reached into my pocket. All I had was a one-hundred-dollar bill. I slipped it to Hussein when I shook his hand—another etiquette breach—but what the hell.

"Oh, no sir, I could not possibly—"

"Hussein," I said, "there are a lot of people here who know me. There are a lot of people here who do not think I am crazy. That little gift ensures they will never know. Right?"

"As you wish, sir."

The party attacked every sense the second I walked through the front door: wall-to-wall people all in festive attire, the mingled aromas of succulent food and too much perfume, traditional Indian music pulsing through a state-of-the-art sound system. Shouts of "Vikram" and "the blushing bridegroom" reverberated from the walls. Someone shoved a samosa into my mouth and thrust a Star of India drink into my hand.

My heart ached.

I glanced into the great room where a crowd hooted their approval as the painters decorated Lita's hands with the traditional mandala flowers and other designs intended to bring happiness and love to our impending union.

My stomach flipped.

Grin and bear it, old boy. There's no turning—

"Vikram!"

The voice, immediately familiar but strangely out of place, made the hair on the back of my head bristle. I turned, hoping I had either imagined it or was suffering a life-ending embolism.

"Haiya," I said, "you look radiant!"

She was dressed in a sapphire blue sari of a most immodest cut. *How can she breathe?* My first thought was that she'd put on weight. Then, I noticed the distribution. *Enhancement surgery.*

Her arms were around my neck and her pelvis uncomfortably close before I could ward off her assault. "How are you, Vikram? I hear you are the toast of the town in the States. Tell me all about it. How long will you be here? When can we have lunch?"

I wiggled out of her death grip and smoothed my jacket. "So good to see you, Haiya. How are you?"

"I am fabulous," she said. "No longer married. It just didn't take." She moved a little closer and faked a whisper. "He did not have either your skill or your natural assets."

I saw a raised eyebrow from one of the older female guests, so I took Haiya by the elbow and guided her outside into the garden.

"Let's start over," I said. "One, good to see you. Two, I did not know you were married. Three, I would appreciate if you did not advertise about our previous, ah, encounters since this is, as you must know, a party in honor of my impending marriage to Lita."

She laughed, an annoying, jangling titter as phony as her implants. "Oh, Vikram, grow up," she said. "Everyone knows you had me. And,"—her voice raised her voice—"everyone knows I broke our engagement because of your serial infidelities."

The voice I heard from my throat was not something I had used in a long time. It came out as a guttural snarl, the sound of a wounded tiger preparing to detach the head of the next creature it saw.

"Don't ever say that again," I said. "You broke the engagement because you did not want to marry a cook. I believe that's how you put it. Well, I am very happily a cook in the United States, in my own place. And I am very happily there without you."

She backed up like I'd slapped her. This time, she shouted.

"No, I will not sleep with you. Lita is my very good friend."

She stormed off as party guests gawked. I turned to make apologies. Lita was fifteen feet away. When I started to explain, she waved me off.

"Anyone who didn't think she'd make a scene here tonight doesn't know Haiya," Lita said and checked her watch. "Who had four minutes?" She saw a hand from across the yard. "You win the pool. In addition, I'm throwing in a bottle of twenty-year-old Macallan. Enjoy!"

The backyard erupted in laughter and applause.

Lita slid her arm around my waist. "I'm a little disappointed in you."

I sputtered. "Lita, dearest." It was a stretch, but it seemed like the right thing to say. "I didn't. I . . . uh—"

"I'm just messing with you, Vik," she said. "We all threw twenty dollars in a hat and bet on how long it would take that shrew to embarrass herself. We all know she is certifiable. If you'd kept her on the hook for another three minutes, I would have won. I had seven minutes."

Lita kissed me on the cheek and flowed back into the house for more tattooing. She was a sweet girl, not a beauty but pretty in her own way. She had an easy manner. According to Isha, the stars said we'd have a long life, three children, and more of the kind of wealth and status our families had enjoyed across the years.

I wish she didn't look so damn happy. Only a total ass would hurt someone like that.

I needed a drink.

CHAPTER 31

TEJ/VIK

THE BARTENDER WAS POURING TWO FINGERS OF 16-YEAR-OLD A. H. Hirsch Reserve over a solitary ice cube when I felt a heavy hand on my shoulder. "See how the mighty have fallen. The legendary Vikram Chatwal, God's gift to women, surrendering to marriage."

"Hello, Amar," I said.

"You know the groom's not supposed to be hanging out by the bar alone," he said.

"Well, I'm not alone anymore, am I, old friend?"

Drinks in hand, we walked out the back and wandered through an expansive garden. We sat on a bench and listened to the thrum of the music. Amar slipped off his jacket and placed it carefully to the side. I spoke into the night. "I can't do this, man. It just isn't right."

He clapped my shoulder. "Jitters, *bhayya*. My brother, it'll be great!" I could feel his eyes on me. "I've never met a groom who wasn't a little freaked. Everything will work out fine." He paused a little too long. "And if it doesn't, you've done your duty to your family."

"That the only important thing?"

Amar looked around. "What do you think, my friend?"

I kicked at a loose rock. "There are a lot of fish in the sea. I think I'd like to troll a little longer. What if someone comes along who wows my sorry ass?"

I could see Harlow's face in my head.

"The price you pay as a son of India," he said. "No matter how it works out."

"You know what," I said. "One of us needs to grow a set of balls, and I nominate you. Be the first modern groom in our family."

"Huh?"

"Stand up to your parents. Tell them you want to pick your own woman. Other families in India are coming around to the twenty-first century. Why not ours?"

"You talk mighty tough for a guy who crumpled like a shoebox in a rainstorm. Rumor has it you caved inside twenty-four hours after you got here."

I nodded. "True, but I have no moral fiber. You, on the other hand—you, bhayya—you can change everything. You can free the men of this family from the tyranny of Isha and everyone like her."

My cousin shrugged. "I'd like that," he said, "but I'm not the family star. We can't all be like you, man, with beautiful women throwing themselves at us." He sipped his whiskey. Hh'd gone more than a few gulps past his limit. His words slurred a little and his eyes wandered.

"Oh, you're not *that* ugly," I said. "Maybe you can find a girl who needs serious glasses."

"Bite me, cousin," he said. He threw his arm over my shoulders. When he breathed, I recoiled a little from the bourbon-based exhaust.

Something was eating on Amar. He drank, but seldom to excess. He loved control too much. He was precise in his work, his manner, his dress, and his demeanor. Tonight, he was close to weepy drunk. Plus, his customary optimism to the point of aggravation had taken the night off.

"What's going on, cuz?" I asked. "I get the feeling you think you met,"—I used annoying air quotes—"the one. What happened? Someone kicked the chair out from under you and landed you on your big ego? You know, since your parents haven't auctioned you off, there's still time for you to have your say. Who was she?"

The voice filtering back to me through the night didn't sound like my braggadocious cousin but like a kid lost in the woods. "There was one girl . . ." His words trailed into the surrounding flowers.

"Where?" Not an inquisition but a prompt.

"New York. It was one night, man. She was serious. Good looking but humble, smart but not irritating. She liked to party, but I was never afraid she was going to go all Lindsay Lohan at any moment."

I laughed at my cousin. "Amar, you're the man!"

"Of course, it was my luck that I had to meet her on my last night."

"Bloody hell. Isn't that always the way? So, it got hot, huh?"

Amar whirled, his eyes intense. "It wasn't like that. We met in a bar and ended up going for a walk. We walked all night, and I mean until the sun came up. Then, she had to go. It was eighteen months ago. I've been out with a lot of women since, but they've all been a waste of time."

"Come on, my friend. Where is she? The world's not that small."

"It was late. We'd had a few cocktails, and then a few more. We were talking and drinking, and then the big yellow ball rises in the east, and she bolts, has to go to class, she says, but she gave me her email."

"Did you write her?'

"I did. Once. Told her exactly how I felt, that I was crazy about her. But things went sideways."

"How's that?"

"I never heard back from her."

"She stiffed you?"

"Not sure. There were a lot of factors."

"Like what?"

"Well, you gotta remember, we'd been drinking. My mind was not the clearest. I was pretty sure I got her email right, but I screwed up and wrote her from my work."

"So?" I asked. "There's nothing wrong with that."

"Well, no, there wasn't. Except, when I staggered into work the next day, one of the admins told me to report to HR. I got fired, man. Security walked me back to my cubicle, watched me pack my stuff, and escorted me out of the business. They took my phone, my computer, they locked me out of the company email, everything. When I reached out to some work people, no one would touch me. I was toxic."

"Damn, *bhayya*, did you steal something?"

"Worse," I said. "I screwed the CEO's daughter."

I buried my head in my hands. "Are you an idiot?"

"She came on to me, bro, and she was smoking hot. She told me she was twenty-five. How was I supposed to know she was still in high school?"

Visions of jail cells ran through my mind. Amar read my thoughts. "Oh no, no, no, she was legal by three weeks. But she'd gone all *Fatal Attraction* on me, and I'd ghosted her. She was psycho. She told Daddy, and Ole Amar's career went ka-boom."

"Let me guess," I said, "you went home and couldn't find the cocktail napkin your dream woman had written her email on, right?"

"No, smartass. It was her business card, and I ran it through the washing machine in my pants."

"You washed your trousers?"

Amar let out an agonized chortle. "Hey, I may be a slob, but I'm not a pig."

CHAPTER 32

HARLOW

THE PARTY BLASTED AWAY ON ALL SIDES. RAUCOUS CONVERSA-tion bounced off every wall. Waiters greased past partiers with stealthy grace. Appetizers evaporated off of trays as soon as a fresh presentation appeared, the revelers descended on it like crocodiles finishing off a wounded fish.

Music blasted from every room. If you didn't like the se-lection in the great room, another song was blaring away just down the expansive hall. Everyone was dressed to the nines.

It's certainly not America. No jeans, no pajama bottoms, no T-shirts, and not a single man wearing a hat. How refreshing.

Lita stood in the middle of the great room, clad in an el-egant saffron sari. The piercing yellow made her light brown skin shimmer. From a luxurious mountain atop her head, her black hair trickled in spiraling rivulets past her high cheek-bones. She smiled extravagantly as two women, one on each side, etched intricate designs on her arms. To the casual observer, she looked happy, almost radiant. But I'd known her a long time. She carried a weight in her eyes she could not hide from me, and now I knew why.

I wandered through my friend's childhood home. Magnificently appointed and decorated with impeccable taste, the house signaled to every guest: We know how to do it right. Every room could have starred in its own HGTV episode.

And these people were not considered the crème de la crème in Indian society.

I shook my head. Unlike America, money did not provide an automatic social promotion in India. I spent a little time talking with Lita's mother, who though busily directing servants and servers and fretting over every detail, took time to meet her daughter's "American friend." She asked all the right questions and paid attention to my answers, but I knew she felt obligated to her other guests, so I did not monopolize her time even though I was starving for some companionship.

A wedding party is a desolate place when you're alone.

No one was in the back room of the house, which contained a small study featuring floor-to-ceiling bookcases, several ornate chess sets, family photos, and a Celestron telescope. I knew that Lita's father had always been fascinated with the solar system. I fondled one of the chess pieces. *The charger, no, that's not right. The knight.*

I put down the piece and moved toward the door when I saw someone in the backyard. Tej—*no, he's Vik now*—was talking to another man. And I knew who it was.

I could hear Lita's voice. "I need to tell you something. One night, I met a boy . . ."

Oh, this could be interesting.

CHAPTER 33

TEJ/VIK

"I WENT BACK TO THE BAR WHERE WE'D MET. WENT THERE every day for two weeks. Finally, I saw a group of girls who'd been with her."

I'd never heard my cousin sound so serious. "They hook you up?"

"Brother, I'm lucky I got out of there alive. They tore me up. Told me I was scum, that I'd treated their friend like dirt, broken her heart."

"Well, didn't they give you a number or something so you could explain?"

"Hell no, bro," Amar said. "They were there with some 'roided up guys—lug nuts, you know—weightlifters. After one of them threatened to pull my pecker out through my nose, I left. I've never seen or heard from her since."

I slapped him on the back. "Chin up, old boy. Things will work out. If it's meant to be, you'll find her, and everything will be good."

Pain radiated from Amar's eyes. "I think that ship has sailed," he said. "It's not in the cards. Trust me, I can tell."

There was a resignation in his voice. He sounded like someone who'd been told he had an incurable disease. He was sad—no, he was lost.

"Well, there is a silver lining," I said. "You can still attract a beautiful woman, even with your bulldog face."

Amar didn't even crack a smile. "I'm sure one day my parents will line someone up, and I will go through with the wedding as I am required, but I will never be as happy as I believe I could have been . . ."

"That's an odd place to stop," I said. "I thought you were going to say her name."

"Well, I could try the old romance novel trope and say she never told me, but in truth, it's a little painful to talk about. You mind if we stop?"

"Not at all," I said. "It's cool."

A waiter approached again. "Are you gentlemen still drinking Hersch?"

"Yes," I said.

A knowing grin. "Excellent choice. Two more?"

"Please," I said.

As soon as the waiter departed, Amar stood abruptly. "I gotta pee. I might go home."

He left before I could say anything. *What the hell is wrong with him?* But I didn't call after him because I noticed his jacket, still on the bench.

He'll be back.

The waiter who'd attended us all evening reappeared with two fresh drinks. When I reached in my pocket, I had a vivid recollection of over-tipping Hussein with the only cash I'd brought. I picked up Amar's jacket.

"Hold on, ah, Radhesh," I said, peering at his nametag.

"It is not customary," Radhesh said, "nor is it necessary." But he did not flee.

I reached into the pocket of Amar's jacket and fished out his wallet. "You have taken very good care of us, Radhesh," I said. "My friend and I would like to express our appreciation."

As I pulled several bills from the wallet, something fell to the ground. Radhesh nodded in appreciation of the gratuity, then bent over. When he stood, he looked at the picture in his hand and smiled.

"Your cousin's lady friend is quite striking," he said. Then he blanched. "I beg your pardon, sir. I should not be so bold."

I shook my head. "No matter, my friend. It may be Old India in here, but out there,"—I swept my arms wide—"out there, it is a new day."

Radhesh handed over the picture, bowed, and scurried away, no doubt terrified I would report his "impudent behavior."

"Like I give a rat's hat," I said. "I love this land, but it is so very backward in so very many ways."

I replaced Amar's jacket on the bench, then opened his wallet to return the picture. I flipped over the photo. Amar beamed at me from a selfie. Next to him, her head touching his, not a beauty, but pretty in her own way:

Lita.

Amar came around the corner. I flicked the picture in his

direction.

"I didn't know, *bhayya*," he said. "Until tonight, I swear to God, I did not know."

CHAPTER 34

HARLOW

I LOOKED AT A TRIO OF CONFUSED FACES. "WHAT WE HAVE HERE
is failure to communicate."

No one laughed. I should have known. After all, how many
folks born in India had ever seen *Cool Hand Luke* much less
heard the line made famous by Strother Martin? Daddy loved
old movies. We watched them all the time, always preceded
by the same four words.

"It's a classic, Lo." I wept during *Casablanca* when Bogart
said, "We'll always have Paris."

"It's a classic, Lo." In the *Graduate* when Dustin Hoffman
said, "Mrs. Robinson, you're trying to seduce me, aren't you?"
Daddy had to explain *seduce.*

"It's a classic, Lo." I thrilled when Roy Schneider said in
Jaws, "You're gonna need a bigger boat." I didn't want to go
swimming for a month.

"It's a classic, Lo." The cheesiest line ever spoken by Hannibal Lector in *Silence of the Lambs* was, "I ate his liver with some fava beans and a nice Chianti."

"It's a classic, Lo." The line every Atlantan knows, loves, and uses, even if *Gone with the Wind* reminds them of times we'd rather forget: "Frankly, my dear, I don't give a damn."

Every line of every "classic" ran through my head while Lita looked at me like I'd grown a third eye. "What are you talking about?" Vik said.

"Okay," I said just before I borrowed a line from *Apollo 13*, "Let's look at this thing from a standpoint of status."

"Meaning?" Lita asked.

"We have four people here," I said. "Two of them are scheduled to be married the day after tomorrow. Two of them are in love. Unfortunately, the happy couple and the in-love couple are not the same people."

Amar shook his head. "So what? Vik and Lita must do what they are expected to do. They must honor the wedding contract. The matchmaker has struck the bargain."

"Well, maybe," I said. "The deal is that someone is going to marry Lita, right?"

"That's half the agreement," Vik said. "My family is part of this as well."

"I get it," I said. "Do this. Everyone close your eyes—no cheating, Vik."

"Why would you think I would be the cheater?"

I looked at the other two. "Which of you thinks Vik would cheat?" They both nodded.

"I thought you were my friend," Vik said. He was looking at Amar.

"I am, cousin," Amar said. "And you have cheated at cards as long as I have known you. You hold in football, and when we play—"

"Enough!" Vik said. "You made your point. Let's just say I am constantly in search of a competitive advantage."

"Yes," Amar said. "You cheat."

The laughter helped everyone relax a little. When everyone quieted, I continued. "Okay, no cheating. Close your eyes."

Three pairs of eyelids snapped shut. Amar lowered his head as if in prayer. Vik rested his jaw on his palms, elbows on his knees. Lita bounced her heels on the ground. She looked for all the world like a four-year-old who needed to go to the bathroom.

I tried to sound calm. "Now, if you are unhappy with the idea of the marriage of Lita and Vik, I want you to raise your hand."

Three palms went into the air so fast someone might have thought I asked, "Who'd like a million dollars?"

"All right, people. Don't lower your hands but open your eyes."

Three sets of eyelids fluttered open. Three heads swiveled. Broad smiles exposed three sets of teeth.

"I'm the newbie here," I said. "But I think there is only one thing to do."

"What's that?" Lita asked, but she already knew the answer.

"The wedding goes on as planned," I said. "But Amar is going to be the groom."

Lita could not contain her exuberance. "That's wonderful!" Then reality stopped her mid-bounce. "What if they say no?"

"You don't have a choice," I said, "but you do have power, assuming you each has courage."

"Meaning?" Amar asked.

"If your parents do not agree, none of you shows up at the wedding."

⟡

I was not privy to all the conversations, but I could hear the one Lita had with her parents. What started as a routine exchange, no doubt between excited parents and their daughter who they figured was "just nervous" gradually escalated both in intensity and volume. Within fifteen minutes, the noise sounded like screeching cats, each trying to claw and howl its way to leadership of the neighborhood street corner.

Lita's father boomed his discontent. Her mother wailed, anguish, embarrassment, and disappointment all rolled into a continual keening. Though Lita's voice remained resolute, she never raised it. To her belonged the calm drone of confidence because the longer the row lasted and the more frantic her parents became, the stronger her understanding grew, "I am completely in control."

When it was all over, Lita rushed into my room, flung herself onto my bed, embraced me, and said, "I'm going to marry Amar."

⟡

Later, I would learn about how it went with the guys.

The meeting with Vik's parents transpired very much the

same way as Lita's except with less screaming and more tears. His father was adamant but melted in the face of Vik's withering logic.

"Baapa, what have you always told me was the most important thing of all?"

"Family, my son. You know this, but—"

"And Amar is the only son of your brother, the only hope for the continuation of Uncle Varun's line."

"But your reputation—"

"My reputation is beyond reproach, Baapa. I will be seen as luckless with the fairer gender. There is no scandal here, and both Lita and Amar will say so. They are simply in love."

"But—"

"But this is family, Baapa. And in your heart, you know it is the right thing to do. I promise I will marry as soon as I can. I have no wish to be a lifelong bachelor, and I intend on making you a happy and doting grandfather."

"All right, my son. But there is one more thing you must do."

"What is that, Baapa?"

"Go over to your uncle's house and get my matchmaker money back."

Amar's path proved less difficult, easy actually. The minute his parents heard he had a chance to marry Lita, he zipped toward matrimony with the speed of a rollerblade racer on a luge run. Mother and father rushed their son to the haberdasher, where they threw money at a confused but delighted-to-be-overpaid tailor.

Twenty minutes before the wedding ceremony started,

Amar's father approached me.

"This is for you," he said. "After all, you played matchmaker."

I looked in the bulky envelope. A thick stack of bills winked at me. I handed it back.

"My gift to the happy couple," I said.

CHAPTER 35

TEJ/VIK

FOR THE FIRST TIME SINCE RETURNING TO INDIA, MY HEART didn't hurt. I wasn't happy, and I wasn't sure I ever would be, but I was not in pain.

The festive mood did little to erase the disappointment in Ma's eyes. She smiled and laughed, but I could tell her heart was not in it. Today was supposed to be my wedding day—her day—the first step in her march toward matriarch status, and one day closer to a brood of squealing, rambunctious grandchildren. Still, I had to keep my life in line with dharma.

My penance had not yet been determined, but my father had agreed with my decision "for the good of the family."

"There is no reason that the wedding you approach with obvious reluctance should shatter three lives," he had said.

Of course, I had to pretend to be devastated by "the ole switcheroo." I played the wounded lover again. And, one more time, I played pincushion to the barbs of gossipmongers. There were rumors about my financial position—or alleged lack thereof—my health, and, of all things, my sexuality. It was not time to defend myself. I stood to the side as Amar and Lita basked in the warm glow of the social spotlight.

Isha swished through the crowd like a social typhoon. She accepted congratulations for "rescuing" a situation about which she had done nothing. She had been a spectator. She acted like she'd singlehandedly won the Ranji Trophy. It had been a very good week for her—fees from my family, Lita's family, and, as I discovered, a handsome bonus for easing out one groom in favor of another.

We gathered in a sea of lights on the sumptuous lawn of Lita's home. Her father played the gracious host, and her mother smiled, waved, and embraced people who greeted her in an endless stream. As Amar's cousin, I was an honored member of the Grand Procession. We sang and danced as the bride's family escorted us to our places.

What could have been a weepy chick-flick disaster developed into a celebration of joy and storybook love. Everyone approved of the welding of two prominent families, even if "Part A" had been replaced by "Part B" at the least opportune moment.

Radiant in a red panetar, a unique silk sari with a white body and red border given by the bride's uncle and worn at the beginning of the wedding, Lita, stunning and demur, stood on one side of the gold and red antarpat. The antarpat was a cloth used to separated the couple at the beginning of a traditional wedding as a symbol of their separate lives. Unlike western ceremonies, Indian brides dressed in modest elegance, with no leg-revealing slits or giggling cleavages. Amar, handsome—almost regal in an emerald sherwani and matching turban—could not stop smiling. The couple's eagerness to embrace pulsed through the crowd like tachycardia, but my cousin and his intended restrained themselves and lent to the moment all the dignity everyone expected.

When they placed garlands around each other's necks to signal the start of the wedding, my ma burst into quiet tears. Amar had been a fixture in our home from the day we moved back from London. People who did not know our family well assumed he was a younger brother. At this moment, he was undoubtedly a more obedient "son."

I caught a glimpse of Haiya near the back. She made a point of licking her lips when I looked at her.

She's nuts. First, she tried to embarrass me. Now she's coming on.

I made a mental note to avoid being one-on-one with her, ever.

Despite my ex-fiancée's bizarre and thankfully unnoticed behavior, everything moved without a hitch. The room felt ancient and good. Lita's mother poured holy water onto her husband's hands. The flow trickled into the groom's hands and then into Lita's. The water represented the continuum of generations, a sacred stream joining two families, one generation to the next and on into the Land of the Eternal.

According to custom, the couple lit the sacred fire. To symbolize both her strength and willingness to overcome any obstacle, Lita stepped over a rock as Amar held her arm. They asked Agni, the god of fire and divine knowledge who safeguards the home, to be the messenger for their prayers for children, health, and long lives together.

After they circled the fire four times, Amar put red kum-kum powder in the part of Lita's hair, marking her as a married woman. They walked seven steps together. With each stride, they repeated traditional prayers for children, character, prosperity, involvement in the world, an industrious life, the seasons of life, and friendship.

We showered the couple with flowers. Through the rain of jasmine blossoms, I caught Lita's eye. Tears of joy streamed from her face. She nodded briefly and mouthed, "Thank you."

I walked over to the bar. It would be a long time before everyone departed. Indian wedding celebrations often continued well into the dawn. I didn't feel like staying, but I figured I'd have one more drink before returning home.

"What kind of bourbon do you have?" I asked.

The bartender pointed to a bottle on the table to his left. "You are in luck, sir," he said. "Mr. Baljekar just brought out two bottles of Pappy Van Winkle. I would suggest having some before everyone else learns of it."

I nodded and held up two fingers. He made a generous pour over a single ice cube and slid the crystal glass toward me. I took a sip. The amber liquid eased its way down my throat like warm honey.

"Pretty good, isn't it, sir?" he asked.

"As good as anything I've ever tasted," I said.

"Well, make sure you come back before it's all gone," he said. He placed the bottle on the counter. "I guess it won't hurt to advertise now that you've had some."

I looked back toward the party and saw Ma. She had stopped to talk to someone, a momentary distraction from what I could tell was her mission. I knew exactly what her intentions were because she was clutching the hand of a young woman of marriageable age, no doubt someone to whom I was about to be introduced. I looked at the guy behind the bar.

"You mind if I take this?" I asked.

"No, sir," he said. "You saw it first. Enjoy."

I walked around the side of the tent and disappeared deep into the garden.

CHAPTER 36

HARLOW

THE PARTY CONTINUED TO RAGE. MUSIC, DANCING, LAUGHING, drinking, and enough food to stock the Atlanta Falcons training table for three complete seasons. I had never seen such abundance or such a lavish celebration.

Maybe getting married to Addison will be fun.

The getting married part wasn't the problem. I was bummed about the *being* married to Addison.

I wandered through the garden alone. The silver dollar moon provided plenty of illumination. Soft lighting fell on perfectly trimmed hedges and pristinely maintained flowering plants. I recognized petunias, of course, lotus blossoms, and rhododendron. I knelt to examine an unusual-looking flower with eight oval petals extending from a center hub. Each petal featured a central "shaft" of lavender surrounded by lighter colors.

"It's beautiful." My voice filtered off into the night air.

I jumped when someone spoke. "It's a leather flower."

I knew the voice. "Vik!"

"Scientific name is clematis. It's one of about three hundred species in the buttercup family of *Ranunculaceae*."

"I'm impressed. But what are you doing here? You should be partying."

He held up a bottle. "This is much too good to be wasted on the rabble. I thought it should be consumed by someone who appreciated its unique attri–atrci–properties."

"Mr. Chatwal," I said, "I believe you might have appreciated the, ah, unique attributes a little too liberally."

"Good point," he said. He extended the bottle. "Wanna belt?"

"You are so very suave," I said. I held the bottle to my lips and took a small sip.

"I never figured you for dainty," he said.

"Nothing dainty about this Southern belle," I said. I glared at him, just a little. *He is so beautiful in the moonlight.* And I took a woman-sized swig.

The 90.4 proof bourbon etched a river of fire down my throat. I coughed a little.

"Smooth," I said.

Vik was smiling. "I was just messing with you, Ms. Kennedy. This nectar is meant to be nursed and enjoyed. It is far too dear to guzzle." He plopped down on a garden stone and patted the space next to him. "Join me. As they say in Atlanta, 'Sit a spell with me.'"

I hitched up my sari. It was a little snug at the hips and thighs. I eased down next to him. I was careful to keep what any Georgia mother thought was a "respectable" distance.

The moon's solitary spotlight reflected off my necklace with a crimson flash.

"That's a stunning stone," Vik said. "Garnet?"

"Ruby," I said. "My father made it."

"You told me he was in the jewelry business. I imagine you have a lot of fabulous pieces."

I touched the stone. "This is the only one I have. Daddy told me it was very valuable. I was almost never allowed to wear it outside the house. Daddy was afraid someone would steal it. I've never had it appraised, but I know it's precious."

"I guess you'd never consider selling it—not to me. I mean, to set up your business."

The suggestion might have enraged me any other time, but the question was sincere, not snide.

"It's all I have of my Daddy," I said. "I'll sleep under an I-85 overpass before I sell it."

We both stared up at the night sky.

"Pretty spectacular, isn't it?" I said.

Vik shrugged. "Just like every other Indian wedding I've ever attended."

"I meant the moon."

He didn't respond. I couldn't tell if he was lost in thought or just hammered. Probably a little of both.

After a while, Vik decided to speak again. "They looked happy, didn't they?"

"Yes," I said. "I've been to a lot of weddings. Not sure I've ever seen a couple that thrilled. After all, they came close . . ."

Shut up, Harlow. You don't need to remind him.

"That's okay," he said. "I came to India single, and I have every intention of returning to my life in America in the same state."

"Why?" I asked.

"Because I have not yet met the, ah, woman of my dreams."

"Not that. I've heard all the talk. I know about the other one, Hermione."

"Haiya," he said. "What's your point?"

"Well, this is the second time you are the focal point of some level of social scandal. The second you agreed that Lita should marry your cousin, you knew people would begin to gossip again. Why did you—"

He grabbed my arm, but it wasn't rough. It was insistent, earnest.

"I did it because of Parul."

CHAPTER 37

HARLOW

THERE WAS A MOMENT WHEN I THOUGHT HE FINISHED SPEAK-ing, that he had shut down. When he began, he stared off into the garden. "I was in love once," he said. His voice was as distant as his gaze. "She was stunning. Her name was Parul. She was three years younger than me. She and her family lived in a hovel outside of Delhi. With five daughters, no sons, and no money for a dowry, their prospects were dim."

"Does birth order matter?" I asked.

"It is generally considered that the eldest daughter will marry first," he said. "And she did. But her husband died of a fever, most likely cholera, leaving her childless and with no financial future."

"Did your parents know about her?"

"They knew I had an impoverished friend. Ma assumed I was just being polite like she taught me."

"And you loved her?" I asked, almost afraid of the answer.

"More than anything or anyone I'd ever known." There had been no hesitation in his answer. "Despite her circumstances, she was wildly generous. She was not educated, but her wisdom was profound. We used to talk for hours. She learned to play chess because . . . well because all high-born Indians play, and she wanted to beat me."

"Did she?"

"In less than a year, I lost all interest in the game. Parul could not prop me up long enough to make me think I had a chance. Any time she wished she could crush me like a grape."

"You've implied she was not Brahmin," I said. "How did you meet?"

"Her grandparents worked for my family."

"Would your parents have approved?"

"You know better," he said. The edge in his voice was sharp, almost bitter. "So, I treated Parul like a younger sister."

"What did she look like?" I asked.

"The face of an angel," he said. "She was small and sickly. She didn't run and play. She couldn't. She'd survived polio as a child. Remember, my country was not polio-free until 2016. As of 2009, India accounted for sixty percent of the world's cases."

"I didn't know," I said.

"Not surprising. Americans are concerned with whatever is right in front of their eyes, whether it's a new virus or the overalls craze."

"I remember those," I said.

"If you ever wore a pair, do not tell me. I might never speak to you again."

"You had some," I said. "I know you did."

He shook his head. "Not with my ma. She still gets upset when she sees me in a polo shirt, and I am a grown man."

"Well, almost," I said.

Silence slid across the evening. It was lovely until it became uncomfortable. You know, one of those moments when if someone doesn't speak, someone else may try something like a kiss.

"So," I said, "you were telling me about Parul."

I saw pain sear his face. "She loved to cook. She had a gift for making *khichdi*, world-class Indian rice and lentil comfort food, favored by Indians when they're ill or looking for a quick, one-pot meal."

"Nothing like protein, carbs, and a little fat for flavor," I said.

"You know your Indian food," he said.

"What I know is that Mrs. Patmore served it on Downton Abbey," I said. "And if you add fish and hard-boiled eggs, you get kedgeree, right?"

"Don't forget the parsley," he said. "Key ingredient."

"Got it," I said. "Maybe I'll just leave all the cooking to you. When did Parul make it for you, the khichdi?"

"I had the flu when I was twelve, didn't want to eat anything."

"Been there," I said.

"Well, my ma must have said something to the kitchen staff because one day, Parul showed up with a bowl of the most delicious khichdi I'd ever had, then or ever."

I watched him go back in time. His face softened. He faked

a cough so he could wipe away a tear. I decided not to mention it.

"It wasn't rice you were tasting," I said. "It was something else."

"I know—" He broke off. It was the first time he'd smiled in a while. Still the grin was brief and wistful.

"Not very many men were interested in Parul because she was frail and poor. No one thought she would be a good helpmate or that she could bear children. That was okay with me. Then, one day, her parents received an offer for her hand."

"That was good for her, right?" I asked.

Dark shadows passed over Vik's forehead. His eyes looked like someone suffering from a debilitating headache. His voice croaked across the night. "An older man approached her parents. He had been married at least twice. His first wife left him. There were rumors of his abuses, but everyone tended to side with the husband in domestic disputes, particularly in those days. His second wife, a young woman like Parul, died suddenly. After a few weeks, her parents moved out of town, apparently with some new-found wealth."

"Did Parul's parents agree?"

"Absolutely. Marriage looked like their chance to improve their station."

"What did you think?"

"I was beside myself," he said. "I knew Parul was against the union, but she was going to do it. She was an obedient daughter. But I was young and impetuous, so I decided to stop the wedding."

"What did you do?" I asked.

"Two days before the wedding, I went to see my aunt. I was determined to rescue Parul. I cajoled my aunt into taking Parul on as a ward. It was the perfect solution. Parul would have a great home, access to better medical care, and a chance at an education."

"Plus, she would be where you could find her after you convinced your parents, right?" I asked.

"Precisely," he said. "After seeing my aunt, I rushed home, got some money, and went to the train station where I bought a ticket for Parul, so that she could go live with my aunt. It was getting dark, but the wedding was the next day. I pedaled as fast as I could to take Parul the ticket. I was naïve enough to believe that everyone deserved to be with someone they loved."

"Did you get there in time?"

"I got there just after nightfall. Her mother was weeping."

"This didn't end well, did it?"

"No," he said. I could barely hear him. "Half an hour before I arrived, a mere thirty minutes before I might have saved who I now know was the love of my life, Parul drowned herself in the Ganges. She was thirteen."

CHAPTER 38

TEJ/VIK

WHEN I TURNED TO LOOK AT HARLOW, TEARS WERE CASCADING from her eyes.

"That's the most horrible thing I have ever heard," she said.

"Unfortunately, there are a lot of similar stories in India," I said. "Not everyone gets as lucky as Amir and Lita."

"Thanks to you."

I didn't want any credit. Helping my cousin, my friend, was not simply a good thing; it was the right thing, and ultimately, the only reason my parents agreed.

The wind stirred the trees, and the pleasant smells of the garden filled my nostrils. The tranquility of the moment dissolved when Harlow sneezed.

"Are you okay?" I asked.

"Apparently, my allergies are not confined to the United States," she said.

She looked regal in her sari and matching silk shawl.

"That's a lovely outfit," I said.

"Well, I owe it all to Lita," she said. "Fortunately, the Indian people do not have the tradition of burdening honor attendants with hideous dresses they will never take out of the closet again."

"There was a movie about that, right?" I asked. "I slept through a lot of it on a plane flight once."

"Yep, *27 Dresses*. Katherine Heigl and James Marsden. Absolutely dreadful movie but, unfortunately, absolutely accurate from a couture standpoint."

"Why have you never married?"

"Not a lot of tact in that question, Mr. Chatwal," she said.

"Hey, you asked me . . . sort of."

Harlow pulled on her earlobe. I'd seen her do that before, a little behavioral tic she had. I pushed a little harder. "It's not like you've never been asked."

"Actually, Mr. Know-It-All, I am strongly considering a proposal while I am on this trip."

"Someone here has already asked you?" I hoped I sounded neither eager nor disappointed.

"No," she said. "Someone in the States proposed before I left. Well, he sorta asked—no, he didn't. Sofia asked for him."

"American matchmaker?"

"No, Sophia is the woman who was married to my father."

"Your mother."

"I call her Sophia."

"I take it you are not close."

"Good guess, Captain Obvious." I saw her jaw twitch.

"Hey, no offense intended. Just asking."

A field mouse scurried past. Most Indian women would have made a great show of fear if for no other reason than to give a man the chance to act brave. Harlow looked at the diminutive creature and giggled.

"He's cute," she said.

"He's probably radioactive like the spider that bit Peter Parker."

She flinched a little and would have completely bought into my lie, except I began to chuckle.

"Shut up," she said.

"Back to your story," I said. "Please."

"Why do you care?"

"You are an intelligent, independent young woman from America. That you are still available confounds me. But it sounds like someone finally snatched you up. Tell me about your fiancé."

"First of all,"—her voice carried a slight hint of fire—"no one is snatching anyone up. I am free to make my own choices in my own good, damn time."

"My apologies." I scooted away from her a little, all for show.

"Second, I have not made up my mind if I am going to accept the *arrangement*. I've known Addison a long time, but not very well. Actually, that's not true. We know each other—"

When she stopped talking, I knew what she wanted to say. "You were lovers in the past?"

She acted like she was going to stick two fingers down her throat. She held out her hand. I gave her the bottle. She took a long pull. "That sounds so gross. We had sex once."

"And?"

"Damn, you're nosey," she said. But she kept talking. "And it was lousy, and it didn't do much for me. Actually, it didn't do anything for me if you catch my drift." The alcohol was getting to her. The words came out in a torrent, slightly mushy. "I didn't know what I was doing. I didn't hear angels singing or waves crashing, nothing but Addison grunting like a pig. He rolled over and went to sleep, and *oh my God*, did I just tell you all that?"

Her hands covered her face and muffled her voice, but I could understand her. "I just told you about my first and only time. I barely know you! You must think I am either a prude or a psycho." She dropped her hands. "And the strange thing is, I don't care at all because I am pretty sure I have had too much Mr. Pappy."

She looked up at the moon and unleashed a wolf howl. When the echoes died away, she looked at me expressionless, but her eyes betrayed a jagged sorrow.

"I've never dated much," she said, "and it's probably because of Sophia."

CHAPTER 39

HARLOW

I WENT UPSTAIRS AT 4:30 A.M. AND SLEPT IN THE CLOTHES I wore to the wedding. Vik and I had talked a long time. Later, I didn't know if I should be more embarrassed about what I'd told him or about what I could remember revealing. The only reason I awoke was because Nivi jumped on my bed. I squinted through sun-blinded, slightly hungover eyes as she bounced up and down.

"Wasn't that the most beautiful thing you ever saw?" Her voice squeaked like a rusty hinge. "Lita was radiant, and Amar looked wonderful. Of course, he's no Vik Chatwal, but oh my god, who is, right? I mean, that guy could be in the movies. Next to him, Saheed Kapoor looks like a hairy chicken. Have you ever seen such eyes? They are so deep. I've never—"

"Nivi!" Her shocked expression told me my tone was a little harsh. "Sorry, but take it easy. It's early."

"Well, someone had a little too much fun last night, I

think. You look like Baapa after he's been drinking beer at the cricket matches all day and all night. Bet your head hurts a little." She rapped her knuckles on the headboard. She might as well have driven a nail into my ear canal. "Soooo sorry," she said as she danced away from my grabbing hands.

"If I catch you, I'll wring your little chicken neck," I said, but she could tell I was kidding because she never stopped laughing.

"Okay," she said, "I will leave you in your misery. Daddy likes his little quiet time too the morning after he overdoes it." She giggled again. Just before she went out the door, she looked at me with oversold innocence. "By the way, it's almost eleven."

Crap! I have a lunch with Vik.

By the time Hussein pulled the Bentley into the drive, I looked presentable, mostly. I vowed to keep on my sunglasses, so the road map in my corneas would not be visible.

"Mr. Chatwal's compliments, Ms. Harlow," Hussein said. "Are we ready for lunch?"

The question sounded a little accusatory, but I nodded and thudded into the back seat. Twenty-five minutes later, we were in an out-of-the-way boit, a place where Tej—*Vik*—was well known by the staff.

Vik was seated at a table when I arrived. He rose and held my chair as I sat. He ordered drinks in Hindi, then turned to me.

"You know, we've had two pretty good talks now. One on the flight and one after the wedding, though I confess I'm a little fuzzy on some of the details from last evening. I know I asked you if you were getting married, but I never inquired as to whether you were dating someone."

"It's complicated," I said.

His dark eyebrows arched. "Seems a simple question to me . Either you are, or you are not."

"Well, Mr. Tej or Vikram or whoever the hell you are—"

"Vik, please, at least in India. Another conversation for another time," he said.

"Well, it's not as simple as you may think. How much of this do you want to know?"

"I am only entitled to the information you choose to divulge."

I took a deep breath. "Well, pull up a chair, my friend. It's quite a tale. It all begins with a woman named Sophia and a childhood playmate turned almost-fiancé named Addison."

The entire recitation took about twenty-five minutes during which we munched on pakora. There were detours, a few laughs, and more than a little embarrassment on my part. "So, when I get back from India, I have to decide if my dignity is only worth five million dollars."

"A considerable sum," he said.

"Obviously."

"And you seem to have few options," he said.

"Again, obviously."

"Because I have not heard you mention any other prospects, and I suspect your friend Ezra is probably gay."

"Okay, stop!" I said. "I'm starting to get depressed."

"Not trying to make you feel bad, just assessing the situation."

I took a deep breath. "To be honest, I'm lonely, and I want to belong to someone, to be a part of something. I came over here on a lark. To be with a friend in an exotic country, to see something unlike anything I'd ever experienced. And I am having a wonderful time. But when I get back home, my life will change. A lot. I'm probably going to marry someone I hardly know, and what I know of him, I don't like very much. It's not love between us. It's just history."

Vik had been gazing at me with his penetrating eyes. Suddenly, he couldn't look at me as if our eyes were repelling each other.

"What's up, Vik?" I asked. "What are you thinking about?"

The smooth oil of sex appeal left his voice. His tone was soft, soothing, protective. "Harlow, I have an idea, but you have to promise not to get mad at me."

The hair on my arm stood at attention. My face flushed, and my thighs got warm. *Oh God, don't ask me to sleep with you. I mean—*. My palm slapped across his shoulder. "No!"

His head vibrated side to side like a startled cartoon character. "I haven't even suggested anything."

"Oh, sorry," I said. *Harlow, take it easy.*

"You know, you might not have a man because of your propensity towards violence." He rubbed his arms a little for effect.

"I've never hit anyone who didn't deserve it."

"Well, if you're going to attract a man over here, that's got to go."

"Who said anything about attracting someone over here? I just mentioned going home to marry Addison."

"My point precisely," he said. "Which leads me to my idea. But, again, before I say anything, you have to promise two things. One, hear me out."

"Okay."

"Two, and this is very important, no more hitting."

I faked like I was going to throw a jab, then smiled. "I promise."

He began slowly, a salesman gently bantering with a potential client before making "the ask."

"Your social life in Atlanta has been a little flat, wouldn't you say?" he asked.

"Deader than Elvis," I said. When he cocked his head, I waved the back of my hand. "Go on."

"You are not fired up about marrying Addison lá Douche. You're not even wearing your engagement ring."

"Check. And I am not technically engaged yet."

"But you wouldn't mind the money your—*Sophia* has promised."

"Double check. I could use it to crank up my jewelry business and to eat, come to think of it, what with no job and all."

He recoiled a little.

"Water under the bridge," I said. "We've already put that one to bed. Onward and upward."

His eyes registered suspicion, but he continued. "You are here in India for a while."

"Well, they gave me two weeks vacay when I started at Legacy. I got special permission to use all of it at once, but they gave me a break since I was traveling to India and all, not like I was going to Macon for the weekend. Anyway, Lita knows I got fired. No, I did not tell her it was you. She still thinks you are the most wonderful person on the planet."

"Thank you for that."

"It was about the noblest thing I've ever heard of, much less seen. I mean, it was some Mother Teresa-type shit, but I digress. When I told Lita about my lack of employment, she told me to stay as long as I like. She's already made arrangements with the airline in case I change my departure date."

"That's very generous."

It took a while before I answered. "It is. And, it means a lot. Not very many people have been so kind to me in my life. It's cool here and everything, but I think I will probably just pack my stuff and head back home in a day or so."

"Let's wait on that decision," he said. "How about we review a few things?"

"Okay."

His expression was serious but not stern. He locked me in his gaze. *Oh, those eyes.* Then he spoke in an almost clinical voice. "Nothing I say is mean-spirited. We're doing a business assessment, okay?"

"Sure."

"You are relationship-less, broke, and currently in a very different culture."

"Yep."

"Where the indigenous population is in the middle of something called 'Wedding Season.'"

I puffed out my cheeks and exhaled. "What's the point?"

"Well," he said, "at this precise moment on the time-space continuum, there are several hundred marriage-crazed mummies hoping to land someone for their sons. While you are not Indian, you have some Indian heritage. Still, you are an attractive young woman, at least by American standards."

"Hey, that's not nice," I said, but I knew what he meant.

"Just stating the facts," he said. "Now, this next part is a little delicate, so take no offense."

"Okay."

"You are light-skinned. Potential grooms will find you extremely beautiful. Mummy will think you are acceptable."

I laughed so loudly his head snapped back. "Jesus Christ on a Ritz cracker, are you suggesting that I pass?"

His face was blank and innocent. "Pass what? We are not in school. There will be no exam."

He was so obviously confused. I felt sorry for him. "Let me 'splain something to you, honey. Decades ago, my people who did not want to keep getting treated like the dirt they cultivated by breaking their backs moved north in the US. When they got to Dee-triot and Chicago and other places, the lucky ones posed as White. They 'passed' as a member of a different race."

Vik's eyes grew. "That's a thing? People were ashamed of their heritage?"

"Ain't nobody ashamed of nothing," I said. I could feel my nostrils flaring. "We are always proud of who we are, but we did what we had to do to get jobs, to get in schools, to have a life. We left behind one type of fear by selecting to endure another one—the terror of being discovered."

There was a long silence, one I was not going to break. Vik licked his lips, then chewed on them, then clicked his teeth together. "No, Harlow, I would never suggest you deny your background any more than I would abandon mine. What I am saying is that your ethnicity will not be an issue in some more open-minded families."

"Go on," I said. My tone was not friendly.

"Brahmin maatajis are very finicky. They almost always insist on someone from the same caste. The next caste, the Intellectuals—professors, doctors, actors—are less stringent."

"Or less bigoted," I said.

"Touché. Frankly, I think it's silly. I would have no problem being with a woman of your—"

"My what?"

"Harlow," he said, "you didn't even let me finish. It's important, especially in India, to listen. What I was saying was that while I would have no problem being with a woman of your distinction, intelligence, and beauty . . ."

Oh, be still my heart. I should be so lucky.

". . . I am not sure my family would approve, but it's a moot point because you and I are merely friends."

Doesn't have to stay that way, buddy.

Vik's resonant voice surrounded me in a warm envelope. "I have an idea. Just a little experiment."

"Go on," I said.

"Since you are going to be here for a few more days—perhaps even a week—allow me to make an introduction."

"A blind date?"

"Oh, nothing of the sort," he said. "A woman of your stature deserves much better treatment. No, I would like to introduce you to Isha, one of the preeminent matchmakers in all of India. You can have a conversation and see what eventuates.

There is absolutely no obligation."

Words bounced in my head like ping pong balls: *arranged, love, shallow, old, pimped, vacuous, convenient.*

Vik looked at me a little sideways. "The idea has some appeal, does it not? You never know. Maybe it's the jumpstart your love life needs. It might be a lark, a story you can tell your grandchildren."

"How I almost married a ninety-year-old Indian guy who met me through a matchmaker only to be rescued at the last minute by a handsome prince?"

Take a hint, dumbass. Or maybe this is his way of getting rid of me. I thought there was a spark . . . was I wrong?

"Not exactly," Vik said. "But you can recount the adventurous spirit. How you stepped into another culture, that sort of thing. Harlow, it will only be for a few days. If nothing comes of it—and, in truth, even Isha would have trouble working that fast—you will have a great experience."

"Let me get this straight," I said. "You want me to use what little time I have left to hire a matchmaker and see if she can work her magic on me."

"Correct. What have you got to lose?"

"You expect me to abandon whatever modicum of self-respect I have and cater to every need of some Indian bim-boy in hopes my innate fineness will so tangle him up in knots that he will use his small brain while he talks his traditionalist parents into allowing him to marry an African American woman?" I heard the volume in my voice increase. "You think I should whore myself out there? 'Hey boys, lookin' for a good time?' And see what jumps up in the old fishing boat. That's what you want me to do?"

And in the meantime, you can explain how this makes me different from Sophia.

Vik shrugged. "Not exactly, but you have the essence."

"I don't know," I said. "I came over here for Lita's wedding, but I also wanted to get away from Sophia and her crazy scheme. I needed time to clear my head, to get out of my own way."

Damn, he has great cheekbones.

"Vik, I don't want to marry anyone for money. I'm a modern woman. I know I can make it on my own. I don't *need* anyone, but I *want* someone to share my life with, my hopes, my dreams, my fears, my joys. I want to love someone, and I want them to love me."

Vik looked at me, but his focus was far away. "Interesting," he said, "I said the same thing to my father many years ago. When I initially objected to the idea of an arranged marriage, he told me how much he had come to love and respect my ma. He was certain the same thing would happen to me." He paused, and we sat in silence for a while. "Harlow, you deserve happiness. You deserve the best. Why not try my idea? You might find what you are seeking."

I took my time before I answered. "Well, Vik, old chum,"— I pressed my face into my palms—"you've got yourself a deal."

CHAPTER 40

HARLOW

"Hullo."

I love the way Indian people say "hello."

Isha was tall, almost majestic, and wearing a deep-green sari. Her dyed silver hair shimmered. She wore it in a chic bob. With perfect makeup featuring kohl-lined eyes and ruby lipstick, she portrayed both sophistication and approachable arrogance. She would have fit in any, old-line, Southern country club. She would have turned heads too. She might have been fifty, but I guessed she was considerably north of that figure. Her beauty concealed her age like a sophisticated cloak.

"Hello." I struggled to sound more confident than I felt as I settled into the gold upholstered chair she indicated with long fingers and a sweeping hand. *Vanna White could take lessons in elegance here.*

"I understand you want to marry." It was not a question. She looked me up and down.

I felt like a broodmare at auction. *Is she going to check my teeth?* "I think. It's sort of a lark. Anyway, Vikram, I mean Mr. Chatwal, suggested you could help me."

"Oh, yes, he has already called. He indicated you are in somewhat of a rush. Is that correct?"

"Yes," I said.

"You are an American?"

"Yes."

"Are there extenuating circumstances?"

"Pardon?"

"Are you pregnant?"

She could have slapped me and gotten less of a reaction. I bolted from the chair and headed for the door.

"Miss Harlow," she said, "please retake your seat." She said, *please,* but she didn't mean it. "I do not mean to insult you. The men and women in India observe chastity and the channeling of sexual energy into spiritual energy. We do not practice it because we are prudish but out of respect for the dynamic and serious nature of the marriage state. We believe it is critical to focus on all the essential elements of life partnership and not just on the joys of temporary, carnal pleasure. Not every other country holds such a custom. Americans can be free with their affections, and I just need to, I believe the expression in your country would be, see the entire playing field. I meant no disrespect."

"None taken," I said, a blatant lie. But I was already itching to leave. I didn't want to be "the desperate girl" looking for the pity marriage. I didn't want to end up with the cousin some family locked in the closet because he tortured small animals.

I preferred to project the image of miraculous availability, to be open to the whims of life and the opportunities they might bring, especially if those included maatas with hot-looking Indian sons who might fall in love with me the moment they walked through the door.

"I see," Isha said. "If you had more time, the Marriage Bureau would be a fine choice. It has proven useful for ex-pats and others who come here seeking life partners. They don't do it in large numbers, but the times are changing. They don't make matches there. They simply supply data about people seeking marriage. Besides, if I may be blunt, at twenty-five, you are a little too old to go that route."

Ouch!

"Still, since Mr. Chatwal vouched for you, I am all in."

There was reverence in the way she said his name.

"I have to warn you, the match will take work. Indian maatajis want an Indian wife, someone shy, modest, respectful, pure, and devoted to her in-laws. Many people have trouble unraveling our ways and traditions. We believe the universe revolves according to the laws of karma. We consult the stars, holy men, and astrologers to ensure we are on the path chosen for us."

"Actually," I said, "I have Indian heritage in my blood. The family name is Diswani."

I handed her a faded picture of some of Daddy's people gathered from the '50s. At the last minute, I'd tucked it in my suitcase, a little way of bringing my father along to the country he'd wanted so badly to see. I felt a stirring in my chest. This group who stared intently into the camera's lens, they were my family too. I had roots in this place of bright colors, over-the-top ceremony, and ancient, time-honored ways.

"I see." She looked closely at my features. "Some people might think you are from Southern India, someone, perhaps, with a family from Tamil Nadu—"

The Atlanta side of my brain started screaming. *Aw, hell no! I may pass the paper bag test in Georgia, but I sure as hell am not going to pose as a Hindu woman for you or anyone else.*

I calmed down before I put my mouth in gear. "Wait a minute, please," I said. "I ain't—I mean, I'm not passing. I am an American. If you cannot help me without a lie, I can't do this."

"Very well," she said. Isha looked at me for a long time. I could see the wheels spinning in her head. "I think this can work. I never lie to clients. Sometimes, I just—how would you say it?—I put a little extra lipstick on the story. But we will go with the truth. You are an American woman seeking to be an obedient Indian wife."

The word *obedient* set my teeth on edge, but I let it go—for now. "I need to know something. How much choice will I have?"

"Miss Kennedy," she said after a stifled chortle, "I do not know what you have heard or what stories you have read, but no one is going to kidnap you in the middle of the night and force you into a marriage against your wishes. Can this happen fast? Absolutely, sometimes overnight. I have,"—she pointed to an ancient Rolodex—"hundreds of names in there, all very eligible men seeking very eligible mates. I do not take on abusive men. I do not take on Neanderthals. First, you will meet every candidate. You will have the opportunity to say yes or no to each one. Remember, they have the same option. You may meet the man of your dreams who decides, for whatever reason, that you are unsuitable. In that case, the process stops."

"For good? I get one shot?"

Isha grinned slightly at the horror smeared across my face. "Do not panic, my dear. If someone is foolish enough to pass on a woman as beautiful and accomplished as yourself, I am sure another will snatch you up before you have time to blink."

Oh, she is good.

"Thank you," I said. "Go on."

"Or this process could take several weeks. You never know. As I already mentioned, if the stars align properly, you could be married this time next week."

My head began to swim. "You don't waste time, do you?" I gulped. "How much is all this going to cost me?"

Isha buried her head in what I assumed was a price list, pulled a calculator from her voluminous shoulder bag and began slapping at the keys. "I understand you wish to return to the States. Atlanta, is it?"

"Yes," I said. "I have my life there. I'm thinking about starting my own business—"

"That is a matter for you and your new husband," she said without raising her head. "We have innumerable American-based clients. Many of them are here for The Season, as you might expect. I will have to make some calls and inquire if any of our Georgia-based clients have come home for a visit. And there are surely men here who would love to move to the

States. Otherwise, we can set something up when you return to America."

"You can do that?" I asked.

"My dear," she said as she patted the Rolodex, "I have some old school ways, but this office connects couples all over the world. India is a hub of computer and software technology." She paused to stab at the calculator a few more times. "The basic fee does not include connecting you with anyone back home. The figure I give you covers only the introductions we will make while you are still here. Should you determine to continue with our service after you go home, we can work on an à la carte basis."

"Fair enough," I said. It was getting a little hard to breathe.

"Excellent," she said. She wrote on a piece of paper and slid it across the desk. I saw the figure and almost passed out: *342,524.* Isha noticed my reaction. "It's rupees, my dear. Do not panic." I tried to do the conversion in my head. Isha saved me the mental gymnastics. "It comes to five thousand US dollars."

Might as well be five million!

"We will take cash, check, or credit card," she said.

"I–I–" I wanted to ask if she had a payment plan, but the words would not come out.

I heard the door behind me open. A starched white sleeve passed my face. A bronzed arm extending from the rolled cuffs made brief contact with my cheek. A hand dropped a check on Isha's desk.

"With the compliments of the Chatwal Family," Vik said.

CHAPTER 41

HARLOW

THE LUNCH WAS DIVINE. LAMB IN A RICH, SPICY SAUCE SERVED with basmati rice.

"This is superb," I said, "but I bet yours would be better."

"Don't think so," Vik said. "This place was always spectacular. The owner and chef is a mentor. He taught me everything I know."

"Can we meet him?"

Vik lowered his eyes. "Sadly, he died last year. His son runs the place now, but he learned his lessons well. In fact, here he is. Fawzi Acharya, it is my pleasure to introduce a dear friend of mine from America, Ms. Harlow Kennedy."

"Dear friend." Not exactly what I'd like, but it beats the hell out of "someone I know."

No two men could have been more opposite. Where Vik looked like a male underwear model, Fawzi embodied every chef stereotype: short, round, balding, with a full face and five o'clock shadow. It was a few minutes past noon. He removed his toque and inclined his head in a stiff, overly formal bow.

"A pleasure, mademoiselle," he said.

"Oh, *vous parlez francais*?"

"Oh, no, no, no. *C'est tres mauvais*. Please, English if you would be so kind," he said.

With a grand flourish, he held my chair as I retook my seat. Before he joined us, he motioned to a server who appeared about a minute later with a bottle of wine.

"Fort Ross, 2016," Fawzi said.

"An American Pinot?" Vik asked. "Your father must be spinning in his grave."

Fawzi looked around with a conspiratorial gaze. "Don't tell anyone, but it was his favorite. Pinot pairs well with the lamb cutlets. It shows cherry, orange peel, and turned earth. With its silky finish,"—he kissed his fingers—"it is perfection."

He grinned at Vik. "More importantly, it is on the house, my old friend."

"Thank you, Fawzi," Vik said.

The chubby man stood, made a grand production of returning his tall toque to his balding pate, then said, "I will leave you two lovebirds alone."

Before either Vik or I could protest, Fawzi headed for the kitchen. Vik's complexion deepened a little.

"I . . . uh . . . I never—"

"Shh," I said. "Don't tell anyone. He might come back and take away our free wine."

Vik and I talked and laughed our way through lunch. He explained how to tell a person's religion and caste by the clothes they wore and how to discern a woman's region of origin from the way her sari hung.

"It's a lot to learn, I know," he said. "But you're sharp. You will get it."

"Hardly matters," I said. "The more I've thought about it, the more I understand this is a frivolous waste of your money. I should head home, marry Addison, take the cash, and serve out my sentence for however long it is."

Vik shot me a withering glance. "Now it is your turn to 'shh' as you so eloquently put it. Karma is an odd thing. Just when you think your life is going in one direction, good fortune can blow your ship a totally different way. You have an entire week. Let this play out."

I was about to protest when I saw Isha at the maître d's stand. "Oh, Jesus on a raft, hide me."

"That means Isha," he said before he looked. "There is no use in hiding. She has more contacts than the CIA. She already knows you are here. If she wants to talk to you, she will come over. If she has nothing for you today, she will leave you alone."

"Well, she's zeroing in," I said.

Vik pushed his chair back, but Isha placed her hand on his shoulder. "Keep your seat, Vikram. No reason to be so formal. You two seem to be having such a lovely time. Isn't this a great place?" We both nodded while she took a quick breath. "Oh, Vikram, I hear you have agreed to serve as a guest chef one evening next week."

Why hadn't Fawzi mentioned that? More importantly, why hadn't Vik? Maybe I'm not as special to him as I hoped.

"It is not official yet, Isha," Vik said. There was a note of reprimand in his voice. "There are details to be ironed out. Please don't activate your broadcast network just yet."

Isha drew an imaginary zipper across her thin, scarlet lips. "Your secret is safe with me," she said but gave Vik a withering gaze. She did not like to be crossed. Then she whirled to me. "Harlow, darling, I have great news."

"Okay," I said.

Isha's smile was non-committal. "There is someone I want you to meet."

Before I could protest, she approximated Queen Elizabeth's wave, and a tall man in his early thirties strolled to the table, a tall, gorgeous man. His tailored white linen shirt clung to his sculpted torso like a second skin. His chiseled face gave no indication of any "work." The good looks had been his since birth. Black wavy hair fell just below his collar.

"Harlow, allow me to present Samir Gupta. Mr. Gupta, this is the young lady we discussed this morning."

"It's nice to make your acquaintance, Ms. Kennedy," he said with a panty-dropping British accent. His broad smile revealed perfect teeth, straight and dazzlingly white.

My God, he has dimples. Winner, winner, chicken dinner.

I felt my knees get a little rubbery.

I picked up Isha mid-resume. "Samir is visiting family in Mumbai and is spending a little time in Delhi with some friends this week. I have the pleasure of knowing his aunt. He is an independent wealth manager."

"Currently in New York," he said. "But modern technology allows me to enjoy a fluid location."

I was waiting for Isha to reveal the long line of insanity in Samir's family or that he'd just been released from prison for murdering kittens. Then the forgotten gentleman to my right broke through my daydream of long horseback rides through the surf surrounded by rainbows and leprechauns.

"Good afternoon, Samir. I am Vikram." Did I detect a little animosity in the voice? "I am a friend of Harlow's from Atlanta. Would you like to join us for a glass of perfectly wonderful Pinot or perhaps a cup of tea?"

The two men shook hands. I had visions of both of them, shirtless, wrestling for the right to woo me.

Who says woo? *No one says* woo. *Harlow, snap out of it!*

"A pleasure, Mr. Chatwal," Samir said.

"Excuse me," Vik said, "but have we met previously?"

"Oh no, sir," Samir said, "but your fame precedes you. Everyone here knows of your triumph in the States. Congratulations on your success. I hope it will continue."

"Thank you," Vik said, although a careful ear would have recognized that Vik meant to substitute *thank* with another word.

The battling Adonises stared at one another, both smiling while wondering if they could stab one another with a fork.

Not sure why Vik cares. He's never shown any interest in me other than as a friend.

I was not about to interrupt the boys' moment.

But Isha was. "Well, that's lovely," she said. "We will let you two get back to your luncheon." She consulted her phone. "Harlow, you are booked tonight. Remember to be ready promptly at seven when the driver comes by. I have arranged for you and Samir to meet on a more formal basis and in a more private setting at the Café du Monde tomorrow. Shall we say two o'clock? I'll have a driver pick you up at 1:30. *Alvida.*"

With Samir in tow, she took off toward a corner table. As he strode away, Samir shot a withering gaze at Vik.

"I don't think he likes you," I said.

"The feeling is mutual," Vik said.

"Why, Mr. Chatwal, I do believe you are jealous."

Vik downed the rest of his Pinot and poured himself another glass. "Don't be silly. I just know a rogue when I see one."

CHAPTER 42

HARLOW

"No self-respecting Indian man would marry someone who does not understand cricket." Vik's voice sounded like cream, smooth and rich. "You must grasp the fundamentals."

"That's the fifth time you've said the same thing," I said.

Lunch had been wonderful—almost a dream—and I had less than no interest in a cricket contest. Or game or dispute or match or whatever it was called but I did in the guy who'd asked me. Besides, the uniforms appealed to my inner fashionista.

"You need to know the game if you intend on attracting someone's attention," he had said. Then he said the thing about self-respecting Indian men for the first time.

"I get it," I said. "It's sort of a miniature version of baseball."

Vik looked like I'd taken off my shirt in public. "Except that it is nothing like baseball," he said. "Notice the absence of four bases. Pay attention to the bat."

"It's flat," I said. "That's not right."

"Only an American would attempt to hit a round ball with a bat of the same shape."

"Well, we had Hank Aaron and Babe Ruth," I said, mentioning the only two Hall of Famers who came to mind.

"And we counter with Sachin Tendulkar, a player of such skill he is virtually a god in India. Unlike your Mister Ruth, Tendulkar never missed two weeks of games because he had eaten too many hot dogs and consumed too many soda pops."

"Good point." Someone threw a ball to someone else. *This game makes no sense.* "What are those sticks in the field? And what's wrong with the pitcher? He can't get the ball to the plate in the air. And why is the batter swinging at such bad pitches?"

I was staring at the field, but I could almost hear Vik's eyes rolling. "First, those are wickets. The bowler—the proper term for what you called *pitcher*—is attempting to knock the bale from atop them. That's why the bowler bounces the ball. It has wicked spin on it. See the small piece?" He pointed.

I nodded.

"That's the bale, the top part. If it is dislodged, the batsman is out. His job is to protect the wicket. He wants to drive the ball into the field."

"It's a circle," I said." Vik took a deep, exasperated breath. Before he could speak, I held up my hands. "It's just weird looking. Don't explain. I'll get it."

"There are similarities to the game, you know, the one I will not mention," he said. His eyes danced when he smiled. "Each team takes turns batting and playing in the field. But the techniques are all different. See how the bowler delivers the pitch?"

He indicated the player with the ball, who took a series of six quick steps, then threw the ball dead overhand on a bounce toward three posts.

"Twenty-two yards at a hundred miles per hour," Vik said. "It's quite a feat to make contact."

"So, when the batter—"

"Batsman."

"Sure, when the batsman wallops the ball, people run."

"A rudimentary understanding," he said.

"And no one has a glove."

"Right."

"I see eleven players on each side, like football."

He nodded begrudgingly. "Must everything relate to some American sport?"

"Well," I said, "it helps keep me straight."

"Okay, just don't say things like that out loud."

"One guy from each team stands in front of the wicket dealio and hits. If he puts it in play, they run back and forth. If one of them makes an out or the stick falls over, he is replaced. How am I doing?"

"Well enough to get by. Nice job," he said.

"Thanks."

I watched the action but went someplace else in my head, someplace warm and dark. Vik and I sat across from one another. Flickering candlelight brought his chiseled face into sharp focus. We sipped wine and fed each other little bites across the table with the intimacy only lovers have. I kept hearing random interjections from around me, but they didn't make sense, and they didn't interrupt my waking dream.

A voice from the right. "That's a beaner, no ball."

Vik led me by the hand. My long silk nightgown trailed behind me. *Why am I wearing a nightgown to dinner?* We walked down a hall and into a bedroom. Rose petals covered the floor. A California king bed beckoned, its silver satin sheets waiting to be rumpled.

A voice from the left. "Give it the treatment!"

Vik turned to me, tipped my chin up with his crooked index finger and brushed the softest lips I had ever felt across mine. He tasted like saffron and peppermint. His cologne filled my nostrils but was not so overpowering as to mask his natural masculine scent.

Someone behind me would not shut up. "LBW, that's an LBW! Leg before the wicket. He's out!"

I felt my knees weaken as he slipped the spaghetti straps from my shoulders, and I stood before him in glistening nakedness. He kissed my shoulder and moved gradually to the trigger spot at the base of my neck. I was overcome with heat and desire—

Vik—the real one—leapt to his feet, applauding. "Oh, he cocked one off the splice in the gully, but that blighter gathered it!"

I stood and clapped, but the players might as well have been wearing clown costumes. I had no idea what was happening or what had just taken place in my mind—and other areas. I sat for fear my "interest" might show through my linen slacks.

"Some play, huh?" Vik said. His face beamed with the wild-eyed fascination of a fan. "Unbelievable!"

"Yeah," I said. "Something else. I really can't begin to describe it." I checked my shoulder to make sure I was still clothed above the waist, then looked back out on the field. anything to keep from staring into Vik's eyes.

He looked at his watch. "I think you have a date in a bit, do you not?"

"It's an appointment, and I already told Isha I didn't want to go. I was supposed to meet someone named Patel."

"Hardly narrows the field in India. It's like meeting someone named Smith in Atlanta, but I fear I know who you are destined to encounter, and I imagine it will be a memorable afternoon. Is his name Goral, by chance? Goral Patel?"

"Yes, how do you know him? Did you take his sister's virtue?"

"No chance of that," he said, "although she's stunningly beautiful."

"Oh, did someone turn down the great Vikram Chatwal?"

"I may be a creep, but I am not a pervert," he said. "She's all of ten years old, I think."

"Finally," I said, "an admirable quality." He sat quietly. I could tell he was debating about telling me something. "What do you know that I don't? Give it up."

"He's a little off," he said. "Goral. He's like that Tom Cruise chap counting toothpicks in the casino."

"Well, aside from screwing up the scene, the actor, and the character, I think I know what you mean. *Rain Man*?"

"Yes, that's the one. Played by . . ."

"Dustin Hoffman," I said. "I'm an excellent driver."

Vik's face was blank. Then, "Oh, a line from the movie? You're full of those, aren't you?"

"We each have unique gifts," I said. "I'm full of movie lines. You're full of bullshit. So, what's up with Goral? Is he Tom Cruise, or does he have to watch Judge Wapner at five?"

"He's the second. A little *challenged.* I believe is the politically correct term of which you Americans are so fond."

"What makes you say that?"

"His Spiderman nightclothes are a pretty solid clue."

"Most of my real serious relationships hold off on the superhero underoos until the magic third date, hoping the PJs will seal the deal. But I knew something had to be wrong with this guy before I met him."

"What tipped you?"

"Well, Isha called me before we got here. She said the family was eager but very selective. They totally trusted her judgment but required the old signature on the dotted line before I ever laid eyes on the handsome prince of India. Can you believe that? They wanted me to enter into a marriage contract, sight unseen."

"Not completely unheard of, but never a good sign," Vik said.

"Isha knows I'm scheduled to have lunch with Samir tomorrow. Why would she line up something with Goral?"

"Isha's not in the happiness business, Harlow. She's a matchmaker. As long as her client meets and marries someone, it's all good to her. What works best is when one of her clients meets another one of her clients."

"Double commission, right?" I asked.

"Exactly."

"Sounds a little heartless."

Vik shook his head. "Maybe, but it's the way we do things. People are rushing to her right now. It's that time of year. She has a very sophisticated system. She wants to maintain her high success rate. But if she were to tell the truth, she would admit that she's more interested in wedding ceremonies than in lasting marriages."

"So, she's showing me to as many possible grooms as possible?" My cell phone dinged.

Vikram pointed. "Check your phone. I will bet you twenty dollars that's from Isha, and she has something lined up for you this evening if you decide not to meet Mr. Patel. Are you going to keep the appointment?"

"And leave a rousing game of guys dressed like jockeys running around a field? Absolutely not."

We watched a few more batsmen. I was beginning to get the hang of it. "Vik," I asked, "will his parents marry Goral off?"

"Without a doubt. And when they do, it'll probably be the biggest fee Isha makes this year—or any year. Unloading the damaged is tough work. But they will find someone who will put up with his idiosyncrasies just to get close to the family money, and it is considerable. The spouse will just have to listen to the same pitiful request every night, the same plaintive line."

"The poor guy's going to have to beg for sex from his wife?"

"Oh no, not at all. They will have sex if and when the wife

says, and only for the purposes of having children."

"Then what will Goral ask?"

"He'll come down every night about 7:30, superhero pajamas on and a helmet if he dresses like Iron Man or Thor. He'll bring his Sony PlayStation Pro and go from one person to the next, asking, 'Do you want to play with me?'"

"That breaks my heart," I said.

"Not as badly as it will break Goral's," he said. He turned and looked at me, his eyes pained and compassionate. "There's something sadly ironic about all this."

"What's that?"

"The name *Goral* means 'lovable.'"

My lip began to tremble. "That's so very sad."

"He'll be fine," Vik said. "They will find someone for him, I am sure." He cheered about something on the field. I didn't see it, and I didn't care. When he sat down, he asked, "So, do we have a bet?"

"Huh?"

"Your phone. Have you checked it?"

"No, but I don't have twenty dollars to spare, and you know it."

"Then, what will you wager?"

"Your twenty against a kiss from me," I said. *Harlow, you hussy.*

"Book it," he said. His teeth gleamed in the late afternoon sun.

I looked at my phone. Sure enough, there was a text from Isha telling me to be ready at 7:00 p.m. As always, she promised to send a driver.

Vik was reading over my shoulder. "Well, well, well," he said. "Looks like I am the big winner."

"Indeed, you are, sir," I said. I stood, bent over, and kissed him lightly on the forehead like a mother tucking in her child. "Now, take me home. I have a date."

CHAPTER 43

TEJ/VIK

WE LEFT THE CRICKET MATCH, WHICH DIDN'T BOTHER ME. Although field hockey is the national game, cricket dominates the news in season. Still, I feel about it like I did about golf. I'd rather play than watch. Besides, after she kissed me on the head, I could think of nothing else but her lips.

Hussein had raised the privacy screen. Harlow was staring out the window.

"I have an idea," I said.

"Hit me," she said without looking around.

"You want to be a proper Indian wife. Can you cook?"

She looked at me with utter disdain. "Honey," she said, "my fried chicken tastes like heaven, you have to watch my biscuits carefully or they'll float right off the plate, and you have not lived until you taste how I bake my granny's red velvet cake recipe."

"I am not familiar," I said.

"And you call yourself a chef," she said.

"So, you color the cake?"

"Aw hell no," she said. Then she realized I was teasing. "Good one. You had me going for a sec."

This is my chance.

"Well," I said, "I've been out of the kitchen too long. I'm going to cook dinner for myself in the guest house. If you'd like to learn a little more about Indian cooking, I would be honored to share what little I know."

"That would be great!" Her face nearly split from her smile. Then, the grin disappeared. "Damn, you know I have a date."

Damn, she has a date. I had forgotten. Her lips. Her full, red lips.

"It's your fault," she said. "You told Isha to put on the full-court press."

"Another baseball reference?" I asked.

She was headed around the corner of the bleachers when she said, "Basketball. You're hopeless."

Hopeless for your lips, Harlow. How am I going to get you to give me a real kiss?

⚘

I was on the phone with Waman when I heard the knock.

"Thank you, my old friend," I said. "And understand this is not a favor. I insist on paying your usual rate."

I hung up and glanced at the clock. *8:48.* I called over my shoulder as I headed for the stove. "Come in, Hussein." I hated to cook only for myself. Flouting convention, I'd invited my driver to join me. When he demurred, I insisted.

"Dinner will be ready in thirty minutes," I said. "Would you care for a glass of wine?"

The voice I heard was not Hussein's. "I'd rather have a Bangalore Malt if you have it."

"Harlow!" I tried to throttle back on the excitement in my voice. "I thought you had a date."

Her face grew stern. Something had gone terribly wrong. "What is it?"

"Guy was a jerk. Let's leave it at that."

I washed my hands and dried them on a dishtowel. "I know who it was," I said. "I saw his name, remember. 'Jerk' hardly covers it."

Harlow's chagrined expression spoke to her unhappiness. "Not real happy that you know everything about my social life. But you're paying the bill, so . . ."

Her voice faded into the corner. When she lowered her head, she swiped at her cheek. Anger spiraled up my throat.

"Did he hurt you?" I asked.

"Just my feelings." The tears were not from sadness. Fury burned in her luscious eyes. "He wanted 'a preview.'"

I stared at her uncomprehending. "Preview?"

"A test drive. He said he'd heard American women did special things."

My jaw unhinged, and the air suddenly grew thin. Harlow did not move. She stood in unbreakable pride and resolute wrath. If I had touched her arm at that moment, my fingers would have come away singed.

"Your marriage system is fucked up," she said. "I didn't realize it was a meat market. Apparently, that guy forgot who wrote the Kama Sutra."

I didn't think this was the time to correct her misconception of the ancient Sanskrit text intended not as a manual of sexual positions but as a guide to the art of living well and other aspects of life and love. The person in front of me was looking for an excuse to "release the Kraken" like in *Clash of the Titans*.

"For what it's worth, I'm sorry," I said. "While many if not most of my gender fall woefully short in the tact department when dealing with women, at least in this country, those of us going through the matchmaking process do everything we can to treat women with the respect and dignity they deserve."

"Well, this one missed a lesson or two in that department," she said.

"No one would have blamed you if you'd decked him," I said. "There's a reason he's still single at forty-one."

Harlow's husky laugh broke the tension. "He claimed he was twenty-nine."

"Did you believe him?"

"Like I believe in the Tooth Fairy," she said. "I thought he was over fifty." She sniffed the air. "Screw that clown. Let's eat."

She opened up during dinner. The tandoori chicken was excellent. I used my own blend of yogurt, spices, and lemon juice to flavor the meat, along with the perfect amount of chile to enliven the palate. My concoction made the chicken succulent and fiery all at once. But honesty told me my culinary skills had less to do with her talkative mood than the malt whiskey. She was on her third.

"It's a good thing I didn't take that guy up on his smarmy

offer," she said. "It would have killed the deal."

"Excuse me?" I said.

"If I'd slept with him, he would have bolted like a frightened filly." She took a long pull from her glass. "I'm not any good, at least I don't think so."

Do I pursue this or take the conversation in another direction?

"What makes you say that? Have there been complaints?"

She tossed her hair to the side. *Oh, I love the way she does that.* I took another gulp.

"As pollsters would say, there is not a large enough sampling size to reflect an accurate position."

"I'm totally lost."

"Vik," she said, "I told you after the wedding that Addison was my first. I didn't tell you the rest of it. Believe it or not, you are looking at an almost virgin."

There was nothing to say. I waited.

She patted her left shoulder with her right palm. "In her entire adult life, Ms. Harlow Anne Kennedy has had sex exactly one time!"

CHAPTER 44

HARLOW

"Goodnight, Ms. Harlow."

I lay back on the bed, the room spinning. "Thank you, Hussein," I said. "I'm a little embarrassed."

"No need, Ms. Harlow," he said. "From everything you said, you had a difficult evening before you came over for dinner. Everyone is entitled to unwind a little.

Oh my God, what did I say on the way home? "Hussein, did I babble on the way home?"

He shook his head. "No, ma'am." He lied. I could see it in his kind eyes. "Would you like some help getting into bed, ma'am? I can summon one of the servants."

"No, thank you," I said. And he slipped out the door.

The evening slowly reconstructed. I'd told Vik everything —how I'd given in to Addison because I was in my middle twenties and had never let a guy past second base.

"Was he kind?" Vik had asked.

"Not particularly, I don't think," I said. "I've blocked a lot of it. There was a lot of noise. Thank God, it didn't last very long."

Vik had laughed, then immediately apologized. "Not exactly a stallion, your Mr. Whitmore."

"More like a firecracker." I held my thumb and index finger about two inches apart. "A little-bitty firecracker."

Vik almost spit out his food. "Ms. Kennedy, you vixen."

Although we laughed, in truth, the story hurt every time I thought about it. Was Addison inept as a lover, or was I uninspiring as a mate? The question had haunted me ever since I'd slipped out of his bed, gotten dressed, and taken an Uber home in the middle of the night.

Just before I walked out, Addison had appeared at the door of his bedroom with boxer shorts and "sleepy-time" hair. "Do you have to leave?" Then he went back to bed.

Alone now, I stared at the ceiling. "Oh, Addison, why couldn't you have asked me to stay?"

The next day Mina gave instructions to the driver in Hindi, and he began careening through the crowded streets.

Every turn, every horn, every pedestrian or cyclist presented possible disaster. Mayhem lurked with every press of the accelerator or slam of the brake.

"Our next stop is the Design Studio," Mina said. "This is where you will select your engagement and wedding trousseau pieces."

"I'm sorry," I said. "Are you familiar with the 'cart before the horse' saying?"

"Yes," Mina said, "but there is a popular Indian expression that supersedes it."

"What is it?"

"'Isha knows exactly what she is doing.'" Mina let go of a belly laugh, totally at odds with her diminutive stature. I put my hands behind my head in surrender.

"Okay, okay," I said. "We're gonna go with the flow. But isn't it a little unusual to have a fashion show before lunch?"

"Think about it," Mina said. "Everyone's trying to meet as many people as possible. Lunches, afternoons at cricket matches, dinners—those are all prime time. No one is going to meet for breakfast."

"Unless the date goes really well," I said. "Then they just nudge one another and order room service."

Mina looked at me in mock horror. "Don't let Isha hear you say that! Chastity, you know."

"Got it!"

Mina pointed to my outfit. "You look fabulous by the way."

"Thank you."

I loved my almost sheer, blushing pink sari. The iridescent tulle fabric in a mirror work pattern reflected the light as sparkles danced all around. A peach-colored drape covered my plunging neckline and made what might have been a provocative ensemble acceptably decorous. A pair of matching Jimmy Choos edged out from the crystal-encrusted hem. I put my hair in a two-strand twist after my shower the evening before. Now my locks fell in lush waves down my back. I'd finished my look with smoky eyes and pouty red lips.

"Your admirer must think a lot of you. That's a pricey ensemble. What lovely accessories too." Mina looked longingly at my chandelier earrings and matching bangle.

"Isha sent it over with instructions to put it on. Lita's mother helped me get it right. Do you know who paid for it?" *Say Vik, please say Vik.*

"I have no idea," Mina said, "but it is not unusual for a suitor to make ostentatious gifts. You have a date with Samir Gupta tonight. Though I do not know for sure, I would assume it is from him."

We pulled up to a warehouse. "Is this the right place?"

"Never let a plain wrapper convince you that what is contained therein is worthless," Mina said.

"Confucius?"

"No, I just made it up," she said. "Pretty solid, huh?"

"Yep."

We walked inside. Huge crystal chandeliers hung from the ceiling. A DJ was cranking out Desi hip-hop. The place was already packed with immaculately dressed men and women of all ages. Long red velvet curtains blocked a stage from which protruded a catwalk.

"I figured we were meeting a tailor," I said. "Didn't know I'd get a show."

"Watch and enjoy," Mina said.

I spotted our location before the usher took us to our seats. Isha was impossible to miss, even in a crowd.

"You look refreshed," she said. "Complexion looks much improved." She grasped my hand. "Your fingers no longer feel like those of a field worker. These next few days are significant. When I consulted the astrologer, he assured me that true love is very near for you. I like the way this is shaping up for you and Samir."

The lights dimmed, music pulsed with the work of fantastic Desi music stars, Nucleya, Shirley Setia, The F16s, Dualist Inquiry, and The Local Train. Gorgeous models strutted out onto the runway, each in an ensemble more fabulous than the one before. The black leather catalog featured designer pieces with dazzling borders, Swarovski crystals, and sequin-encrusted bustiers. A sea of salmon pink, tangy orange, and searing red gave way to a pearl-white silk lehenga with silver and diamond accents. The heavy under-blouse featured exquisite embroidery in an ancient motif.

"With your figure, you would look fabulous in that, my dear," Isha said. Her eyes never left the models. She noticed every nuance of every outfit.

For whatever reason, my focus wandered momentarily, long enough for me to spot a bevy of young women clustered around Vikram Chatwal.

What is he doing here?

Standing nearby, vigilant and eager, a gaggle of maatajis chirped among one another. I could imagine the conversation.

"He is such a catch."

"My Lakshaya looks so very good on his arm."

"Is it proper for her to throw herself at him so blatantly?"

"I imagine you want her to step aside so your daughter can squeeze next to him."

Mina tapped me on the shoulder. "Isha is speaking to you," she said.

I tore my attention away from Vik and his harem. Isha's focus remained riveted on the stage. She never turned her head. "It is not seemly for you to stare at Mr. Chatwal, my dear," she said.

How can she tell where I am looking?

"Now, pay attention. We need to select a few items. Your time is very near. My astrologer is never wrong."

A willowy model toured the stage wrapped in a midnight blue sari. She'd accessorized with tulle veils and gold temple jewelry. Each model seemed more beautiful than the last, each outfit more desirous.

My heart craved the seductively draped dresses, capes in vibrant colors, timeless hand-woven jackets, and metallic braided hairpieces. My wallet shrieked disapproval of every imagined purchase. Hand-painted skirts sang a Sirens' song and drowned out any semblance of fiscal responsibility. In my head, I saw how I could put my own twist on the magnificent traditional clothing, how I could craft the perfect accessory piece.

Isha read my thoughts. "Pay no mind to the expense," she said. "Your handsome benefactor has already assured me he will cover whatever you need."

That must mean he paid for this gorgeous dress!

CHAPTER 45

TEJ/VIK

I DESPERATELY WANTED LAKSHAYA TO LET GO OF MY ARM, BUT every time I stretched, she reattached like a barnacle. My head hurt from watching Harlow out of the corner of my eye. She stood a full head above most of the attendees and looked beautiful.

She could be on stage. She would look much better in every selection than the models.

The women around me clamored for attention.

"Don't you like that one, Vik?"

"Do you think that color would go well with my complexion?"

"How much longer will you be here? We should set up a lunch."

If they had all been naked and covered in baby oil, I would not have been interested. I did not want vacuous fortune chasers whose only interest lay in snagging a husband. My desire was for someone with more talent than beauty, more ambition than avarice. I wanted more. I wanted special.

I wanted Harlow.

After ninety minutes, the show wound to a merciful end. The music stopped. The crowd swelled in a crescendo of gushing compliments. Everyone had been overwhelmed by the annual spectacle.

Across the way, Isha beckoned, not to me but to a cluster of my contemporaries—cads every last one of them. They tumbled over one another in their drive to meet the mocha-colored beauty on Isha's arm.

I headed toward Harlow, intent on staking my claim, but a stampede of marriage-crazed maatjis swam toward me like Indian Ocean hammerhead sharks rushing a bloody steak. I heard endless repetitions of the same sentences.

"You remember my daughter."

"Vikram, you look wonderful."

"Mr. Chatwal, I know you are very interested in finding someone worthy of your position."

On and on, each comment more self-serving than the last. I smiled and nodded and did the best I could not to offend anyone, though I wanted to scream and race from the building. But my parents had reared a proper gentleman, so I endured the onslaught, answered every question, responded to every greeting.

By the time I fought my way clear of the feeding frenzy, Harlow was nowhere to be seen.

CHAPTER 46

TEJ/VIK

MA, I HOPE YOU ARE HAPPY.

I looked across the table at Ursi. She was anxious, eager to impress me. And she only mentioned marriage in every other sentence. It was my duty as a son to play the part of an active suitor, to pretend to be hunting for a bride as long as I was home.

I had hoped the Lita debacle would pour water on the flame of my mother's matrimonial intentions for me. Instead, it doused the fire with gasoline. The community marveled at Maji's endurance, the quiet patience she exhibited for her son, who *could not land* a wife. Though I was twice scorned in the public's eye, my ma was thrice revered.

Arranged marriages benefitted individual families but not necessarily the individuals in the family. Spouses were select-ed like broodmares—good bloodlines, outstanding stock, childbearing hips, proper discipline. The idea was to continue the creation of solid families and stable communities.

"The times are changing," I said.

My father's response was brief but abundantly clear. "But not in India."

This date was a "two thumbs down" disaster, but I knew it would be. I'd picked Ursi out of the pile on purpose. I checked the box of "meeting a prospect" without ever endangering my bachelorhood. Ursi smiled easily. She had all her teeth. She ate with the correct fork. She made pleasant conversation. But she was the wrong caste and from the wrong region. Even if I'd loved her with the passion of Lancelot for Guinevere, Maata would wave this landing off before I began my final approach.

In India, marrying someone from "the wrong side of the tracks" was not the same as a North Carolinian wedding someone from Texas in America. Ignoring class distinctions could have disastrous results. Not everyone wanted to maintain the social distinctions of the subcontinent. The Indian government reserved a specific number of spots in the universities for members of the lower classes and set aside government jobs as well. Allowing people the chance to get ahead meant a lot in a land as ancient and strangled by tradition as my homeland.

But there existed no charity among the upper reaches of the upper class when it came to marriage. Who would bear whose grandchildren represented a preeminent position. In my case, an "eligible" woman meant one who was "qualified" by my parents' standards.

My strategy was flawless. In less than a week, I could look my mother in the eye and say, "I tried. It just was not in the stars. I will try again on my next visit."

I approached the marriage game like a business proposal. One: know every part of the deal. I perused Isha's list before we scheduled any rendezvous. Two: I'd been very compliant with my parents then I'd made my position abundantly clear to Isha. I was running the show and would have the final say. The old way might have worked for my parents hundreds of years prior, but I would steer this process. Three: Anticipate and maneuver toward the desired outcome. I had left Georgia without a wife, and that's the way I intended to return.

Oh, bloody hell. Pay attention, Vik.

"I'm sorry, my dear, the waiter made a lot of noise just then and I missed what you said." I locked eyes with Ursi. She ignored the blatant nature of my lie. One could have heard a blade of grass growing in the near-empty restaurant.

"I said, I hope we can meet again soon," she said.

Be careful, old boy. Dharma compels you to protect women like this.

I saw them all the time, watching me, trying to attract my attention, then acting shy when I looked their way. I always waved. I never winked. I was trained to be gracious and never duplicitous. Leading women on was bad for my karma.

I felt a bolt of self-flagellation shoot up my spine. I might be a rogue, but I was neither cruel nor insensitive and never with the defenseless. Uris was scholarly and earnest. Her preparation for our meeting was evident in her meticulous makeup and pristine wardrobe.

She deserves better than me.

"Ursi," I said. I could tell she knew what was coming after

I called her name, but she never looked away. *Man up, Vik!* "Someone will be fortunate to have you as his bride. I wish you all the happiness in the world."

A socially acceptable, upper caste Brahmin shoot-down.

She pushed her thick glasses up and smiled. "Thank you for your honesty," she said. "Not everyone I meet is so courtly."

I paid the bill and escorted her to her car. When I paused, unsure what to do, she shook my hand and drove away without another word.

Three steps across the parking lot, Hussein pulled up in the Mercedes. He opened the door. "Home, sir?"

"Isha's office, please," I said.

I beat myself up all the way.

CHAPTER 47

HARLOW

IF I HAD EATEN ARMADILLO SCRAPED FROM THE HIGHWAY, I would not have known. I couldn't remember the last time I'd been so disinterested in food—or so nervous. Samir sat across from me. His smooth skin gave no indication of the blistering heat; not one drop of perspiration dripped from his chin to his perfectly tailored linen suit. The top three buttons of his pale-pink silk shirt were undone. His chest looked as smooth as a hardwood floor.

I thought about Steve Carell's character getting his chest waxed in *The Forty-Year-Old Virgin* and him yelling, *"Kelly Clarkson!"* I choked a little on my mulligatawny and tried not to spit it across the table.

"Are you all right, my dear?" Every time Samir spoke, he was so suave. I remembered Henry Higgins' diatribe from the musical *My Fair Lady* I'd watched with Daddy: "Oozing charm from every pore, he oiled his way across the floor."

"I'm fine," I said. "A little just went down the wrong way."

"As I was saying," he said, "the investment landscape in New York is a little crowded. I've been thinking about moving my operation to the American South. I understand the landscape is as stunning as you are, Harlow."

This guy must practice his lines before every meal.

"And the people are reportedly quite friendly."

Before he could say something cheesy like, "I've never met anyone quite like you, Harlow," I changed the subject.

"Do you like cricket?" I asked.

A look of utter amazement spread across his face. "Of all the women I have dated, and there have been a considerable number—but none as charming as you, I might add—you are the very first ever to show any interest at all in cricket. Yes, I enjoy watching it very much. But I love to play it even more. At one time, I thought about becoming a professional, but I tore my ACL when I was in my early twenties and, well, *poof!*"

He clapped his hands back and forth like a Vegas blackjack dealer at the end of a shift. For a moment, he looked a little wistful, and I realized this had not been a boast intended to impress me. He had, in some small way, opened up.

"Do you miss it?" I asked.

"I do indeed, like something inside of me has been surgically removed." He paused, then swallowed hard. "But enough about me. Tell me about Harlow Kennedy. What interests you?"

I started talking about movies, and sports, and my dreams of opening my own jewelry design business. I had no idea I'd been prattling on, but suddenly I looked around and realized we were the last patrons in the restaurant.

"Oh goodness," I said, "I must be boring you silly. Everyone else is gone. We should probably let them clear the table so they can get a few moments off before the dinner hour."

Samir stood and helped me from my seat, a true gentleman.

Well, that'll play well in Atlanta.

He offered his arm in a very Old-World way and escorted me to the parking lot where Isha's driver opened the door for me. Before I stepped into the back seat, Samir raised my hand to his lips and kissed it gently.

"Until this evening, my dear," he said. "Would it be acceptable if I picked you up?"

I did not know how to answer. The Indian people had stringent, arcane rules of conduct. I knew where to draw the line about physical intimacy but was totally out of my depth regarding dating protocol. Behind Samir's shoulder, I saw the driver give the slightest of nods.

Okay, that's clearance from Isha.

"Certainly," I said. "What time should I be ready?"

Samir's smile was blinding. "I cannot imagine you require any time at all to prepare. You even looked radiant this morning at the fashion show."

"You were there? I didn't see you."

"I stayed out of sight," he said. "But I must say, you looked most elegant in the dress I bought for you."

He gave me the dress. Not Vik.

I cried most of the way back to Lita's house.

CHAPTER 48

TEJ/VIK

NOT EVERYONE WOULD HAVE BEEN ALLOWED TO SIT UNAT-
tended in Isha's private office. But not everyone was the son of
one of India's wealthiest men. The surroundings were somehow
opulent and understated at the same time. The furnishings likely
cost more than a mid-sized American home.

"The wedding business is good," I said. I let out a sigh of
relief when I looked over my shoulder. The door was closed.
"These people already think there is something profoundly
wrong with me. Twice dumped by a potential bride."

The office afforded a welcome respite from the noise of
India. Triple pane glass reduced the clamor of the streets to
a mild buzz, like the evening sounds of cicadas in the American South. I slumped into a Pollaro leather chair. Visions of
Rati drifted into my mind—her sumptuous figure, her willing
smile, her tiger eyes, her skilled hands. Slowly, the face atop
her naked body began to change. The sharp features softened.

The crow's feet disappeared. The years fell away.

Harlow!

I jumped from the chair, instantly awake. For a moment, I did not know where I was, but as my orientation returned, so did a feeling I'd been fighting since my trip across the Atlantic.

"Harlow," I said.

What was I thinking? I put her together with the preeminent matchmaker in all of India. Someone will snatch her up. She is a prize. I only wanted to keep her here for a little longer.

"Vik, you are an idiot!" The sound of my own voice made me jump, and I realized I was pacing around the office.

My attention fell on Isha's desk, a solid surface design I recognized as Italian—Viadurini—and outrageously expensive. It looked like an *X* swirling from the floor. Customized in Isha's signature light pink, the piece, though not my style because I needed drawers and more area, the desk spoke to the matchmaker's obsession with all things contemporary.

Except in the institution of marriage.

I lowered myself into a matching executive chair, Eames, I suspected. I'd been considering a new chair before I'd opted for a standing desk. Besides, I did not wish to spend almost five grand for a place to rest my backside. The only items on the tabletop were a computer, her legendary Rolodex, and a small stack of file folders. I recognized them immediately.

Bride profiles.

Oh, the allure of forbidden fruit. I fairly salivated to see what delectable morsels I might uncover, what weaknesses I could emphasize to extricate myself from each pair of grasping hands, one after another. And there, on the very top, a name I could not—would not—resist: Harlow Kennedy.

The paperwork drew a picture of an accomplished and interesting woman. Public school in Sandy Springs, undergrad at Emory. Fluent in French. Jewelry maker. Loves vinyl records, 80s rom-coms and classic sci-fi novels. I had a brief vision of sitting in front of a fire, feeding samosas to her as we listened to whatever the hell she picked.

Hmm, interesting. Harlow has Indian blood. Father's side, from Maharashtra, the western part of the country. Family name, Daswani. Ma will know.

I heard voices outside the door. After returning the folders to their original position, I raced back to the overpriced but very comfortable chair in front of the desk. I tried hard to look like I'd just awakened from a catnap when Isha breezed in.

"Mr. Chatwal, how lovely to see you. I'm so glad Mina got you situated. How was your luncheon?"

"It's a hard pass, I am afraid," I said.

Isha's cheery façade broke for a moment. "As if you did not know before you went," she said. Then, back to Madame Sunshine. "Honestly, Vikram, you should let me help. I promise to line up someone who will make you forget every other woman you've ever met. Right here on my desk I have the names of a number of very eligible women."

"Thank you," I said, "but I am quite comfortable with our current arrangement. I will continue to pick and choose. I have pledged to my parents that I would try to meet someone before leaving. I did not pledge to try very hard. When next I return, if I am not wed, which will probably be the case, I promise to turn you loose in all your matchmaking glory."

She extended her hand. "A bargain then, to make up for the last two."

Ouch! I'd never given much thought to how much face Isha had lost because of me. First there had been Haiya, a situation that continued to look like my fault. Now Lita, who made me look flawed. This time, when I left India as a single man, the gossips would have a field day with Isha. They'll say, "She's lost her magic touch, " or "She can't even find someone for the most eligible bachelor in Delhi."

And with me. "I heard he was a brute. That's why Haiya wouldn't go through with it," "Well, someone—I won't say who—told me he is *teda*, that he prefers men," "It doesn't surprise me. After all, he lives in Atlanta, a most immoral place," and "His poor maaji must be devastated."

Isha was still talking. "After all, your circumstances have been, shall we say, a little unusual."

"A thousand apologies," I said. "I will make amends in good order. Right now, though, I have some significant issues at home requiring my full attention."

"Something interesting, I trust. And profitable?"

"Yes, on both accounts," I said. "You may know I am launching an entire line of Bombay Baby frozen foods, like nothing anyone has ever seen. It will be a taste of India in your home freezer."

She smiled, but I could tell she was unimpressed.

"You don't quite get it," I said. "Here in India, cooking is culture, a time of fellowship, of reverence. In a great deal of America, it is simply a necessary evil. Everyone rushes all the time. It is not the bustle of the streets. In the States, people do not go to the market. They race to meetings. At dinners, they are less interested in communication than they are in commerce."

Isha looked horrified. "The food must be awful."

"Not all of it," I said. "Some Americans, men included, take the time to prepare meals properly. To others, adding something as simple as a spice or two is nothing more than a waste of time. I want my food—I'm sorry *our* food, the food of this marvelous country—to reintroduce the joys of adventure and zest. I believe it will be a smashing success."

"What else?" she asked. Now, she was genuinely interested, not just because of the money.

"I've been asked to consider serving as a guest chef-in-residence at some restaurants in major cities in the US, a celebrity appearance, as it were."

"That would be significant," she said, "both for your business and your self-esteem."

She almost said ego but caught herself just in time. In the end, she never forgot her place in the social pecking order.

"Thank you," I said. "So, as you can see, spending any more time here than is absolutely necessary is not something I can do. I would not have come at all except for my mother's medical condition, which I now know was not as dire as was originally presented."

"I understand, Mr. Chatwal," she said. "May the gods grant you safe passage and look favorably on all your endeavors."

I had my hand on the doorknob when Isha spoke again. "She's quite lovely, isn't she?"

"Who?" I asked.

Isha stood behind her atrocious desk and slowly fanned herself with a folder. She held up the large envelope. "Miss Harlow. Quite lovely, indeed." She stopped my protest with a shake of her head. "Vikram, I knew you would look. Your interest in the woman is obvious. Do you really think I have gotten this far in business by randomly leaving confidential information on my desk?"

CHAPTER 49

HARLOW

Now I'm really confused.

I'd been certain things with Vik were going to take off romantically Monday evening, but after I told him about the "test drive" request, I guess he figured making a move was out of the question. He didn't know I was ready, willing, and—*Kama Sutra* or not—able, at least to do my best. Still, dinner passed without incident. We finished a post-dessert brandy, and Hussein drove me home.

Maybe I wasn't Vik's type. I'd seen pictures of his dates. How could I miss them? His sculpted face was plastered all over the society pages of the Sunday *Atlanta Journal Constitution* at least once a month. The captions all ran together in my brain: Tej Mayur with such-and-such heiress, Super-Hip Restaurateur Escorts Star Guard From WNBA, and my favorite was Flavor of the Month for Indian Entrepreneur. His date was a world-famous supermodel. They didn't even have to print her name in the caption.

After last night with Samir, I wasn't sure what to do. We hadn't done anything more than I had done on a high school or college date, but somehow, I felt I'd made some sort of commitment with my conduct.

"What the hell, Harlow?" I said after I slammed my coffee mug down on the counter. I looked to see if I'd cracked what I was sure was something I could not afford. Fortunately, no crockery was harmed during my brief tirade. I was meeting Samir again on Thursday, and I had dinner plans tonight with some guy named Maktar or Mubar or Motown or something. I didn't care.

I should ask Isha to refund Vik's money, at least part of it. This is getting way too complicated.

I looked at the clock. "Damn, 9:45." I had to book it to meet Vik at the market. His dinner on Monday had been so divine, at least from a culinary point of view, that I requested more of his cooking. And I vowed never to set foot in a kitchen as long as he was around. The boy flat out knew his way around a chopping block and stove.

I stepped to the curb just as Vik strolled across the street. The market teamed with noise. Aromatic spices poured into my nostrils with every breath. Shoppers scurried, baskets on arms, while vendors hawked their wares. It was a human ant farm.

"Close your eyes," Vik said. He held something underneath my nose. "And it is?"

"Clove," I said. "But anyone who's ever made mulled cider knows that. You gotta step up your game, man."

Another.

"Cumin."

Another

"Turmeric."

He seemed genuinely impressed. "The girl knows her spices. Hang on, one more. If you get this one, I will buy you anything you want in the market under a thousand dollars."

"Pretty sure of yourself," I said.

"We will see," he said.

I closed my eyes. I felt the air move. "Why are you flapping your hand in front of my face?"

"I don't want you to look."

"Unlike you, I do not have a reputation for cheating at cards and the like."

"Not going to let that go, are you?" he asked, but there was no malice in his tone. "Ready? For a thousand-dollar gift . . ."

"Vik, if you just want to give me a thousand dollars, I'm not too proud to take it." I sniffed and laughed. *God in heaven, I hope he knows I'm kidding.*

"What is your guess?"

"Everybody knows what cinnamon smells like."

He buzzed his lips. "Wrong, O Great Oracle of all things India. It is not cinnamon. No soup for you."

"Liar," I said with laughter in my voice. "Liar, pants on fire." *I knew someone whose pants were on fire, but I wasn't going to tell him.*

Vik waved at a vendor. "Excuse me, Saab? My friend is new here. She is sure I lied to her about this spice. She thinks it is cinnamon."

"Oh no, *guruji*. Your lady friend, though quite stunning, is incorrect. She does catch a whiff of cinnamon because this spice is fresh, a telltale sign. But it is not cinnamon. It is cassia bark."

"Mother—" I caught myself before I humiliated my host. "Mother McCree," I said. "Thank you, sir, for your informative lesson." I glared at Vik. "Don't look so smug. You only won on a technicality."

The rest of the morning was a tutorial. "Traditional meals vary from region to region," Vik said. "Southeasterners like healthy foods: fish and vegetables and salads. For them, the focus is on the sides like pickles, chutneys, and sambar."

"Hey, slow down. Remember, unlike you, I am a native of Georgia. What the heck is sambar?"

"An Indian hot soupy vegetable dish, it goes with all kinds of things." The longer he talked, the more relaxed I felt, the less on display. I realized I had been trying to audition as if Vik were somehow on the "menu" of available grooms. If he'd wanted sex, he would have tried something after dinner. He obviously wasn't interested in anything other than a little companionship. So, I decided to go with the flow, and I began to enjoy everything.

I was not Indian by any stretch of the imagination, but I had roots here from long, long ago. The entire morning deepened my appreciation and understanding of my father's people. Vik talked, and I soaked it up, a thirsty sponge lapping water. This place, this incredible land with its odd mixture of the ancient and the hyper-modern, overflowed with tradition, customs, and spectacular food.

Vik was in full lecture mode. "Northern India has withstood countless invasions. Each new conquest brought something new, another dish, another flavor. The Mughals introduced Persian influences. Travelers from distant lands taught the Indians how to incorporate new fruits and nuts into dishes. India features mustard and coconut."

By the time we started back to the guest house, about a mile's walk, I felt I'd experienced a graduate-level class in India. And I was richer for it.

The heavens opened. Buckets of rain fell before we could make it to shelter, so we surrendered and sloshed through the deluge. When we stepped through the door, we were soaked to the skin.

We toweled off, and I caught a vision of my rapidly curling hair in the bathroom mirror. *Eek! Oh well, nothing I can do about it.*

We unpacked our treasures. "Any chance we get some sunshine today?" I asked.

Vik peered out the window. "Not likely. The clouds are low, heavy, and unmoving. It will be wet all day."

I pulled at my blouse and hoped it did not cling too much. I was not suffering from an over-abundance of undergarments.

"So, what's on tap for tonight?" he asked. "Another fabulous lecher?"

My ebullient mood crashed, and I sighed. "Vik, I may tap out,. I think it's a great tradition, and the matchmaking thing makes sense in some ways. It's like an analog version of an online dating app, but I don't think it's going anywhere.

How much of your money do you think you can get back from Isha?"

Vik's shoulders slumped. "I'm sorry to hear that, Harlow, but I don't think you've given it much of a chance. In truth, you've been hazed a little, tested by Isha."

"How's that?"

"First Goral. That's always Isha's opening salvo. If she can get someone to bite on that, she gets a big payday. Tonight's date obviously does not excite you. And let's not forget Monday night's creep."

"Ugh."

"Those were little tests. She knows you are serious. That's why she put you together with Samir. He's a step up, candidate-wise, wouldn't you say?"

"I guess," I said.

"You still have time. Don't rush it. Let the game come to you, as you Americans are fond of saying."

"Okay," I said, "but if anyone else wants to check under the hood, I'm on the first flight out of here."

"Fair enough," he said. "How about some lunch?" He led me to a cutting board. "Chop the chicken, then toss them in some lemon juice."

I did okay. When he critiqued my technique, he stood behind me and guided my hands. I resisted the urge to push back into him. My throat tightened, and I got a little lightheaded.

I listened to his explanation of the proper method for roasting cumin seed and for stirring in the ginger and garlic. I diced onions, then mixed paprika and chili powder with the tomatoes. He showed me how he made his garam masala,

which was a warm spice blend made with cumin and coriander seeds, cardamom pods, cinnamon, cloves, and pepper-
corns.

He talked as we worked. "Early on, the food critics in
Atlanta were brutal, especially the old school guys. They ac-
cused me of betraying my heritage and my traditions. They
wanted every Indian meal to end with fresh fruit. I preferred
to offer rum-soaked cake, something I used to sneak from the
kitchen when I was a boy. Americans prefer something sweet
after dinner, so I used my judgment. The writers scolded me,
but the diners praised me. I went with the paying customers.
I had more business than I could handle in less than three
months. And it has stayed that way."

"Good for you," I said. I realized that the pace of my stirring increased whenever he got close. *Easy on the throttle.*

"Gently," he said. "The chicken is already dead."

His manner was easy, non-threatening. He instructed
without condescension. When he told me something, I felt
informed, not belittled.

He dipped a spoon into the sauce I'd made. As soon as it
touched his lips, I went weak in the knees. *Lucky damn spoon.*

"What do you think?"

A look of sheer joy spread across his face. "Absolutely delightful. You have a gift."

"Thanks," I said. "You have a little schmutz on your face."

"Schmutz?"

I reached with a dish towel and wiped the tiny river of
sauce traveling toward his chin. *He's going to kiss me! He's going to kiss me!*

My phone dinged four times in rapid succession. Vik took the towel from my hand.

"You better check those texts," he said. "Sounds like someone is excited."

I looked at the screen. "It's Lita."

"Ah, the blushing bride," he said. "What does she say?"

I read Lita's text. *Having a wonderful time in Bali. Everything is beautiful here. Well, I think so. We've barely been out of the room unless you count doing the nasty on the balcony as "out." LOL. Girl, you should totally do this. Find you a man and get busy. TTFN!*

"Sounds like she's having a large time," Vik said. His eyebrows raised slightly, and he flashed a knowing grin.

To save face and to change the subject, I began rattling off what he'd been teaching. "Okay, let me see if I have this right. Any respectable Indian wife needs a flat metal pan called a tava for flatbreads and a kahdhai, the Indian version of a wok for deep frying. Is that right?"

Sensing my embarrassment and desperation not to discuss sex outside a hotel room, Vik let any further discussion of the honeymooners drop.

"You got it," he said. "But do not worry. Any well-stocked kitchen will have such basic items." A brief pause, then, "Are you busy Thursday afternoon?"

"I don't think so." I checked my phone. "Tomorrow, Isha has scheduled me for a spa. I think it will take the better part of the day. Then, I have dinner with Samir."

"I have a better idea," he said.

I poised myself for the invitation. I was ready. *It's going to happen.*

He put a hand on my shoulder. I could feel myself preparing to move into him. Then, he said, "Tomorrow night, my parents are insisting on having a little event in my honor. Actually, it's my birthday. Why don't you and Samir come to the party?"

CHAPTER 50

TEJ/VIK

I KICKED MYSELF ALL EVENING.

Why in the world did you encourage her to come with that guy?

None of this made sense to me. First, despite what I told my parents, I was determined to leave the country the same way I came: single. Second, not only had I encouraged Harlow to give the Isha method a shot, but I had also funded the excursion. Third, I didn't know anything about Samir, but my foolproof asshole detection system had pinged like crazy when I met him. Fourth, Harlow. Fifth, Harlow. Sixth, Harlow.

I went out for the evening after lying to Ma with a straight face. "I have a date."

"Who is it with, my son? I imagine I know someone in her family."

"I'm not sure, Ma." Not a lie since I had no engagement

for the evening. I just needed to be somewhere quiet where I could spend time telling myself how big an idiot I was. "But we will talk all about it tomorrow."

"Well," she said, "maybe the day after. Tomorrow I will be spending all day with the final preparations for your party. It will be—I believe the word is *groovy*."

I did not have the heart to tell her that she was only about fifty years behind on the hip lingo.

"You are too kind, Maata. The more I think about it, the less enthused I am about the whole idea. I don't guess there is any way to—"

I had gotten farther into the sentence than I thought I would. "Never! We cannot call off the paartee now. It would be humiliating. Besides, my son does not turn twenty-nine but once. We will all have a wonderful time. Won't we?"

There was steel in her gentle eyes. When it came to entertaining, Maata did not play.

"Yes. I promise. I will be the life of the paartee."

I spent the evening in the seedier part of town. Nothing dangerous but not the type of place I usually frequented. Since I was neither overdressed nor boisterous, no one bothered me. I didn't make a scene by yelling, "Next round is on me," or anything of the sort. I sat at a back table, sipped on a middling Scotch, and ate some very fine aloo chaat in phyllo cups. As always, the distinguishing feature of the appetizer was the significant contrast of colors and the delightful opposition of spicy chutneys and lightly sweetened creamy yogurt. The brilliant red pomegranate pearls were exceptional. On my way out, I mentioned the dish to the barman.

"Thank you, sir," he said. "My maaji makes those every evening. They are the house specialty. All my regulars love them."

I gave a brief outline of Bombay Baby. "I'm always looking for new recipes. That Chat was the best I've ever had. Do you think your maaji would share her secret?"

He hesitated.

"I'm sorry," I said. "I will most assuredly compensate your maji. I meant no disrespect."

"No offense taken, sir," he said. "I simply do not know anyone brave or foolish enough to ask my maataji to divulge a secret that has been in her family for generations."

"I understand," I said. And I did. Some people are very territorial about family recipes. To press this good man would have been dishonorable. "Thank you again. They were a delight."

"I will give your compliments to my maataji," he said. "The other part, I will take to my grave."

He smiled broadly, and I waved as I departed. I spent the rest of my time wondering what Harlow was doing.

CHAPTER 51

HARLOW

HARLOW, WHAT ARE YOU DOING?

I had not made out with a guy in a car since high school. The situation was borderline hysterical. Two full-grown adults trying to crawl all over each other in the front seat of an Alpha Romeo 4C Spider defied the laws of physics, geometry, and practicality.

Samir and I had enjoyed a fabulous dinner. The quality of the service was exceeded only by the succulence of the duck Madras. Though technically a British-Indian concoction, the blend of curry leaves, onion, ginger-garlic paste, turmeric powder, Kashmiri chili powder, fennel and tomatoes brought out every nuance of the perfectly cooked and diced duck legs. The concoction paired perfectly with the bottle of Valbuena 5° 2015 Tempranillo the sommelier recommended.

Samir was the perfect gentleman throughout the entire dinner. I could not remember the last time anyone other than the little Cub Scout on Peachtree Street had held a door open for me, but after we left the restaurant, he turned into a horny octopus. We'd gone for a drive, a magnificent experience in the speedster.

"She'll do zero to sixty in four-point-one seconds," Samir said. He downshifted and floored it. The car shot down the road and topped ninety before I knew what was happening. Samir knew how to drive, and he handled every turn with elan. We drove for about fifteen minutes. I guess he believed the old myth that fast cars rev up a woman's libido because he pulled off the side of the road and leaned in, leading with his face. His hands followed close behind.

His kissing was a little on the overly eager side, not as slobbery as Addison, but less refined than I would have thought. What he lacked in smooching technique he more than made up for with hand speed. He was everywhere. When I eased his palms off my chest, he immediately moved to the small of my back and tried to hoist my blouse up over my head. I moved sideways to loosen his grip only to feel his fingertips inching their way from my knee toward the inside of my thigh. All the while, he kept me in a lip lock that inhibited breathing and positively baffled any attempt to speak.

When he managed to undo my top two buttons, I pushed away hard. "Samir, take it easy." I leaned back against the door and refastened my blouse. "One dinner does not entitle you to a walk on the wild side."

"You are captivating, Harlow," he said. He reached for me. I stiff-armed him with a move that would have made any college running back proud.

"Take a breath," I said. "I know I need a few."

"Harlow." His voice carried the husky tone of a dude who had things on his mind other than Bible reading. "I've never met anyone like you. I think we should be married. The sooner, the better. We can return to America and live a life of luxury,"—he paused, then pressed toward me)—"and unending passion."

I shook my head. *He said* married. *I know he did.* "You can't be serious. We've known each other three days tops."

"But I have been looking for you my entire life. And karma has brought us together. You are my destiny. I must have you tonight." His hands moved, this time away from me.

"If you touch your belt, so help me, I will get out of this car and walk to town," I said. "Calm the heck down, and let's just talk for a while."

CHAPTER 52

HARLOW

It was good to have a day off. No dates, no lectures on cooking, no cricket. Nothing but time for me. Best of all, there would be no wrestling match with Samir and no quasi-marriage proposals. When he'd dropped me off at Lita's, he'd been a little overly formal, but I passed it off as embarrassment about the overabundance of his enthusiasm.

Mina's voice broke through my recollection.

"It's called the Lotus Flower," she said. "Absolutely the best spa in all of Delhi."

The city bustled outside the car's tinted windows. I watched children clutching parents' hands and youngsters playing games in the dirt outside merchant stalls. Beggars sat at the side of the road.

"Stop the car, please," I said.

The driver locked the brakes, initiating a cascade of horns and shouts. I pointed to a man with a basket.

"Is he going to do what I think he's going to do?" I asked.

"If you believe the basket holds a cobra, then you would be correct. The man is a *sapera*. What you would call a snake charmer. They live together in a place called Mollarbandhgaon, the community of snake charmers."

Sure enough, the man placed the basket on the ground, took off the lid, sat, and began to play a wooden flute. Within seconds, the frightening specter of a hooded cobra rose like a slithering mist and swayed in rhythm to the tune.

Passersby stopped, non-Indian every one of them. The locals continued on their routes, paying no more attention to the eerie spectacle than I would to a homeless man in Atlanta.

"There is great controversy," Mina said. "Animal rights activists want the tradition ended. Proponents of human rights believe the sapera has every right to practice both his trade and his religion."

"Religion? Like snake-handling evangelicals in the States?"

Mina made a small gesture, and the driver began to move. "I know nothing of your American religious sects, but snakes are believed to be divine incarnations and are treated with great reverence and care, many times like members of the family."

"Fascinating and scary."

"Here's something interesting," Mina said. "People make *kajal* from the snakes' venom."

"And that is?"

"Eyeliner," Mina said. "I don't use it,"—she shuddered a little—"but others swear it wards off eye disease." She shifted in her seat. "We're almost there, and I know what you're thinking."

"Am I that obvious?"

"You ask the same question every time we do anything," she said. "You want to know about paying, and the answer is always the same."

At the same time, we said, "Mr. Chatwal has taken care of everything."

"Same answer for a tip?" I asked.

Mina tried to look disgusted, but she cracked and giggled. "Yes, of course."

Ten minutes later, we passed through an ornate doorway into a luxurious reception area complete with a flowing water feature filled with tiny orchids. The speckled marble floor stretched more than a hundred feet, an expansive gray desert broken occasionally by tufts of lush green vegetation. Soothing music played through hidden speakers. Massage therapists, aestheticians, nail technicians, and assistants glided along the corridors, their steps muffled by thick, white socks. Everyone wore pristine black wrap tunics. This was Shangri-la, only mere steps removed from the traffic and dust of downtown Delhi.

Mina led me to reception. "Checking in for Harlow Kennedy," she said.

The young woman behind the desk, a petite Burmese wearing makeup of surgical precision, said, "Of course. Isha has scheduled the full-day bridal prep package." She looked at me with a neutral expression. She was paid never to react. "Your beauty consultant is Yamini. She's one of our most highly requested."

A tall, slender woman bowed from the waist. She wore the uniform du jour. "I am Yamini," she said. She did not attempt to shake my hand. "Follow me, please."

A set of wooden doors opened to a private dressing area. Once we had settled in the dimly lit room, she pulled out a clipboard and began making notes.

"Do you have any allergies?" she asked. "Skin or food? Our Ayurveda treatments are all natural. Our elixirs are made from precious and rare healing minerals. We work with the three doshas, Vitta, Pitta, and Kapha, for inner calm and balance. We want to de-stress and detoxify you."

"No allergies," I said.

"We will start with body brushing, then a bath filled with rose petals and essential base oils of almond, coconut, and acai. We distill pure essential oils naturally and mix in ghee daily."

Ghee? Are they going to de-stress me or baste me?

Yamini continued. "I reviewed the information you provided, and I think we should focus on balancing your Pitta, or water essence dosha."

I wasn't entirely sure what a dosha was or why it needed balancing, but I had come this far.

Yamini's voice was as smooth as the music. "You have sensitive skin, so something soothing and relaxing to calm you makes sense. We will follow up with a gold dust scrub to help with oxygenation and the rejuvenation of your skin. It also works wonders with aging skin."

How old do you think I am?

Still, it all sounded luxurious. Yamini moved on to the hair treatment. "We will cover your hair with a hydration mask, then finish with a rinse, a blow-dry, and a de-frizzing serum. Do you have any questions?"

I shook my head.

"Beauty is more than external," she said. "Lasting beauty is about peace and happiness, the whole of our existence, not just parts of our anatomy." She peered at my face like a doctor perusing a surgical field. "Overall, you have a lovely complexion, but I see some dry, irritated patches. I can soothe those out. Our faces and complexions manifest our thoughts and emotions. Ayurveda deals with the whole person."

The droning went on, very little of which made sense. Still, it served a purpose. Yamini's practiced voice flowed across my ears in a most relaxing way, inflection-free, almost hypnotic. I looked at a large gold statue with eight appendages.

"What is that?" I asked.

"That is Chymunda," Yamini said. "The legs and arms represent the different qualities that a woman needs to achieve true beauty."

Chymunda was adorned in jewels and sitting serenely atop a fierce tiger as other miniature goddesses stood at her feet. "She is several goddesses in one, embodying three aspects of a woman's being," Yamini said. "Saraswati represents knowledge, Kali represents courage, and Lakshmi represents wealth and prosperity. Chymunda herself is the slayer of evil. Everyone needs wisdom, courage, and power to ride the back of a tiger. We achieve true beauty when we develop all aspects of life."

I thought a lot about what she said and realized that any

future husband would have to see beyond the simple descrip-
tion Isha had published in her matrimonial posts. He would
have to look into my soul. I wanted a kindred spirit. I wanted
a soul mate. And . . .

. . . I wanted too much for a woman with very little time
and less money. *This is a frickin' waste of time.*

I would have left, but departure seemed rude in the middle
of the balancing milk and honey massage. When it was over,
my muscles were dewy and weak. When I stepped off the table, I was light and undisturbed. Yamini said something about
anti-cellulite lymphatic drainage and blood circulation. She
could have been discussing nuclear fission and a colonoscopy
prep, and I would have nodded. It had been a long time since
I felt this good.

She led me to the mani-pedi room. I settled my feet into a
tub of scented water with floating orchids. Before she pulled
the privacy curtain, I noticed two young women in the adja-
cent space. Even with the partition closed, I could hear them.
I made no effort to avoid eavesdropping.

A nasally voice said, "I asked Papa to talk to Isha again
because I think I'd be a match for him."

A breathy, obviously fake, voice countered, "Well, he is
hot, I'll give you that. Strong features, very successful. But I'm
not sure if you'd want that match."

Nasally said, "Why not?"

Breathy asked, "Do you want to live in America?"

"It could be worse. You know Nakula had to move to Ger-
many," Nasally said.

Both voices chorused, "Ew."

Then Breathy said, "Well, the family money would be nice. And it would make Preethi shut up. She thinks she is all that because she married a doctor in London."

"Did you see his picture? Donkey face," Nasally said.

Both laughed. "Ew."

Breathy said, "It's not a bad idea, although I think he has issues."

Nasally asked, "Who cares with that body and that wallet?"

"Good point, but there has to be a reason he's still single," Breathy said. "And it's not like he hasn't had chances. You don't get dumped as many times as he has unless there is something terribly wrong."

Nasally said, "You might be right. But I'm willing to take my chances. No one that gorgeous can be bad in bed. Even if he is, I'll just use his money to underwrite my numerous love affairs."

"You are a shameless slut, you know."

After a long, annoying cackle, Nasally said, "Maybe, but the minute we finish here, I am calling Daddy and telling him I want Isha to line me up with Vikram Chatwal."

My skin crawled inside my cozy faux-fur robe. What did these little witches know about Vik? He'd told me about Haiya and her refusal to consider being part of his dream. And I was the one who'd come up with the marriage swap idea. I shifted in my seat. Time to get up and give those harpies a piece of my mind.

Yamini noticed my movement. "Is the water too hot, Miss?"

"No, no. Everything is great," I said.

She moved her head a quarter turn to the right. She didn't believe me. Then I felt my grinding teeth and clenched jaw. "I promise, everything is fine."

"The purpose of today is relaxation," she said. It was a reminder, not a chastisement. "Serenity is the watchword."

I closed my eyes and melted into the chair. I awakened when Yamini began toweling off my feet. When she pulled the curtain back, the next cubicle was empty.

CHAPTER 53

TEJ/VIK

"My friend, I have bad news and worse news."

I'd known Waman since grade school. He was quiet, dependable, honest, and one of the finest private investigators in Delhi.

"They haven't . . ." I could not bring myself to say it.

"No, not yet at least, old friend," he said. "They steamed up the car windows the other night, but there is no evidence that Samir has breeched Ms. Harlow's fortifications as of yet."

"You have such a way with words," I said. "And where was Harlow's chaperone?"

"Ms. Kennedy is an American," Waman said. "She has no one here to act in that capacity. And, from what you have told me, she would refuse to cooperate with anyone so assigned."

"True," I said. "What's the worse news?"

"He has no interest in her," Waman said.

I could scarcely contain my glee. "Why would that be

worse news?"

He thumped me on the temple with his knuckles. "Use your head, Vikram. He has no interest in her romantically. In fact, my operatives tell me he is bedding three others in town. After he made out with Ms. Kennedy, he dropped her off, then spent the night with one of his paramours."

I grimaced. "Has anyone used that word since 1940? Paramours, really?"

"Vikram, I may be in a sleazy line of work, but I remain a gentleman," he said.

"Okay, I still don't get it. If he's not serious about her, there is no problem."

"That's where you are wrong, old friend. He has no romantic interest in her. I did not say he was not going to use her to his advantage."

"What do you mean?" I asked.

"It can be summed up in two little words."

"Ah." I nodded. "He's gay."

"No, not at all. I told you he had three other lovers."

"You did not specify they were women."

Waman released a long sigh. "You are still a smart ass, Vikram, just like when we were in school. But, no, the two little words have nothing to do with his sexuality."

"What are they, green card?"

"That's part of his problem because his visa runs out in about a year," Waman said.

I knew a lot about US immigration requirements. My visa had taken a while to be approved, and the restrictions grew tighter almost every month. "Ten to thirteen months to qualify for a green card after marrying a citizen," I said. "So, he marries Harlow, lives with her—"

"Reaping the considerable benefits of same," Waman said.

Damn, he could have gone all night without mentioning that.

"But that's not the real issue," he said. "You didn't get the two words right."

"What are they?"

Waman looked left then right, as if someone might be listening.

Who would care? I guess it's a PI thing.

"Flat broke."

My mouth dropped open like a surprised guppy. "What do you mean? The guy's wearing designer clothes. He's got a $75,000 Tag Heuer on his wrist. I ought to know. I've got two of them. He's a big-time wealth manager in the States."

"No," Waman said, "he says he's a big-time money manager in the States. I've looked. My operatives have searched. We can't find a single client. He's been in the US for five years. He's lived in five different cities—Los Angeles, Chicago, Denver, Jacksonville, and now New York. I pulled his bank records—"

"How did you get those?"

"Don't ask, my friend," he said. "You want to maintain what the Americans call 'plausible deniability.' Anyway, I got 'em, and he is up to his well-tailored rear end in debt."

This didn't make any sense. "Why would he be interested in Harlow? She doesn't have any money."

Waman tapped the side of his head with his index finger. "Think, my man, think. First, he gets close to her, talks her into marrying him. Won't take much effort for him to find out her Social Security number. He fills out a few applications. *Bing, bang, boom.* He's got a hundred thousand dollars in credit cards all in her name. He can go 'livin' la vida loca' for a while with that kind of scratch."

"Doesn't make sense," I said. "Maybe he has a big time for a few months, but after a while, the money will tap out and—" I stopped. The entire plan appeared in my head. "He's seen Isha's files. She undoubtedly told him everything about Harlow and her family."

"Precisely," Waman said, "which means . . ."

"He knows about Sophia."

CHAPTER 54

TEJ/VIK

Waman slipped away into the darkness and left me with my thoughts and the sound of his words banging around in my head.

"He lives off Harlow long enough to get close, then sets about conning the rich old lady. He cons her out of her money, probably after he's talked her out of her panties, then he scoops up everything he can. Maybe he runs the same credit card scam. Maybe convinces her to let him manage her money. However it goes, about the time his green card comes in the mail, he disappears and leaves the two women to clean up a load of debt and an ash heap of heartbreak. That's the whole taco," he said.

He'd used the wrong idiom, but I hadn't bothered to correct him.

Music from the party wafted through the night. People were having a good time at my birthday party even as I agonized over a woman who was slipping further away from me by the second. I couldn't talk to anyone. If I said, "I think I'm falling in love with a woman," they would rejoice. Adding two little words—*from America*—would turn their glee to gloom. Calling Miguel had proven futile. When I called, he was either partying or recovering from a night of debauchery.

I'd begged my parents not to make a fuss about tonight. They promised not to mention the reason. No one in India needs an excuse for a party. But, as I had feared, the celebration was over-the-top annoying. A parade of BMW, Mercedes, Jaguar, and Maserati automobiles rolled through the gates of the estate and deposited couples dressed to the nines bearing gifts. Valets parked the cars of those who did not use a driver. Uniformed hostesses escorted everyone to large tents where most of the maatajis wasted no time in presenting the merits of their not-yet-engaged daughters to my parents.

Energetic partygoers mingled ever so politely with their competition. A few industrious single men prowled the crowd hoping to pick off the limping antelope of a desperate, upper-class woman too tired to be selective in her search for a mate.

Maybe Ma will gang up on one of them and lose track of time before I go back to the States.

I watched as my mother moved among friends, often laughing with her hand over her heart. Her joy, I knew, came from the prospect of getting closer to finding my bride, the sooner, the better. I cursed fate for not giving my parents the large family that they'd wanted. I was the only one. Like all Indian maatajis, mine had dreamed of a string of weddings.

I was sure she longed for a lap full of little ones bearing the family name. Had there been a sibling, Ma would not have let up on me, but she might have been a little less laser focused.

My parents had spared no expense on the Bollywood-themed gala. The lawn overflowed with partiers as they mingled under twinkling lights. The air teased every nostril with hints of ginger, roasting lamb, and cumin.

I scanned the crowd for Harlow and spotted her hanging on Gupta's arm at the far corner of the pool. When she threw her head back in response to a humorous comment, my heart skipped a beat. She looked sublime, a vision in blue with turquoise beading. She'd caught her hair up in a loose side braid with ropes of sparkling crystal gems entwined throughout her long, dark waves. I'd never seen anything as breathtaking in my life.

She laughed again. Her apple-colored lips parted in the kind of joy that made me wish I was sharing the space with her. I thought about what I'd told my mother about the moment when you knew you had found perfection. There wasn't a set of rules you could follow to make your life amazing. "Parfait" always slipped in on silver heels when you least expected it.

Gupta was tall and elegant in his unmistakable masculinity. His hand settled in the center of her back, protective and territorial. His dynamic presence dominated everything within the sound of his voice. I watched the cluster of those around him. The men envied him. The women, even the happily married ones, hated Harlow.

A waiter approached. "Mango lassi, sir?"

"Bring me a Johnny Walker Blue, please," I said. He nodded. "Make it a double."

He acknowledged my order and eased through the crowd toward the bar.

Despite the crowd, I recognized my ma's voice in the rumble behind me, just like all children can.

"Vikram, there you are. Don't you agree?" she asked.

"Certainly, Ma," I said. I might have just agreed that all men in India should be neutered. At that moment, whatever she was talking about did not interest me at all. I could not take my eyes off Harlow.

Ma turned to the tall woman standing beside her dressed in flowing gold and blue. "There you have it, Sundari," she said. "I told you he would go. His father and I have raised a most honorable man. Your daughters will be well taken care of with Vikram at her side."

Bloody hell. What have I done? Whoever the hell she was, Sundari seemed pleased and drifted into the sea of guests. "What did I just agree to do?"

"Sundari's girls, Nalini and Maya, want to visit an ailing cousin in Shahdara. They certainly cannot travel alone. I assured Sundari you would be most pleased to serve as an escort."

"I have a great deal to do, Ma," I said. "I have a limited number of days left in my visit. I want to spend some time with you and Baapa. I am standing in as chef one night at Fawzi's place, my old friends have asked me to play cricket, and I have not so much as touched a bat in two years. I need some practice. I have a list of calls longer—"

She interrupted with the certainty of all mothers who

know what is best for their sons. "Well, we thought the two of you would hit it off—"

"Wait a minute. How old are these girls?"

"Nalini is but a child: thirteen, I think. Maya is a little older."

"How much older?"

"She is nineteen."

"So, this is not a good deed. It's a set-up."

Ma tried to look penitent. She failed. "I have a duty to you and our family. There is nothing wrong with helping you a little in your quest for a bride."

She thinks it is a quest. I think it's a game of dodge ball.

I was not lying about anything. My reputation as a skilled batsman would take a serious hit if I attempted to play without some preparation. More importantly, my status as a "world-class chef"—Fawzi's idea of publicity, not mine—would be shattered if I did not take time to perfect the blend of ground nuts, yogurt, red chilies, and coconut I intended to use for the chicken chettin and I'd promised to present.

"Mother," I said, "I am overbooked. I am two days behind on calls to Atlanta. We are still launching the frozen food line, and there are many details to be discussed. One of my business partners just inked a deal for a full-color cookbook. I am to be prominently featured."

Ma looked on the verge of tears.

"I will honor the promise you tricked me into making," I said. "But no more. Everything from now on is local and brief. Nothing longer than an hour. I need your word on that."

She smiled broadly. "You have it. And thank you, my son."

CHAPTER 55

HARLOW

VIK'S MA EMBRACED HIM, AND I SAW HIS FATHER NOD FROM several yards away. Every child knows that nod, the one from a proud parent when they witness their child embodying the lessons of youth. What had transpired between mother and son, I did not know, but I figured it had something to do with the overdressed woman Mrs. Chatwal had hauled across the yard to speak with Vik. Logic told me the conversation had been about someone's daughter, an available, unmarried daughter.

Just as I felt Samir's arm around my waist, Vik looked at me from across the pool. I leaned into the forearm on my back. I felt oddly guilty and smug all at once. I was there with a stunning man. The great Vikram Chatwal, the man running so hard from who he was that he'd lived for two years as Tej Mayur, stood at a party in his honor accompanied only by his mother.

Samir reacted to my movement by bending close and

whispering something. My focus was so intent on Vik that Samir could have claimed to be the lost Crown Prince of the Romanoffs, and I would not have reacted. But I threw back my head and laughed as if I were attending a live Dave Chappelle show.

I interrupted my staring to respond to a comment on my dress. When I looked back, Vik was gone. Moments later, Samir leaned in again, "Would you like another drink, my dear?"

"Sure," I said. "But see if you can find something stronger than this fruit punch, please."

"Vodka? Gin? Bourbon?"

"Scotch," I said. "Preferably something older than fifteen years. Straight up."

"I love a woman who knows her mind and her Scotch," he said. He unleashed a devilish grin, excused himself, and strode toward one of the dozen or so bars scattered around the property. Ten seconds later, a server passed.

"Excuse me, please. Where is the ladies' room?" Armed with instructions, I moved toward the palatial house. I walked under the porte-cochère, mounted the half dozen steps, passed through the mammoth portal into the marble entrance hall, and turned left. I was so fascinated by the ornate tapestries on the wall that I ran directly into someone.

"Vik! So nice to see you." *Don't sound so damned excited.*

"Harlow, I need to talk to you," Vik said.

"Well, it's nice to see you too, Harlow," I said. I made no attempt to sound pleasant. "How have you been, Harlow? What have you been up to, Harlow? Are you having any luck,

Harlow? Are you having a good time at my ridiculously extravagant party, Harlow?"

He stepped back and bobbed his head. "I am sorry. It is always wonderful to see you. I have missed our lunches and talks. I know you've been very busy with Samir."

Ah, keeping tabs, are we?

A servant approached. "Mr. Chatwal, your parents have requested your presence. The buffet is now ready, and the guests have been invited to dinner."

"I'll be there momentarily," he said.

As if on cue, the very essence of India blew in through the open front door. I could detect freshly baked flatbread with sautéed yellow squash and a curry bar with choices of goat, lamb, shrimp, fish, or tofu. A gorgeous, hand-decorated henna-inspired birthday cake topped with a rose stood in the middle of the buffet. There would be enough to feed the Army of Luxemburg.

Vik returned his full attention to me. "I need to talk to you."

"Well, I need to talk to you as well," I said. "Three days ago, I was ready to go home and tell you to get your money back from Isha, but I have to tell you, she has done a marvelous job. I understand her plan now, like someone selling you a house. Show you the dregs first, then *bam*! They hit you with your dream home. Samir Gupta is the real deal, Vik. He is kind and funny. And I don't guess I need to tell you that he is just about the best looking, eligible man in India." *Don't say it, Harlow.* "Present company excepted." *Damn, Harlow, you weren't supposed to say it.*

He paused for a moment.

"What is it?" I asked.

"There's no way to come at this delicately," he said.

"Are you pregnant?" I asked.

He did not react to my goof. He always reacted when I said something outlandish. But this time, his face remained stoic, jaw set, eyes steely, and they did not stray.

"Harlow . . ."

"Out with it, Vik. We've become good friends. No secrets."

He took a deep breath, then released a string of sentences in such a torrent as to challenge my ability to comprehend. I caught snippets. ". . . not what he claims . . . marriage of convenience . . . trio of girlfriends . . . immigration issues . . . money problems . . . con game . . . Sophia . . ."

When he finally stopped talking, a high-pitched hum swelled in my ears, a constant ringing so insistent I could barely think. I put my hands to my head and closed my eyes. As the ringing subsided slowly, I lowered my hands and stared at Vik. "How do you know all this?"

To his credit, he did not hesitate. "I hired a private investigator."

I didn't hesitate either. I drove my knee directly into his groin. "Damn you, Vik."

CHAPTER 56

TEJ/VIK

I FINALLY UNFOLDED FROM A FETAL POSITION. "WAS THAT TRULY necessary? You could have just punched me, you know."

"Don't get up, or I will," Harlow said.

Moving very gingerly, I sat and wrapped my arms around my knees. "This okay?"

"Whatever." Her eyes blazed with something other than anger. She wasn't pissed. She was hurt.

She already knows. "I didn't tell you anything you didn't already know, did I?"

Her breath came in ever shorter gasps. She was about ten seconds away from a full-blown meltdown. Her shoulders began to heave up and down. She turned her head, sniffled, then collapsed on the ground about five feet away. I groaned, struggled to my feet, and took a tentative step in her direction.

Her head snapped up. "Touch me with whatever you don't mind losing," she said, the snarl of a wounded animal.

The sound of distant music mixed with the occasional hoot of a barn owl and Harlow's muffled sobs. I stood for about ten minutes. I was not going to leave.

"Harlow?"

"What?"

"I did not tell you anything you didn't already know, did I?"

She looked up, mascara dripping down her cheeks. "No. Well, I didn't know it, but I was pretty suspicious. I may be desperate, but I'm not stupid."

"Talk to me," I said.

She patted the path next to her. "Sit down. But the no-touching rule is still in effect."

I lowered myself to the ground just outside arms' length. "When did you begin to suspect something?" I asked.

"Oh, on our dinner date. He was all over the map, talking about how much he admired me and how he would love Atlanta and had always wanted to live there. He always talked about how much he liked to tip people, but I never saw him give anything to anyone. He boasted about this car and that boat and this house and that ski chalet. I never saw so much as a picture."

"Did he . . . ?"

She made a face. "How big a slut do you think I am? We made out a little in his car, and he tried to get me in bed. When I reminded him about being chaste, he backed off. But he called it 'a quaint tradition observed mostly in the breach.'"

"Harlow, I'm so sorry."

She'd been staring into the night. Now she looked at me

with reddened eyes and a quivering lip. "I'm going to ask you something. Don't get any ideas."

"Okay," I said.

She stretched her arms. "Can I have a hug?"

I scooched over so fast I almost ripped my pants. I wrapped my arms around her. She melted into me and sobbed. We didn't move for a long time.

Finally, she pushed back, wiped her eyes, and stood. "Okay, even though I was with a total phony, I had some good times and some fabulous meals. I didn't surrender my virtue. And I am ready to jump back in the pool. Where's Isha?"

"Don't," I said. Standing up was not as easy or painless as I made it look.

"Don't what?"

"Don't jump back in the pool."

She tossed her hair and ran a quick hand over her cheek. Suddenly, she was radiant, full of life, feisty, the old Harlow.

"Why not?" she said. "I got close to the fire, didn't get burned. I'm here for three more days. Might as well enjoy them."

I stared at her, afraid to speak, afraid to say the words that had been burning in my head since—*damn*—since the plane ride. I knew then what I wanted to say now, but I was frightened. Not of her significant self-defense skills but of running her away, of never seeing her again.

"Vik," she said. "I'll just have a little fun. Why the hell not?"

I spoke before I thought anymore. "Because I love you, Harlow."

CHAPTER 57

HARLOW

I MUST HAVE LOOKED LIKE A STARTLED COW. "OH NO. YOU DID not just say that."

"I did," he said.

"Right now, at this very moment?"

"Yep."

"After what I just told you?"

"Seemed as good a time as any."

"What is wrong with you?"

"Nothing, just being honest."

"Your timing leaves a little to be desired."

"Sorry about that."

"No, you're not."

"You gonna cry again?"

"Nope."

"You gonna yell at me again?"

"Nope."

"You gonna curse me again?"

"Nope."

"You gonna injure me again?"

"Nope."

"Well, what are you gonna do?"

I kissed him, and it was wonderful.

CHAPTER 58

TEJ/VIK

Baapa's voice remained calm, but turmoil tossed in his eyes like a squall-tossed ocean.

"This is very troubling, my son," he said. "And you knew it before you came in to see me."

I looked around the room I knew so very well and breathed in the smells of my younger days. The dusky odor of books, well-read but carefully preserved. The lingering aroma of my baapa's aftershave absorbed in the upholstery of overstuffed chairs. Cherry pipe tobacco, a habit my mother tolerated but made clear was to be confined only to this relatively small area of the expansive house. The distinct scent every son knows— the smell of a father—a mixture of sweat, sweetness, authority, tradition, age, and station. Indescribable but so distinctive that every child can detect it with closed eyes.

There was no anger on my father's face. But I saw a deep questioning. First, a question about me. "What has possessed my boy to act this way?" Then, a more profound query. "Did I do something wrong that he would act this way?"

The sins of the son may not be visited on the father, but a child's missteps weigh heavily on every parent. And I could tell while I might not have wounded my beloved baapa, my profession of love for Harlow upset him.

"This is very troubling," he said again. "You must not forget the position of this family. Nor can you abandon your obligation to our traditions."

"I mean no disrespect, Baapa," I said. "And I am not trying to humiliate you or Ma in any fashion."

"I know, my son," he said. "But let's review. You were engaged to Haiya, an arrangement I now realize was neither wise nor advantageous. Since her marriage to another, she continues to act in ways that bring shame and disrepute to her family. Though you have taken a beating from the gossips, I know you did nothing to bring about the end of the engagement. Haiya has shown herself to be an individual of low character. In truth, to use the vernacular, she may be a little, as you younger people say, cray-cray."

I could not help myself. I laughed so hard I felt tears coming to my eyes. The contemporary expression, though properly used, fit my father's personality like a ill-fitted suit. When I regained my composure, I wiped my face.

"You have judged correctly, Baapa," I said. "Haiya is a troubled woman. She made a scene at the engagement party, the one for me. I mean, the one that was supposed to be for me but turned out . . ."

I saw a rueful look. "You are making my point for me,

my son," he said. "It's hard to keep track. Lita is also a fine young woman, and she would have made a wonderful wife and mother. Correction, she *will* make one, just not for you."

He raised a palm when I took a breath. "I know, I know. I agreed with the arrangement you made, and I am proud of your willingness to sacrifice *your* happiness, but I am now worried that you are blind to the possibility of crushing your ma's hopes and dreams."

It was not time for me to speak.

"So, my son, what do you have to say?"

Now, it was time.

"Something you have never heard before," I said.

"Which is?"

I stood, took a cleansing breath, and looked him in the eye. "I am in love with Harlow Kennedy."

The only sound was the office's pocket door sliding open. Then I heard my ma's voice, thin but resolute.

"If she is good enough for you, my beloved Vikram, then do as you feel you must."

CHAPTER 59

TEJ/VIK

THE MORNING BROKE WITH SUNLIGHT AND POSSIBILITY. When Harlow had not answered the phone, I sent her a WhatsApp text. *Quick morning trip, acting as a chaperone. Don't worry, they are ugly. Meet me at the cricket field at noon.*

Hussein got us to the train station to buy tickets and get settled in first class in plenty of time. I'd told a small lie. While Maya certainly could not match Harlow's beauty, the nineteen-year-old was attractive. Way too shy for my taste, but after I finally coerced her to talk, she impressed me with her understanding of world events and the depth of her literary knowledge.

"I am particularly fond of Nectar in a Sieve," she said. "The theme of hunger as a threat to dignity is particularly telling. I plan to attend the Institute of Science on Karnataka as I begin my journey toward a doctorate in biology."

"To what end?" I asked.

"Over 180 million of our fellow citizens, almost 14 percent, suffer from malnutrition. I intend to lead a team in search of ways to eliminate the problem."

She was engaging and articulate. Her little sister sat and played with a doll. But I could tell she was listening. "And what do you like to do, Nalini?"

"I play football."

"Why do you like it?"

"Because I am better than all the boys, and it makes them cry."

I looked at Maya, who nodded. "It's true. She's a killer striker."

Nalini wasn't finished. "I wish you two would kiss. It's the only reason I came on this trip. Our aunt is not sick. Mummy made it up, so you would come on this stupid train ride, fall in love with Maya, and get married. So, kiss her and let's get this over with."

Maya buried her head in her hands. I thought she was crying, but when she finally looked up, her face was contorted in amusement. "She plays football the same way. Flat out all the way." She composed herself. "I am so very sorry. This was supposed to be a very hush-hush sort of thing."

I searched for the appropriate response. "Well, ah, you see, ah, there's another—"

She interrupted. "Don't worry. I'm not the least bit interested. You're very nice and all, and quite handsome, but you're not my type."

I steepled my fingers. "Oh, is that so. What, pray tell, is your type?"

She wasn't any less direct than her little sister. "Quite handsome men who do not know they are quite handsome."

"That's rather brutal," I said. "Are you calling me conceited?"

"Answer one question," Maya said, "as quickly as you can."

"Okay," I said.

"Are you handsome?"

"Uh, well, it depends. Okay, you made your point. Let's get back to literature. Have you read *The Palace of Illusions*?"

"Loved it," she said, "but what self-respecting, feminist Indian girl wouldn't like the tale of the woman who married all five Pandava brothers?"

We had a delightful time, including a lovely ninety-minute visit with Aunt Indira, a feisty octogenarian who served tea and gulab jamun that was so good, I begged her for the recipe before we left.

"You can have it when I die, young man," she said.

"Then I hope I never receive it," I said.

The trip home was uneventful, just full of more stimulating and humbling conversation. It was a very good morning.

CHAPTER 60

HARLOW

"WE'RE GOING TO BE HERE HOW LONG?" I DIDN'T REALIZE I'D raised my voice until I saw people looking, turning in our direction. I switched to a whisper. "Listen, last night you blew me away. You told me you loved me—"

"Well, you kissed me," Vik said.

"That's beside the point," I said. "You don't tell a girl you love her, then say, 'Hey, come sit in the hot sun on a hard, wooden bench and watch me run around in a bright yellow suit for *six solid hours.*"

Vik pursed his lips. "Well, I don't think those fellows are very accomplished. This could be over in as little as four, four-and-a-half."

I smiled. "I don't care. It's just wonderful to be here. But if you look over here and don't see me, just know it's because someone has taken me to the hospital to treat the heatstroke."

Vik kissed me on the head, then trotted out to the field,

where his presence was greeted with cheers and slaps on the back.

"He's quite good, you know."

It was an older man seated behind me on the bleachers. He sat under an enormous golf umbrella. "Would you care to share my chhatri?" he asked, looking up at his umbrella.

"Don't mind if I do," I said. I scooched up a level and sat next to him. He didn't offer his name, but he did pour a cup of cold water for me from a large thermos.

"Thank you," I said. "You are most kind. I'm—"

"I know who you are," he said. Somehow his interruption was soothing instead of rude. "You're the future Mrs. Vikram Chatwal."

I hoped he did not hear my gasp. "What makes you say that?"

"Word travels fast on the Delhi grapevine," he said. "Rumor has it there was a fascinating event at the Chatwal estate in the far reaches of the night." Before I could reply, he pointed to the bowler. "They're beginning. I prefer to watch cricket in silence."

♦

Although I still didn't grasp all the nuances of the game, I could tell Vik was a stellar player. He roamed the pitch with a grace usually associated with ballet dancers. He caught everything hit near him and unleashed throws that would have made a major league scout reach for a radar gun. He hit the ball with savage ease, regularly crushing it out of the field and tallying six runs at a time.

About two hours into the game, my umbrella-sharing com

panion nudged me with his elbow. I looked at him. He maintained his reverential silence but nodded to our left. I saw Samir strolling toward our location.

"Good afternoon," he said as he stepped up the bleachers. He leaned in to kiss me. When I turned my head, he looked startled. "A little public affection is not forbidden, even in India." He sat next to me.

The second his seat touched the bleachers, I stood. My voice was dispassionate and flat. "Samir, unless you are meeting someone, there's no reason for you to be here."

For a moment, I could tell he thought I was kidding. But his jovial countenance faded when he studied my expression. I neither smiled nor frowned. I intentionally narrowed my eyes, not squinting but carefully avoiding anything he might interpret as enthusiasm regarding his unannounced attendance.

"Are you on a date?" he asked.

"She is." It was the old man. "She is here as my guest and companion for the afternoon. If you are a gentleman, sir, you will kindly depart so we might enjoy the game in peace and tranquility. Should you continue your rude interruption, I imagine I will have to use my walking stick and give you a lesson in manners."

The old man never took his eyes off the game. In fact, in the middle of his threat, he applauded a stellar play by one of Vik's teammates.

"Are you serious?" Samir asked me. "Or are you just desperate?"

"The only sign of desperation would be ever going out

with you again," I said. "I know about you, about what you do, about your questionable business practices, and about your inability to keep your pants on. So, if you would be so kind, please leave and never bother me again."

Samir rose, and I sat and looked toward the field. He stepped down from the bleachers and headed for the clubhouse. He never looked back.

Three hours later, the game ended. My companion and I had not exchanged another word. The old man collapsed his umbrella, retrieved the sterling cup from which I had been sipping, and nodded curtly. I stood and kissed him on the cheek. Then, he walked away with the confident stride of a man who had once been able to compete on the field of athletic competition with the likes of Vikram Chatwal.

CHAPTER 61

TEJ/VIK

Harlow's enthusiasm always shone through.

"You played great," she said.

I shook my head. "Seen a lot of cricket matches, have you?"

"Today was my second," she said. "But you look rather dashing in your uniform."

"You know we lost, right?" I asked.

"Not until someone told me," she said. "Did I mention the uniform?" She paused for a moment, then asked, "So, what's for dinner? I'm starving. I mean, really, they can't sell burgers or something?"

"Harlow?'

"Yes."

"We're in India. Burgers are not a thing. Sacred cows, remember?"

She grimaced. "My bad. But the fact remains, I'm hungry."

"Lucky for you that I know someone who is reportedly a

world-class chef. If you play your cards right, he might—how do the cowboys say it in the old movies?—rustle you up some grub. How about a nice serving of Punjabi vegetable curry?"

She slipped her hand into mine as we walked toward the club. "Well, even as hungry as I am, it will be a lot easier to enjoy my food if you don't smell like the animal you are about to sacrifice on my behalf."

"Not over-fond of my new cologne?" I asked. "It's called 'eau de stink.'"

She laughed, the sound of wind chimes in a summer breeze. "How much time do you need?"

"Twenty minutes," I said. "I've got a room on the second floor, number 210. I'll leave the door unlocked. For propriety's sake, give me a good head start, then come on up."

She raised an eyebrow. "Is this the 'Oh no, you caught me coming out of the shower' routine?" She was kidding, but I saw a glimmer of suspicion.

"No, no, no," I said. "I'll shower and change in the bath. By the time you get there, I'll be ready to go, fully dressed. Cross my heart."

She slapped my shoulder. "Then get going, buster."

I trotted across the lawn, entered the clubhouse, and hurried to my room. After grabbing my bag, I stepped into the shower. The warm spray pelted away some of the aches and pains in my shoulders and thighs.

You've got to get in better shape, old man.

I started toweling off, feeling refreshed. I decided to let my hair air dry. I put on my boxer briefs and had my trousers halfway on when I realized I'd left my linen shirt hanging in the closet. Not wanting to embarrass Harlow, I scooted into the room, clutching my pants at the waist, and yanked open the closet at the exact moment I heard the room door open and feet shuffling across the floor.

"Okay," I said without turning, "I am running back in there,"—I pointed to the bath—"and act like you did not come in before I got fully dressed.

From over my shoulder, the voice of a tigress. "Don't hurry on my account, lover."

I closed my eyes. *Haiya.* Paralysis and embarrassment riveted me in place. *Wake up, buddy. This is a very bad dream.*

I turned. No, this was reality. Haiya was standing in the middle of the room, balancing on black, six-inch stilettos, and wearing a lightweight, thigh-length rain jacket. She slipped it from her shoulders in one smooth motion to reveal her naked torso. She took an intentionally exaggerated breath that made her chest swell. I stared at her nakedness in horrified admiration.

She took three long strides across the room, threw her arms around me, and attacked my mouth with her tongue. When I put my hands on her shoulders to push her away, my pants slid to my knees.

"That's a good boy," she said in an exaggerated purr. Her head moved downward. I would have pushed her away, but I was paralyzed by the sight of Harlow coming through the open door. She was looking for something in her shoulder bag.

"My God, this place is amazing. If I were you, I'd never leave—" She heard Haiya moan and looked up. "I—" Harlow didn't finish.

Whatever noise came out of my throat didn't sound like my voice. It was thin, strained, and—the worst part—echoed with guilt. "Harlow," I said, "It's not—"

Hurricane sirens wail less than Harlow's scream. "Don't you dare! Don't you dare say, 'It's not what it looks like.' It's exactly what it looks like, you asshole!"

Haiya, now on her knees, looked over her shoulders and tossed her head back to accentuate her near-perfect bust. She stared straight at Harlow but was speaking to me. "Honestly, Vik, you said we had time."

I finally unglued my feet and stepped toward Harlow, but my pants wrapped around my ankles, and I pitched forward, hands flailing. Haiya stood just enough to break my fall. My left palm settled on her breast.

"Okay, baby," Haiya said. "If you think she's into watching, I'm all for it."

I had seen steamed rice with more color than Harlow's face. Tears streamed from her eyes in a torrent. "You knew ... we were going ... I thought you ..."

She pivoted. With Haiya clutching my hand on her bosom with one hand and her other on my crotch, I know my explanations sounded ridiculous. "Harlow, don't—let me explain."

But the door shut.

And Harlow was gone.

CHAPTER 62

HARLOW

THE FLIGHT LEFT INDIRA GANDHI AT 4:05 AM. I'D PUT MY phone in my suitcase on purpose. I didn't want to hear any lame excuses, any apologies, or any explanations. I knew what I'd seen, and I knew what it meant. Like Daddy always said, "All men are scum, except for me."

I chose *The Agony and the Ecstasy* for my first in-flight movie. How Rex Harrison had gotten an Oscar nomination for his portrayal of Pope Julius II escaped me, but he looked like the greatest actor of all time in comparison to Charlton Heston's jaw-clenched, wooden interpretation of Michelangelo. I got about halfway through it before the two Ambiens butterflied their way into my brain, and I fell into a sorrow-filled sleep.

I was too wobbly to walk to the next flight at Charles de Gaulle, but so out of it that the wheelchair didn't embarrass me at all. A sympathetic flight attendant poured me into my first-class seat and patted me on the arm. "They always break your heart, honey," he said. "Don't worry. You won't feel a thing as long as Damien is on the job."

Damien didn't lie, and he made a terrific whisky sour. I lost count somewhere around the fourth one.

Just shy of thirty hours later, after I'd slept through another half-dozen miserable old movies, my feet touched Georgia dirt, and I was home. After another ninety minutes, I thanked the Uber driver, opened my apartment door, said a silent prayer of thanks for working air conditioning, then fell into bed and slept for a day and a half.

♦

Even when she was happy, Sophia's voice lacked warmth. "That's wonderful, Harlow. Addison and the Whitmores will be very pleased with your decision."

"Not like I have a spectrum of choices," I said. "Thought I'd gotten lucky in India, but that crashed and burned."

"Did you have your heart broken again, dear?"

Why does that sound like a urologist asking, "Does it hurt when you pee?"

"No, Sophia, nothing like that. I just—oh, never mind. It was nothing."

"Well," she said, "I will call Judith Whitmore immediately, and we will get this party started."

I hung up, looked at my phone, and said, "Probably ought to be awake."

I'd barely gotten my bra unfastened when the phone rang. "Hello, Addison."

"Dollface," he said, "I'm so—"

"Let's get one thing straight, Mr. Whitmore, you will never call me Dollface again, especially not in public. If you do, you will immediately be able to wander into First Presbyterian downtown and apply as the soprano soloist."

A pause. Then, "In what universe do you imagine I would ever set foot into that place? They are so, so . . ."

"Egalitarian?" I asked. "Unbiased? Inclusive?"

"Oh, come now, Doll—I mean, Harlow. You know I am all about PC and letting everyone in the pool. After all, you and I are getting married."

"Well," I said, "my ring finger looks a little naked right now."

After one of his annoying chortles, sounding like a pig with a sinus condition, he said, "We can remedy that this afternoon. Springdale's at three sharp. Be there or be disappointed." He hung up.

I looked at the clock. *1:45 p.m.* "Hell, it's 11:15 p.m. in New Delhi." I went to the cabinet, pulled out a bottle of Casa Amigos Reposado, and took a shot.

Armed with a bit of liquid courage, I called an Uber and headed to the jewelry shop. Three hours later, a four-carat, pear-shaped, yellow diamond sat in a box on the counter.

"She's a beaut," Addison said.

I think it's gaudy. "It's lovely, Addison. But aren't we missing something?"

He looked around for a cue card or something, any hint of what he should do next.

"Think this through, Addison," I said. "We looked at the rings . . ."

"A lot of them."

"We selected a ring . . ."

"A very pretty one."

"You paid for the ring . . ."

"And how, I mean I *really* paid. That's not some cereal box thing. Didn't come out of a gumball machine. I mean—"

"I get it, Addison. It cost a lot of money."

"Did you notice I paid with an Amex black card?

"Yes, very impressive."

He stood there, waiting for the return of Haley's Comet.

"Addison," I said.

"Huh?"

"Looked, selected, paid, and now it's sitting in a box on the edge of the counter without a recipient."

"Oh! Right, right." He swept to the floor with the grace of an exhausted rhino, rested on one knee, and took my hand. He looked up at the clerk. "Hey buddy, little help here. He held out his hand for the box. "Thanks." Still on one knee, he looked at me like a guy perusing a new set of irons at Edwin Watts and wondering how well he might play with them. "Harlow, you want this?"

I struggled through my excitement enough to say, "Sure," and he jammed it on with the gentle touch of a pipefitter.

"There. We're engaged. I expect you are all atwitter."

"Positively giddy," I said.

"You know, a girl gets a ring like that, you'd think there would be some appropriate appreciation expressed."

"Thank you very much, Addison," I said.

"I had something else in mind," he said. He made a crude

gesture with his tongue on the inside of his cheek.

"Addison," I said, "in this deal, you get what I want to give and only when I want to give it. Shove anything in my face at your own risk."

"She's got claws, this one," he said. He pawed at the air like a hissing cat and shrugged at the clerk who looked like he'd rather be a patient in an ICU.

"It's better if you remember that I have teeth, and I've read everything ever written about Lorena Bobbitt."

A little of the smugness disappeared from Addison's face. "Look, Harlow. I know this isn't exactly the knight in shining armor scenario you had envisioned, but I think we can make this work. We can be a good team, you and me. I've got plans, and the further I go, the further you go. We'll do great. Let's just try to get along."

I nodded. "Fair enough, as long as you remember, I am an equal equity member of this partnership."

His head bobbed enthusiastically.

"And, I am the *only* other member of this partnership."

His head stopped bobbing.

"I'm serious, Addison. Your screwing around might not bother me, but I don't want to contract whatever one of your little Trixies might be hauling around in her honey pot. So, as long as we are in this arrangement, keep it zipped up tight until I decide otherwise. Understand?"

"Got it," he said. "Ah, can I at least kiss you in celebration of our engagement?"

"Absolutely," I said. "But if your tongue touches me, you'll need stitches."

CHAPTER 63

TEJ/VIK

THE NOISE OUTSIDE MY BEDROOM WAS APPALLING. I RETREATED into my bathroom. Maybe I could think in there. My phone leered at me from my palm. "Come on, Golden Boy, think of something clever. Dazzle the girl. Use the ole Chatwal charm."

I was fresh out. My charm meter was on empty.

I started typing. *Dear Harlow*— That's no good. *Dearest Harlow*— Worse. *Yo Harlow*— Give me a break.

I settled on her initial.

I typed, *H, I hope time has offered some perspective. You walked in when I was trapped in a vortex of unwanted advances. I have no interest in Haiya. I only want you, now and for—*

"Oh my God," I said, trying to make myself heard above the thumping from my den. "You're not Boris Pasternak, and this isn't *Doctor Zhivago*. Just write the girl."

I typed out a text and hit send.

Then another.

And another.

I put my phone on my bed and walked out into the mael-strom.

◊

"Tej, bro, this party is lit!"

The music thumped so loudly I could barely hear Miguel, but one look at his eyes told me everything I needed to know.

Bet he's not drinking the cheap stuff.

Of course, I didn't have any cheap stuff. Nothing but the best for the notorious Tej Mayur, Atlanta's celebrity whatever the hell I was. I looked around at my condo.

Who the hell are all these people?

More than fifty bodies crowded my expansive great room, eating, drinking, dancing. Everyone knew better than to bring drugs into my place, but I bet at least half of them could not have passed a blood scan. The place was awash with half-but-toned, silk-shirted men and stiletto-wearing, Lycra-encased women.

The attitude was festive, but there was something artificial about the mood. I didn't feel any of the genuine joy there had been at Amar and Lita's wedding. While every guest in my home smiled—well, a few of the white guys were biting their lips while they raised their hands over their heads and point-ed, the required Caucasian dance move—the grins lacked warmth. They looked more "painted on" than the garments most of the females wore.

It wasn't the debauchery of *Animal House* or the infamous disaster at Jake's parents' place in *Sixteen Candles*. No one was dry humping on the couch. Nothing was broken. I didn't mind anyone having a good time. My question was, Is anyone here really enjoying themselves or are we all just killing time before the next event next week at someone else's pad?

A part of me wanted to go over to the sound system, shut it off, and ask everyone to leave. But Tej Mayur's party-boy reputation could not take such a severe hit. I needed to keep up the image, pump up the façade. Everyone who came to one of my bashes would talk about it for days, then bring three or four or twelve guests to Bombay Baby because "Everything Mayur touches is epic."

Who were these people? They were not my friends. They were my past, present, and future customers. So, I let the music rattle the walls and nursed a drink in a corner chair until the last guest, always Miguel, looked outside and saw the Uber driver waiting.

"Later, dude," Miguel said.

"You need some help getting downstairs?" I asked.

"All good, Tej," he said. "Thanks for the evening. As always, it was dope."

"Night."

"Night."

He made it to the elevator, managed to push the button, and stayed upright at least long enough for the lift doors to close behind him. Once he was out of sight, he belonged to the poor schmuck waiting downstairs to take him home.

I cleaned up a little. A few guests had been considerate enough to bag the garbage and load the dishwasher. There were a few glasses scattered about, but nothing my housekeeper couldn't manage. I took out my wallet, slipped a fifty under one of the bottles at the wet bar (a little tip for the extra work), made sure the Spharon Excalibur system was powered down, and went to my bedroom.

Even though it was dark, I knew my way around, so I went into the bathroom, turned on the shower, put my clothes in the hamper, held out my hand to ensure the water was the right temperature, then stepped under the warm waterfall. Fifteen minutes later, I toweled off, brushed my hair, and headed into the bedroom. I switched off the light and heard a voice.

"I thought maybe you'd fallen asleep in there."

I turned on the bathroom light back and squinted. The shape in my bed wriggled from under the covers. Kiara stood in the dim light just as I remembered her, 5'8" of sex appeal.

A black mesh bodysuit accentuated her perfectly sculpted brown body. Her long dark hair cascaded across her chest and somehow made her seem less clothed and more tempting. She ran her tongue across her pouty lips and purred.

"You look tired, baby. Don't worry. Just relax and enjoy. I'll do all the work."

🔥

Sometime later, after a long talk, Kiara stood at the elevator doors. She was still crying.

"Are you sure?" she said.

"Positive."

"And you don't want one last fling?"

She still had not managed to wipe away the raccoon eyes of her running mascara. With her topcoat securely buttoned, which happened within ten seconds of my coming out of the bath, she looked sad, pitiful, and a little brittle. For the first time, I could read insecurity in her blue eyes.

"Kiara," I said, "our times together have been wonderful, but I changed during my trip home. It's time for me to grow up a little." The light turned green, the bell pinged, and the doors opened. I kissed her lightly on the cheek. "I've already called down. Elliot will see you to your car."

"If you change your mind, you can always call me, you know."

"I know." The doors closed. I sent Kiara one last text before I erased her from my contacts and blocked her phone number. *Please tell all your friends that I now go by my given name: Vikram Chatwal.*

CHAPTER 64

HARLOW

ANOTHER DAY IN ATLANTA, ANOTHER TRAFFIC JAM. I WANTED to be home. I wanted a gallon of Cherry Garcia and a blanket. I wanted to be in bed alone.

No, not really. But the guy I want won't ever be in my bed.

The Uber driver mashed the brakes. "Sorry, ma'am," he said.

"That's okay," I said. "I live here. I understand."

He misinterpreted my response as an invitation to a conversation. "Just get back in town?"

"A day or so ago," I said. I wasn't sure what day it was.

"Where from?"

I didn't feel like chatting. "India."

"Great place. Hoosier Country. Love that movie, great message for kids—"

"No, India. The place next to Pakistan."

"That so? You come home with the runs? Everyone I

know who's ever eaten over there comes back with a case of Gandhi's Revenge."

"I'm fine, quite enjoyable, really." *Well, except for finding the man I thought I loved getting busy with his ex-fiancée.* I didn't need to give a travelogue. I needed quiet. I needed a place to cry. "Beautiful. Unique." *A place to break your heart.*

"Were you there for business or pleasure?"

"I went there for a wedding."

His smile grew wider, interested. "You got married, ma'am?"

Thoughts raged. No, yes, I mean, engaged. *Not the guy I want—* The phone interrupted my internal rant. Sophia.

"Hello, dear," she said.

My stomach flipped. I clenched my jaw to avoid throwing up. "Sophia, you win. I got engaged yesterday." I swallowed hard and tasted the bile.

"I heard. Why else would I call? We need to do some shopping. How about this afternoon?"

Just get the damn thing over with. "Fine, but I'm tired."

There was a huff. "Well, take a quick nap, drink some coffee, and take a shower. I'll see you at Monique's in three hours."

I looked at my reflection and shook my head. "Make it four."

♦

Sophia stood just inside the door when I entered. She made a grand motion toward a saleswoman sitting at a French Provincial table. The woman, a little overdressed, with a spectacular cascade of hair, stood and extended her hand. "Harlow, what a pleasure. I'm Precision." I must have jumped a little because she laughed. "That's okay. Everyone thinks it's weird. My father was a racing fan. He always wanted a boy. He named me Precision."

"Oh."

"Her last name is Gere, Harlow, like the actor."

I felt the smile smear across my weary face. "Precision Gere. I bet you've wanted to kill your father most of your life."

Sophia slapped her hands together like she was reprimanding a bad doggie. "Harlow!"

Precision giggled. "At least you told the truth. Most of the stuffy people in here try to act like there's nothing wrong with my screwed-up name. But I never worry about people forgetting it."

My cell dinged. I reached for it. Sophia squeezed my arm. "Manners, Harlow," she said.

I dropped the phone into my purse, but I saw the texter's name.

Vik.

My pulse quickened. I got light-headed and stumbled. Precision held me by the elbow. "Are you okay, Harlow?"

"Yes. Just tripped."

"I understand," she said. "All brides get a little clumsy. Must be the excitement."

I liked her. Despite the stuffy atmosphere and outrageous prices for everything, I enjoyed my time as we sorted through blank invitations, wording, fonts, linens, table décor, and a host of other things about which I did not care. After three hours, too many finger sandwiches, and more than a few flutes of champagne, we were done.

The room spun a little as I reached for the door.

"You're *not* driving, are you?" Precision asked.

"Uber," I said. I knew better than to try to converse. Alcohol, combined with my fatigue, made my mind mustier than the Bat Cave. "Thank you."

Sophia leaned into the Uber. "Tomorrow, one sharp, Julian's Bridal. Once we have the dress, we are set."

I fell asleep in the car and never checked my phone.

CHAPTER 65

VIK

MY CELL PHONE SHATTERED AGAINST THE FAR WALL.

"Answer a damn text!"

Bishal picked up what was left of the electronics. "Want me to get a new one, boss, or will you just smash that too? You know, our profit margins aren't big enough to keep popping a grand every time you get pissed."

"Sorry," I said.

"Something I should know about?" he asked.

"Absolutely not."

Bishal stared at me, his head turned to one side. "You haven't been the same since the India trip. You're a little off your game. And people are beginning to notice."

"What do you mean?"

"Well, the staff decided on a little test the other night. They overcooked the naan, put it in a basket and walked it right past you. You never flinched."

I bolted out of my chair. "Fire whoever served it. I will not—"

He didn't let me finish. "I know, I know, you will not tolerate anything less than excellence. Relax. It went straight into the trash. They were just checking, and when you didn't notice, they were concerned. Your people love you, boss."

I slumped into my chair and buried my head in my hands. "I'll be okay. Just a little worn out from all the travel and dealing with things at home."

"Is your maji feeling any better?"

No, she's sure she will die without ever seeing a grandchild from me.

"Much better," I said. "Thanks."

♦

Ninety minutes later, Bishal knocked.

"Come on in. You know my door's always open to you."

"Just making sure there aren't random electronic devices flying through the air. Self-preservation, you know."

His laugh was genuine. Mine was not.

"Here's the newest iPhone. All set up, charged, and ready to go. Everything is transferred from your old account."

"Thanks," I said.

As he walked out, he called over his shoulder. "That one has a shatterproof case."

I heard him cackling all the way down the hall.

Bastard. I stabbed at the keys. Voicemail. I sent another text, the shortest one yet. *H, please call me.*

I placed the phone very gently on my desk, then stared out the window at the rain.

CHAPTER 66

HARLOW

I SHRIEKED WHEN I LOOKED AT THE CLOCK THE NEXT MORN-
ing. *11:30!*

I toweled off but did not take time to dry my hair. Sophia
noticed other omissions as soon as I walked in the dress shop
door.

"Did you misplace your makeup, dear?" she asked.

"Overslept," I said.

"Good thing Addison's mother declined my invitation."

Only Sophia would invite a future mother-in-law to something as "mother-daughter" as shopping for a wedding dress.

Three hours later, I sat to discuss my choice. Sophia looked
regal in a wingback chair.

"Have a seat," she said. "I want to show you something."

I sat. Sophia fished into her expansive Louis Vuitton bag
while I waited. When she extracted her left hand, I could
barely see.

"God Almighty, Sophia! That has to be four carats."

Sophia admired the ring. "It's almost six. Vincent is very proud of it."

"Vincent?"

"Vincent Allemande," Sophia said. "A few years older than I am."

"How did he make his money?" I asked.

"The old-fashioned way," she said. "He inherited it." A coy smile crept across Sophia's face. "What makes you think he has money?"

"Honestly," I said, "what other reason could you possibly have?"

I saw something in Sophia's eyes I'd never seen—ever. Sadness.

"It's the same reason I always have, dear," she said. The pain spread across Sophia's face. "Harlow, how much do you remember about my leaving your father?"

"Just that one day, you packed your bags and took off. Before I knew it, Daddy told me you had a new husband."

"It wasn't quite that fast," she said.

"Seemed that way. I was only five when you walked out."

There was an internal collapse. I could see if just as surely as I could smell the overwhelming presence of vanilla scented candles in the store. Sophia's wall—the stoic barrier she'd erected between us and maintained like a twelfth century monk preserving a holy relic—was crumbling.

"Child,"—Sophia had not called me *child* in decades—"I didn't walk out. I didn't have a choice."

CHAPTER 67

SOPHIA

"Everyone who knows me calls me Sophia. To the world, I am Sophia Carter Kennedy Ellison Bashelder."

"Don't forget Allemande," Harlow said.

"All in good time, child, all in good time," I said. "But that's not my real name."

"Huh?"

"Honesty, Harlow, can't you do better than a grunt?"

"Huh?" she said. But this time, she was grinning.

"My real name is Lorelei Turner. I was born in 1964, a few months after President Kennedy died, just outside Tuscaloosa, Alabama."

"Roll Tide," she said.

"Roll Tide," I said. "My mother worked for the Baldwin family. They were fine people. I don't mean good. They thought they were fine, thought their bathroom business smelled like roses."

Harlow nodded. "Lotta white people like that."

"The Baldwins owned most of the county. They always talked about how their family had worked the land for generations."

Harlow's phone buzzed. She clicked it off without looking. "Bet they had some relatives who helped. You know, darker-skinned cousins, the kind who didn't get paid."

"Absolutely. Plow the fields, wash the clothes, tend to the chillins, and other things." Harlow understood.

"Just lie back, don't say nothing, don't tell the missus, and if a baby shows up, I don't know anything about it."

"Tell it, sister," I said. "My relatives' bones rest in a plot for coloreds in one of the back fields of some sagging plantation house where the residents can hardly afford the electrical bill now. Seems they're not so adept at working the land when they have to do it themselves."

Harlow's laugh contained no humor. "What's so important about the history lesson. You're not telling me anything new. You know, the ugly underbelly of *Gone With the Wind*."

"But, as they say, the devil is in the details," I said. "Here's a news bulletin. You never knew your grandfather."

"Sure I did," she said. "I loved Pappy Carter. He was my favorite. He used to keep those little cinnamon candies in his pocket and sneak one to me when you weren't looking."

I laughed. "Like I couldn't smell those things on your breath. Come on, Harlow."

"Well, we tried."

"I know, child," I said. "But you never knew your grandfather."

Harlow tilted her head to one side like a confused cocker spaniel. A scowl moved across her brow. Then, slowly, a terrified light of recognition radiated from deep in her eyes and moved across her stunning—and stunned—face.

"Pappy Carter wasn't your father," she said.

"Your Grandma Lizzie was a beautiful woman," I said. "And from what everyone says, the woman could sew like no one you've ever seen. If she'd had the resources and lived anywhere other than the Deep South, she could have become a famous designer. Women came from miles around. She made ball gowns and wedding dresses. If she were still alive, there's no way in the world she would stand still for your buying your wedding dress in a salon like this. She would have made something that would put everything in here to shame."

"Wow," she said. "You never told me." Then she paused. "Go on, you haven't gotten to the main point yet."

"No, I haven't," I said. "You see, the Baldwin's had a son, Spencer—"

"The son of a bitch raped Lizzie!"

I shook my head. "No, it wasn't like that," I said. "But they were involved. In some versions of the story, they were secretly married. Not sure, but either way, they were in love—happens, you know. When Mrs. Baldwin found out that Lizzie was 'in the family way,' as she put it, well, let's just say Spencer was suddenly accepted to a prestigious university program in Europe, and Lizzie's services to the family were no longer needed."

"They kicked her out?"

Tears formed in Harlow's eyes. Her beautiful jaw clinched hard enough to crack a handful of walnuts.

"Harlow, people make choices all the time—good and bad. Some people are strong, and some have the character of al dente spaghetti. Spencer made a choice: a woman and his child or family money. He chose, and your Grandma Lizzie moved on."

"When did she marry Pappy Carter?"

"I was five years old when she met your grandfather. They got married, moved to Atlanta, and never said a word about my birth father. Pappy Carter was lighter-skinned, so no one suspected anything. Three years after they moved here, Lizzie was delivering a dress to a lady in Buckhead when a high school junior driving some souped-up car after nipping a little too much from his daddy's liquor cabinet screamed through a stoplight and rammed her car. She died on the way to the hospital. No one was ever charged with her death."

In all her life, Harlow had been talkative. Not now. She stared straight ahead in silence that was almost reverential. She chewed on the inside of her lip, a sure sign she was fighting tears. I continued with the story.

"Your Pappy Carter was a good man, kind, gentle, and honest. He didn't have any training of any sort, but he could fix anything.

"He built me a dollhouse, remember?"

"I do. It was about the last thing your Pappy ever did."

"Well, he lived a long time after that."

"Ten years or so, not long enough for me, but he was pretty old when he married my mother. But he couldn't work at all after he developed arthritis. You saw his hands every time he slipped you one of those candies. What did they look like?"

Harlow pursed her lips. "They were gnarled. Fingers crooked. I remember he always held the candies between his knuckles."

"The poor man could barely walk, and those candies were about the only thing he could hold. He could scarcely lift a fork. Had to grip it in his fist. If you think back, I always cut up his food for him."

"I remember."

I reached in my bag and took out a linen handkerchief. "Here, child. Honestly, I don't know why you young people never carry these."

She dabbed at her eyes and blew her nose. When she extended the handkerchief to me, I shook my head. "Consider it a gift, Harlow. Just take good care of it. Those are not cheap."

"So, what does any of this have to do with Daddy?"

"I met your father when I was at college. I had a full scholarship to Spelman. We had a mixer with Morehouse. The minute I saw your Daddy across the room, I didn't even consider dancing with anyone else. I sat and waited for him to ask me."

"Daddy was handsome."

"Oh, child, that is not the word for it. Your father was the best-looking man in any room at any time, and every woman at Spelman thought so. I did not know until much later that many of them knew him. Let's just say that they were far more acquainted with him than I was."

I took a sip of water. The clerk came over. She'd been hovering. "Have you ladies decided?" she asked.

"We'll take the Vera Wang," I said. I slipped her my card. "Deliver it to this address by tomorrow afternoon, please."

CHAPTER 68

HARLOW

WE SAT IN THE LIVING ROOM OF MY CHILDHOOD HOME.

"You haven't been here in a while," Sophia said.

"Not much reason," I said. "You've fixed it up."

In my mind, the stately old Victorian was always a little tired looking. Something always needed fixing—a loose shutter, some chipped paint, a leaky faucet, an electrical outlet. Daddy was handy. He could repair anything. But his jewelry business took a lot of his time, so by the time he finished one job, two more things had broken. He couldn't ever catch up.

When Sophia moved in, she hired everything out. She acted like she hardly knew which end of a screwdriver to hold. More likely, she saw any sort of manual work as "beneath her station." So, after Daddy passed, in addition to the men using the revolving door of Sophia's matrimonial commitment, we always had a parade of folks coming through the kitchen door for "the help," as Sophia explained. They were replacing this wire or tightening that sconce.

The house had always smelled of food: Aunt Izzy's crawdad etouffee, Dad's homemade brisket. When I got a little older, I tried my hand at all sorts of things. When things went well, I was praised. When I had a disaster, no one fussed at me. Izzy simply baked a batch of cookies. The aroma would cover the acrid smell of what she labeled my "learning experience."

"I've had a little work done," Sophia said.

I didn't take the bait. Too easy. "Why are we here?"

"Time to clear the air," she said. "And let me begin with an apology."

"For what?" I asked.

"For everything," she said. "But for starters, for being a terrible parent."

I saw a sincerity of which I did not know Sophia was capable. She looked tired, an intrepid warrior who'd fought one too many battles and who, despite all odds, was preparing to enter the arena again. Because she knew no other way.

"I wasn't a bad mother early on," she said. "I doted on you. I spent every waking hour with you. I had no social life, but I did not care because I could not stand to be away from you ever."

"Didn't seem to bother you when you left."

"Your father ran me off," she said.

The words were out of my mouth before I had time to think about them. "Because you were whoring around."

Sophia let the accusation linger in the air for a while without saying anything, like when you are in a group of the socially elevated who refuse to acknowledge that someone has discreetly broken wind. She massaged her brow with her thumb and index finger, then began.

"You have it backward," she said. "Someone cheated in our marriage. That much is true. But the party who was guilty of infidelity was your beloved father."

CHAPTER 69

SOPHIA

I let my words settle. I knew Harlow wanted to argue, but she suddenly seemed incapable of speech. The silence stretched for a while before I spoke.

"Your father was not what you thought," I said. "I've never told you, but I was pregnant when your father and I married. He was the only man I'd ever been with. He was so, so smooth. He could charm the skin off a snake. And he certainly charmed me right out of my panties."

Harlow grimaced a little, but I was not going to stop.

"Everything was great for a month or so after the wedding, but as soon as I began showing, the passion your father had for me deflated. He didn't kiss me in the mornings after breakfast; he spent long hours in his shop; he went out at night, came in very late, and never came to bed before he'd showered. Still, I did the laundry. I could smell perfume on his shirts. Whenever I would ask what he'd been doing, he always told me he was consulting with customers about a special piece of jewelry."

Harlow's eyes locked onto me, a penetrating gaze. She'd always had that look, and she could always discern the truth. She was a human lie detector. I knew if I strayed from the facts one little bit, she would know, and I would lose whatever small part of her heart I had forever.

"Didn't Daddy do well in business?" she asked.

"Yes and no," I said. "Your daddy always drove a nice car, and he was some kind of a clothes horse. That man was pickier about what he wore than almost any woman I have ever known."

"He had a lot of money, didn't he?"

"He *looked* like he did," I said. "Always carried around a big roll of bills. Of course, it was a single hundred covering a stack of ones and newsprint. By the time the man died, he was in hock to every credit card company in America and every loan shark in Atlanta."

Harlow looked like a kid who'd just discovered her parents playing Santa on Christmas Eve, a look of total disbelief and disappointment.

"But he had all those stones, all that gold. He made all those lovely pieces."

"He did," I said. "And how many of those have you seen since he passed? Nary a one. The day after we put him in the ground, Big Daddy Lassiter, Roscoe Freeman, Dakota Calhoun, and Isaac Goldstein walked down into his workroom and decided who got what. They took the rest and paid off your father's bills to about a dozen or so credit card companies that had been hounding him for months about late payments. It was the only way to prevent you from being thrown out on the streets."

Harlow's eyes bulged. Her hand flew to her neck. "That's why—"

"Yes," I said. "That's why you never wore that spectacular ruby necklace outside the house. No one could ever see it. If the loan sharks had spotted it, someone would have snatched it. If you had tried to stop them, they would have hurt you."

"Wait a minute," she said. "If Daddy was the one catting around, how come you were the one who left?"

"That's a good question," I said. "Remember I told you I was pregnant when we got married?"

She nodded.

"Couldn't finish school. So, when you came along, I didn't have a degree. I was completely dependent on your father. Hourly jobs didn't pay enough. I would have lost money if I'd paid someone to watch you. Besides, I didn't want to leave. You were the most important thing in the world to me."

"But you left."

CHAPTER 70

HARLOW

SOPHIA'S FACE WENT BLANK, AND I COULD TELL HER MIND WAS traveling back in time. The closer she got to her target, the more anguish I saw etched on her face.

The words dragged out of her, a verbal car towed against its will. "It was a terrible night. I confronted your father about his infidelity. I knew about all the women. I suspected there might be other children around, but I never discovered any. I found out later your father had paid for at least three abortions. He said a lot of terrible things, projected all his sins on me. He called me awful names, suggested I have been having affairs when he knew it wasn't true. I told him he had to stop, to give up all his girlfriends. That's when he told me to leave."

"Why did you go?"

"I was fine with leaving. I had a bag packed for you. But your father said he had no intention of giving me any money. I thought that was fine, my name was on all the accounts. I could access enough to get by, and I told him so."

"What did he do?"

He laughed. He'd removed my name from everything. The accounts, the house. He forged my name on a quitclaim deed and got a crooked Notary to endorse it. I owned nothing. He told me in no uncertain terms that he would not give me anything, even if I took you with me. When he told me, I knew I couldn't take you because I could not take care of you."

She wiped a tear away, a rapid flick of her hand like she was brushing away a gnat. I could not remember ever seeing Sophia cry.

CHAPTER 71

SOPHIA

I KNEW I WOULD REMEMBER THE FIRST NIGHT AWAY FROM MY daughter for the rest of my life. Her father and I had not had much of a relationship for a while. I could not get revved up for romance with a man who reeked of another woman's perfume and regularly called me by someone else's name, by accident or not.

But not having Harlow crushed me. I'd brushed her beautiful hair every night before putting her in bed. It was a little ritual. One hundred strokes. Then, she would brush mine. It was a little rough before she got older. I had to stifle a lot of screams when she yanked the brush through tangles or beat it into my head like she was hitting a kettle drum. But the time together was worth a few bumps and "ouchies."

I read her stories every night, and we sang "Twinkle, Twinkle Little Star" while looking at the Georgia night sky. When lightning split the darkness and thunder shook the house, and the wind bent the trees, we sang even louder, a defiant lullaby sung to an approaching summer storm.

I could see the face of the child in the young woman across from me, the same beauty I'd seen the day she came into the world, except the beautiful eyes had changed. Where once they were hopeful and trusting, now they looked guarded, suspicious.

Did she need the entire story? How would she react when I told her I spent the first five months in my car? I looked for work everywhere, but the economy was in a tailspin. Though I picked up a little day work here and there, every time I found an opening for a decent job—something at a diner or cleaning houses—I was always in line behind more qualified people. Hell, I couldn't even find work bussing tables.

I learned where it was safe to park, where I wouldn't be bothered either by the police or by the perverts. After one particular scary encounter with a deranged man, I took to carrying a razor in my bra. Sometimes I beat the other street folks to the restaurants before the leftovers went in the trash. Sometimes, I had to dumpster dive. After more than one hundred fifty days on the street, I had one decent pair of pants, two shirts—everything else had worn out or been stolen—and no hope.

I didn't want to, but I went to Mama Jasmine's. I only knew about the place because Harlow's father talked about it all the time when he routinely complained about my lack of bedroom skill, or at least, my unadventurous nature. No man was going to pay for whatever I might do for them, and I sure as hell was not going to do what they wanted to pay for. Would

Harlow believe I had not degraded myself for money?

The night I staggered through her backdoor, I could not remember my last shower. I'd cut off my hair with an old pair of scissors I'd liberated from someone's trash. The only reason I could stand my own smell was because I stood outside in the rain for twenty minutes while I worked up the courage to knock.

Jasmine's reputation was of a woman who knew what men wanted, but she was also kind to those who came to her for help. She never forced anyone into anything, but if a girl wanted to earn serious cash, Jasmine explained everything: what to expect and how the money worked. Her splits were generous: 60-40 in favor of her "girls." She took care of doctor bills and food. The girls stayed in the house if they wanted. Jasmine even had a nursery in the back.

But there were others, like me, who could not bring themselves to enter the world's oldest profession. So, Jasmine put me to work gathering and laundering soiled sheets and scrubbing floors. She took out a modest amount for my room and board.

Did I think about asking if Harlow could live with me? Every day. Mama Jasmine would have allowed it. But Harlow's father would have raised unholy hell, and there was not a judge anywhere in Atlanta who would go on record as approving of a mother who kept her daughter in a whorehouse.

I stayed for six months, got rid of most of the "street crazy" I had developed. My hair grew back, and my self-respect returned—at least most of it. One night, Mama Jasmine approached.

"Time for you to leave," she said.

Terror seized my throat. "I can't go back on the street."

"I won't do that to you, Sophia," she said. "I have a better way."

For the next month, she tutored me. We couldn't work together every day. I still had my chores, and Jasmine had her hands full. But whenever she had a moment, she taught me about men: what they wanted, what they needed, how to please them, and, most importantly, how to control them.

"You're special," she said. "You are college-educated and refined. For the most part, you have not led a hard life. There are no canyons of regret on your face. You still have a chance."

"I won't be a whore," I said.

"No." She laughed. "I am going to teach you how to make men your bitch."

I told Harlow everything, walking her through my past until Mama Jasmine changed my life. "His name was Sterling Ellison. He was sixty-seven when I met him."

"When was that?" Harlow asked.

"About a year after your father kicked me out."

"He was a regular at Jasmine's, but he knew I didn't work there. Mama made that clear to him. Much to my surprise, he asked me to marry him."

"Seems a little fast," Harlow said. "Something you want to tell me."

I knew what she was after. "It's exactly the opposite of what you think, Harlow. He had to buy the cow first."

Harlow choked on her iced tea. "I never thought I would hear you refer to yourself as a cow, Sophia."

"If I was going to whore myself out, I would have worked for Mama Jasmine," I said. "Believe it or not, I still had some self-respect."

"Did you love him?"

"Not in the slightest. But I knew he had money, and I knew he wanted me. His eyes were the size of silver dollars every time he saw me. After we went out a few times, he realized he was not going to get to the Promised Land until he said, "'I do.'"

"So, you got married."

"He bought me a Givenchy dress for the occasion. We got married at the Court House and went right down the street to a big fancy hotel where he got what he paid for. I wasn't in that dress for more than ninety minutes. Never wore it again.

"Were you happy?"

"I was better than happy," I said. "I was safe. All he wanted to do was dress me up and show me off. He didn't have a lot of stamina, so we only had sex about twice a month. He swore I was going to kill him, but he said he would die happy."

Harlow's face contorted. "I could have gone a long time without hearing that."

"You want the story or not?"

"Okay."

"He liked my body, but he wanted me to have a heavier chest, so he paid for implants. When he decided my butt needed a little tightening, I did that too. I did some lipo and a few Botox injections to make him happy as well."

"Did it help his libido?"

"I thought you didn't want TMI," I said.

"Well, in for a penny, in for a pound," she said.

"Fact is, he was more into watching than anything else. He liked me to dance for him, strip, actually. It got his blood pumping. One night, I put on my tightest, sexiest dress and my tallest stilettos and reenacted the famous scene from *9 1/2 Weeks*, complete with 'You Can Leave Your Hat On' blaring in the studio. I copied the moves exactly."

"What happened?" she asked. "Or do I want to know?"

"Well . . . it was interesting," I said. I had her on the hook, might as well draw it out a little.

"Go on," she said.

"It killed him," I said. "Massive myocardial infarction. About the time I was standing with nothing on but a fedora, he was knocking on the Pearly Gates."

Harlow slid out of the chair, tears in her eyes. "Oh my God, Sophia, you stripped a man to death?"

"I did indeed," I said. "He'd wanted me so badly that we'd gotten married without a prenup. I inherited a bundle."

"So, why did you keep getting married?"

"I was never going to have happen to me what happened with your father. I wanted to make sure I would never live on the street again."

There was a long pause. Harlow wanted to ask me something, but she was hesitating. "Go ahead, child. What is it?"

"Sophia," she said. "Why have you been so mean to me my entire life? You've been cold and distant. You've treated me like I was a stranger. Even when you moved back after Daddy died, you kept your distance. You were too busy finding another husband or getting rid of the one you had. You never had time for me."

The question didn't surprise me. I'd been asking myself the same thing most of my life. I'd loved this child so intensely. We'd been Twinkle, Twinkle buddies.

"It took me a long time to figure that out," I said. I swallowed hard. Now was not the time to dissolve in tears. "While you were in India, I went through the house and found some old photos. I looked at them for a long time. The more I looked, the more I understood. "

She moved back into her seat and gazed at me with her terrible emerald eyes, the sparkling green lie detectors. "What, Sophia? What was it?"

I walked across the room and held out my hand in invitation. "Come with me." She took my hand, stood, and walked as I guided her toward the mantle. Before we arrived, I said, "Close your eyes. I won't let you fall. I promise."

She did as I instructed, and I maneuvered her to the middle of the hearth and turned her toward the gilded mirror hanging over the fireplace.

"When I tell you to open your eyes, tell me the first thing you see. Do you understand?"

"Yes, ma'am," she said, ever the obedient and polite Southern child.

"Okay," I said. "Open your eyes and tell me."

Her lids shuttered open, and she gasped. "Oh, God, it's Daddy. I look exactly like him."

CHAPTER 72

HARLOW

WE TALKED WELL INTO THE NIGHT. WE LOOKED AT ALL THE old pictures she mentioned. Sometimes we laughed, and sometimes we wept, but the tension and animosity slowly faded, shed like a snake's skin, abandoned and useless.

About three in the morning, we were giddy with exhaustion and decided to go to bed. At the bottom of the stairs, Sophia turned me toward her and put her arms on my shoulders. "Answer one more question before you go to bed."

"Okay."

"Do you love Addison Whitmore?"

My hesitation spoke louder than any answer.

"Okay, then," Sophia said, "tomorrow, you need to go see him and slow things down. Take some time to figure out if he will make you happy. After a while, you will know, and I thoroughly believe you will make the decision that is best for you."

"Okay," I said.

"Goodnight, Harlow," she said.

I kissed her lightly on the cheek.

"Goodnight, Mother."

CHAPTER 73

HARLOW

THE NEXT MORNING AFTER NINETY MINUTES OF ATLANTA traffic hell, I sat in the backseat of an Uber and stared at the entrance to Addison's condo complex. I ran through the various conversations in my head.

We need to pump the brakes a little. I'm not breaking up with you, but what do you think about waiting six months for the wedding? No. You know I care about—

"Miss Harlow." It was Nevin, my new best friend who'd entertained me on what seemed like a ninety-hour drive by telling me about how he was a "Film Maker."

Just tell me you want to make movies because no one really likes film.

He said he was killing time while some people over at EUE Screen Gems were looking over his "treatment."

Gag.

"Miss Harlow," he repeated. "We're here. We've been here

about five minutes. You okay?"

My head snapped up. "Yeah, Nevin, sorry. Just thinking about a few things." I held out a twenty. "This is for the extra trouble and time."

"Not supposed to take that," he said as he reached.

"Who am I going to tell?" I said.

I pulled on the door handle and stopped. Addison was coming out of his building. He held open the door for a tall, leggy blond wearing a skirt that would get her arrested if she bent over.

Sunlight always rats out the panty-less.

I looked again. Addison wasn't following her. He was still holding the door. An elderly woman using a walker tottered out and nodded to Addison, surely telling him, "What a nice young man you are. Your mother would be so very proud."

Okay, all good.

Except Blondie had stopped about two feet from the curb and turned. Her hands-on-the-hips pose told me she was waiting for Addison, who let go of the door, walked directly to her, and stuck his tongue so far down her throat he could tell what size shoe she was wearing.

"Mother fuc—"

"I'm sorry," Nevin said. He was shoving the twenty back at me.

"Not you," I said. I pointed. "That!"

Nevin turned. Blondie ground her thighs against Addison, a frickin' lap dance on the sidewalk. He disengaged, opened the door of the waiting car, let her in, and popped her on the ass.

"Go," I said. "Go now! Slow but don't stop."

Nevin reacted like an Atlanta Dream point guard spotting an opening. "Drive-by," he said. "Got it."

Ignoring honks and screeching tires, he pulled into traffic and cruised alongside Addison's ride. I rolled down the window and leaned out up to my waist.

I used my best "girlie" voice. "Hiya, Addie, baby! You're lookin' so fiiiiine."

He looked up and was greeted by my smiling face and extended middle finger. I kept looking at him as Nevin rolled to the corner and started into a right turn. Addison was still staring at me when I dropped his engagement ring into the storm drain.

Nevin roared in laughter. "Damn, girl, you're cold blooded."

CHAPTER 74

VIK

"All set?" I asked Dinesh.

"Yes, sir," he said. "Opening right on time, just like always. Every table is full. We are booked solid for the next month."

He smiled with satisfaction. "I knew you could do it, sir."

"Dinesh," I said. "Please call me by my first name."

"No, sir," he said. "Old school, remember?"

I looked him in the eye. "Stellar work. I mean it. You've been the champ, my friend. You steered well while I was away. And I have not been myself for a few days."

"You've been looking at your phone more than usual," he said. "A lot more than usual. Are you expecting to hear from someone?"

I hesitated.

"Are you *hoping* to hear from someone?" he asked.

Without an answer, I walked across the restaurant and greeted the first of the evening's guests. They always loved to see the great Tej Mayur, Mr. Entertainment himself. My greeting was genuine. After all, these good people were getting ready to spend their hard-earned money in my establishment. But the smile felt forced, and before long, I handed greeting duties off to Bishal and retreated to the sanctuary of my office.

A business on fire, even on a rainy night in Atlanta, and all I could do was stare at a blank phone screen. *Why won't she answer?*

Benny came in with a dish for my approval. The tamarind sauce with chilies would be perfection over rice. I nodded in a disinterested way. "Fine," I said. My response did not invite further conversation.

My phone dinged. I nearly dropped it in my haste to look at the screen.

A weather alert: high winds expected.

"That's just what I need," I said. "A power outage. Maybe the roof could collapse and bury me alive. That would make it a perfect day." I shook my head at my morose sarcasm and decided to text Harlow again. *What is this, the tenth time? Twentieth?*

I'd lost count. But I knew exactly how many responses I'd gotten. Zip!

Serious had not worked. *Please, can we talk? I promise, it wasn't what you thought. I need to talk to you.* All those had resulted in a blank screen.

Another approach. *This text is redeemable for free refreshments and one signature cocktail at Bombay Baby. The chef recommends a small plate of malai kofta and a Cosmopolitan. No reservation required.*

If I could just slip a tiny taste of chicken meatball between her lips, watch her savor the blend of onions, spices, and tomatoes, I'd be a happy man. I wanted to show her Bombay Baby, introduce her to the staff, take her out to my condo, and slow dance to Aretha while I pressed my face into her soft hair.

The customary "Delivered" notification did not appear. I sent it again. Nothing.

"I'm blocked," I said. And I banged my head against my desk.

Dinesh peered into my office. "Sir, you don't look well."

Get it together, dude. "I'm fine, Dinesh. But thank you."

He said nothing. His eyes saw everything. "Why don't you take the night off, sir? We've got this. No problem."

I took off without any argument. I stopped at a local market for yellowfin tuna and pinot noir on my way home. The crowds had cleared out as the rain increased. I ducked under an awning to wait out the downpour. Passersby scurried along, either carrying umbrellas or with jackets pulled over their heads. Then I saw her. Tallish, toffee skin, drenched tresses, a soaked flowing skirt.

"Harlow!"

No response. I lengthened my stride.

"Harlow!" I touched her elbow, and she turned, a look of complete bafflement. I backed up so quickly, I almost fell. "I am so sorry. I thought you were someone else.

Sarcasm creased her face. "That's okay," she said. "You folks all look the same to us too."

CHAPTER 75

VIK

THE BELLS WOULD NOT STOP. A FIRE ALARM, A CLOCK, AN AIR raid. Visions swirled in my head. I swatted at them without effect. They kept ringing. When I rolled over, I realized it was my phone.

"What?" I said.

"Dude." It was Miguel. "Are you drunk? I've been calling for two hours."

I sat up in bed, then immediately buried my head in the pillow. Icepicks of pain shot from the base of my skull.

"Tag? Tag?"

"I'm here," I said. "At least most of me."

"You tie one on last night, brother?"

I remembered the encounter in the rain, the sneering rebuke, my retreat into a bar. And I remembered the first three tequila shots — or was it five? "Might have been a little overserved."

"Bet you smell good," he said.

I cracked an eye open and winced at the light. "My mouth tastes like the Kentucky Derby."

"Well," he said, "take a shower, gargle with some peroxide, put on deodorant, and get your ass over to Annie Alice's Bakery ASAP."

My stomach did a backflip. "Oh God, man, I don't have any interest in a pastry."

"No doubt," Miguel said. "But I guaran-damn-tee you'll be interested in a macaron."

◊

Forty-seven minutes later, I staggered through the door of the bakery. The "Customer's Here" jangle of the bell felt like someone stabbed me in the eye. Miguel sipped coffee at a small table in the back corner. The oatmeal raisin cookie in front of him could have fed a kindergarten class.

A woman wearing a floral apron scurried over to the table as I sat down. She put a small cup in front of me. "Mr. Mayur, we are so honored to have you at Annie Alice's. Cappuccino on the house for the *International Master of Eclectic Taste*. I saw the spread in *The Journal-Constitution* this morning. Can I have your autograph?"

I nodded and reluctantly took off my sunglasses. Temporarily blinded, I groped for a pen inside my jacket. I scrawled my signature on what I thought was a menu.

I might have just signed over Bombay Baby.

I took a sip of the coffee. "This is excellent." I forced a smile. I thought my face would break. "How's the bakery business?"

"Pretty good, to tell the truth, although we've been slow this week. All the rain, you know." She frowned at the window even though it was sunny. "The storms this week have even scared the regulars away."

"You have a lot of return customers?" I asked. My interest increased. I was always willing to "borrow" someone's marketing ideas.

"Yes, we do," she said. "Quite a number of people stop in several times a week for 'Triple A.'" I must have looked blank because she continued, "Afternoons at Annie Alice. We feature coffee and a plate of macarons for $5.99. It's a little better than break-even, but it brings people into the store, and they almost always buy something else to take with them."

"Good idea," I said. "Very clever. I hope you are wildly successful."

She beamed. "That means so very much, Mr. Mayur. I mean, you are such a celebrity. And for you to say something nice like that is just the best thing I could ever hope for."

Miguel was bouncing up and down like a kid who needed to use the bathroom. "Ask her about her Lemon Lady."

"Huh?"

The owner did not wait for me to ask. "Oh, her. The Lemon Lady. We call her that because she comes in every afternoon at 5:15 on the dot, only wants lemon macarons. She won't eat anything else, so now we save some for her every day."

"That's nice," I said.

"Oh yes," she said. "She is so friendly and kind to everyone. We love The Lemon Lady—Harlow."

I was silent for a long time.

"Did I do something wrong, Mr. Mayur?" she asked.

"No, not at all. Everything you told me was fascinating. In fact, would be so kind as to do me a huge favor."

♦

The next day, I was in the kitchen so often, and with so many opinions, that Dinesh finally ran me out.

"You've given six sets of contradictory instructions," he said. "Wherever your mind is, it's not here. Kindly go to your office and don't come out until we open for guests. All you get to do tonight is say hi, then back into your cave until you get over whatever is wrong with you, sir."

Four o'clock came and went. 4:05. I re-read every article in *The Journal-Constitution* online edition.

4:47.

I played canasta on my phone. Three games, lost all.

4:59.

I watched YouTube videos of guys doing stupid things.

5:16

The phone rang. "She's here. We are ready to execute Operation Restoration."

"Go!"

I watched the scene unfold in my head. Annie Alice's owner approaching Harlow, putting down a cup of coffee and a dozen lemon macarons. "On the house."

Now she was handing Harlow *The Atlanta Journal-Constitution* folded open to the personals, one circled with a red Sharpie.

Miserable, sad Indian gentleman seeking ideal wife. Prefers long curls and a sassy disposition. Must know how to make a killer red velvet cake. Understanding of cricket and jewelry designing skills considered plusses. All other cooking skills can be negotiated if applicant looks adorable while she stirs the sauce. Mother issues welcome because gentleman has them too.

Would love to meet, talk, and dine on fine Indian cuisine.

The longest six minutes of my life passed before my cell phone buzzed. "What happened?" I asked.

"She's crying," the owner said.

"Damn," I said.

"Oh, no, sir," she said. "This is good. Very, very good."

I was having trouble breathing. "Did you give her my other message?"

"Not yet. Want to hold on?"

"Yes."

The seconds moved like a turtle. Then, "You can expect Miss Harlow Kennedy to arrive at Bombay Baby tomorrow night at eight."

I made no move to wipe my face. Tears had never felt so good. "Thank you. Thank you very much. You eat free at Bombay Baby for the rest of your life."

"That's very gracious," she said. "But unnecessary. Owning a business is tough enough without cutting into your margins. I'm just glad I could help."

"Well, thank you again."

"Any time, Mr. Mayur," she said.

I hung up.

Not anymore. Tej Mayur is dead and buried. From now on, I am the real deal. I am Vikram Chatwal.

CHAPTER 76

VIK

THE STAFF STOOD DUMBFOUNDED. ONLY DINESH DARED TO speak.

"Did I hear that right, sir?"

"Yes," I said. "No seatings after six. I want the place cleared by eight. Every employee stays, all-hands on deck, at double time and a half. That should make up for any loss in tip revenue."

"You are the boss," Dinesh said. "It will be as you instruct."

Naima scanned the reservation list with a look of hopelessness. "I'll have to make a lot of calls. And some of these folks will be very unhappy."

"Sorry about the hassle," I said. "Please convey my apologies and assure everyone they will receive a twenty-five percent discount and a free bottle of wine when they come in next time."

Naima looked a little relieved.

"Just make sure they understand the wine will be one of my choices," I said. "No 2014 Zampa Insignia."

Dinesh looked up. "Five thousand a bottle is a little over the top, even for you, sir."

"That will be all," I said. I walked away, but I halted after two steps. "I'm sorry. You people are my friends, my family. You should be in the know."

They gathered around.

"This is not just anyone tomorrow. I will be dining with someone important." I saw a few hands go up. "We're not going to play twenty questions. It's not a sports figure or politician. No, it's not my maji."

Nervous laughter. I heard someone say, "Thank God."

"No kidding," I said. "We don't want that kind of pressure. Still, this is someone equally important. It's a special lady I want you to meet."

I had enjoyed drinks with innumerable beautiful women, friends and dates. In all my time, I'd never dined alone with any female at Bombay Baby.

The room broke out in cheers.

I heard Dinesh next to me. "Oh, happy, happy day!"

As I expected, the next night, the staff members responded, but something was different. Instead of their usual bustling efficiency, I saw . . . joy. Within forty minutes after the last patron left, my crew transformed the entire back quarter of the restaurant into Bollywood. Purple, green, and jasmine silks hung from the walls. Busy hands had covered the bench of a large plush booth with vibrant pillows. Handmade elephant print parasols were suspended from the ceiling as if they were floating on air. An abundance of peach roses crowded gold potted floor planters. Faint whiffs of incense floated through the air, and Master Ravi Shankar's sitar filtered through the speakers.

When Dinesh escorted Harlow in, the only light in Bombay Baby came from a sea of flickering candlelight washing across every surface.

"A lovely lady here to see you, sir."

I drank Harlow in, a mixture of bashfulness and fire. Flaming red lipstick accented her full lips. An embroidered black tulle dress with a plunging neckline highlighted every curve. Her curls were set in deep waves and swept over to one side, exposing her graceful neck.

I held out my hand, a request to touch her arm. She nodded. Shots of electricity zinged up my fingers when I felt her velvet skin. I breathed in her familiar jasmine smell.

Her face leaned in, framed by my hands. She moved toward me, closer , closer. Our lips touched, trembled, backed away, then lingered in a long, soft kiss. It was an apology

It was an explanation.

It was forgiveness.

It was a beginning.

"Thanks for coming, Harlow," I said in a voice I'd never heard before.

She leaned toward my ear. "I've missed you, Vik."

My thumbs pushed away the tears from her cheeks.

We walked toward the table, slowly, hand in hand.

"How did we get here?" she asked.

"Once upon a time," I said.

She chuckled. "Original."

"My story," I said, "my introduction." She nodded. I started again. "Once upon a time, I had some time to kill, so I got to know a girl in India. I spent a lot of time teaching her how to be a wife. But all my lessons were a waste of time."

She halted mid-step. "Watch it." But her eyes were playful.

"A waste of time because she was already perfect."

"Nice recovery," she said. "Vikram Tej Mayur Chatwal—Mr. Smooth—never at a loss for words."

I motioned to the table. "I meant every one of them."

We sat. One of the servers started over with a wine bottle, but I shook my head.

"I need to explain something," I said.

"Yep, you do."

"My beautiful Harlow," I lifted her hand to my lips—"I am sorry. I knew I loved you the day I was introduced to Lita. The room was full of people, but you were the only one I saw."

Silence. Then, "Don't stop now, mister."

"You rushed out of India after the unpleasantness at the Cricket Club."

"You do know your way around a euphemism," she said. "But I knew that little scene wasn't your fault before I was halfway home. By then, I was embarrassed."

"When I realized you'd left, I was frantic. I went to my parents and told them everything. I was expecting a huge fight. I was all prepared to battle accusations of abandoning my people, my heritage, and my family. Baapa was a little stiff-necked, but Ma told me she had known it was you all along."

"I knew she was a smart woman the moment I met her," Harlow said.

"Harlow, I cannot live without you." I slid out of the booth and sank to one knee. I pulled a ring box from my pocket. When I opened it, she gasped. I started to explain. "It's—"

"I know Alexandrite when I see it," she said. "I make jewelry, you know. Vik, it's stunning. I also know it's mined in India."

"Yes," I said. "This ring has been in my family for three generations. My grandmother left it to me. Harlow, I love you so much. Will you marry me?"

She breathed in hard. "I love you, too. Absolutely yes!"

I slipped the ring onto her finger, gently squeezed her hand, and sat next to her. Dinesh appeared like a genie with a bottle. The cork popped. The champagne fizzed.

"A thousand blessings to you, Ms. Kennedy," he said.

"Thank you."

"Look at us," I said. "We did not miss wedding season after all. Will you need much time to prepare? I want to marry you very soon."

"Well," she said. "I don't need as much time as you might think. Long story, crazy, actually." Her giggle was nervous, a little creepy. "You see, Sophia, my mother, and I already bought a dress because—"

"I don't need the reason," he said.

"I'll tell you everything, but first, you need to kiss me."

"It has been a very long time since the last one," I said.

"Yes," she said. "And I suspect you can do better."

"Will I be graded?"

"Let's—"

She did not have a chance to finish. My lips pressed against hers, tenderness laced with pent-up passion. Her mouth opened, and we kissed until we heard the staff beginning to shuffle.

"Not bad," she said, but she was a little breathless. "Not bad."

"Glad you approve."

"Well," she said. "There will be many more tests before I determine your grade."

"I hope so," I said and moved closer.

She put a finger to my lips. "Those guys over there—the waiter dudes—they're thinking we should either order or get a room."

"Do you have a preference?" I asked.

"Yes," she said. "But I am also starving, so I will suffer through this presentation while I deny myself the pleasures of the flesh."

With that, I raised my hand, and the servers swarmed the table like locusts.

The appetizers arrived. We ate and talked. Sumptuous dishes came and went. We kissed and ate. Plates, dishes, glasses, and linens disappeared. We talked and kissed. The candles went out one by one, and the staff retreated and left us alone. I heard Dinesh's voice from the door. "Goodnight, sir. Congratulations. And remember to lock up."

My response was to kiss Harlow again, for a long time.

She ran her hand gently through my hair. "I have so much to tell you. You won't believe what happened with my mother and me."

"I'm all ears," I said.

She buried her face into my neck. Energy pulsed from her tongue to the base of my spine. "Mister, right now, your ears are the very last thing I care about."

HARLOW

Even though Vik had started his story with "Once upon a time," it would be a while before we got to "happily ever after."

While my mother almost broke her hip when she stumbled after jumping for joy, the Chatwals were more reserved. It seemed the longer they had considered Vik's profession of love, the more their enthusiasm waned. Their reserved reaction stung a little.

Over the next four days, Vik spent hours with his folks on video calls. What started off as easy chats soon deteriorated into an icy standoff. Things finally reached a breaking point. I heard every word. I was sitting next to Vik but out of the camera's view.

"You are a man," Mr. Chatwal said. "You can do what you want but must know our initial enthusiasm has cooled somewhat after several hours of consideration."

Mrs. Chatwal's expression gave no indication of any thought, feeling, or emotion. Mr. Chatwal continued.

"You must know that we are no longer caught up in moment of drama. My son, we have changed our minds regarding Ms. Kennedy's suitability. Next wedding season, you will come home and find an acceptable wife. If you do not comply with our wishes, there may be significant consequences."

Vik did not respond at first. He chewed on his bottom lip so long that I began to fear his response. "Baapa," he said, "do not go there. Let's not say anything we will both regret. My devotion to you and Ma is unending, but I adore Harlow. And, as you said when I was home, love will find a way. I have finally found the one. And I am at peace in my heart."

He took a quick breath. "I hear your implied threat to disinherit me. It is both cruel and trite. I know you are a traditional man, but you have not risen to your position of influence by staying anchored in the past. Times have changed. I want to be happy. I know deep down you want that for me."

Mr. Chatwal began to speak, but Vik held up his hand. "Respectfully, I will finish, then we are done with the discussion. Know this: the family fortune does not factor into my decision. Certainly, I do not want the Chatwal empire to diminish. I want the family to flourish. I would love it, and I am only human. I know your financial backing would enable me to expand my dream, perhaps all over the world. That being said, I am going to succeed with or without your help. So, I am going to marry Harlow, my beautiful American woman. She is of another country, and she is of another race. I love India, but the United States is the country of my choosing and I intend to live here with Harlow. For once in my life, I am truly happy, and I am going to stay that way."

He pulled me into the camera's view. There was a slow but unmistakable change in Mrs. Chatwal's expression. And for the first time in all the conversations I'd witnessed, she smiled. She whispered into her husband's ear for a long time. I saw the man's face begin to soften. He leaned into her and spoke. We could not hear what he said but Mrs. Chatwal's reaction was one every husband knows. It said, "You need to rethink that, my dear and rethink it now."

Mr. Chatwal stared at the screen for a full three minutes, lost in thought. Then, he nodded. "Your mother has always provided an unerring compass to my life. She feels very strongly about this."

I held my breath.

"So, it is settled, Vikram, and this is the last time we will discuss it," Mr. Chatwal said. He smiled broadly. "You will marry Miss—you will marry *Harlow*, and she will be our daughter. Your ma sees the light in Harlow's eyes. It is not the gleam of avarice. She says it is the beam of love. Your mother and I have come to love one another across the years, but she just pointed out how much easier it might have been for us had we started in a different place, a place of affection."

Vik leaned in to kiss me. I closed my eyes, then heard his mother gasp. When I opened my eyes, Vik was sitting ramrod straight like a schoolboy who'd been reprimanded and his mother was looking at him with suspicion. She said nothing, but her eyes said, "Remember your training. Some things are always private."

"Outstanding," Vik said. "We do not want to wait. We plan to be married next weekend. That gives you twelve days to make arrangements to be here."

His mother leaned toward Vik's father. More whispering.

"We will not be in attendance," Mr. Chatwal said, "but not for the reasons you might suspect. Your ma, while better, remains too weak to travel. It is, as you know, a very arduous journey."

Vik's eyes reflected a flash of sadness, then the mask of indifference appeared. Vik's eyes went hard until Mr. Chatwal resumed. "We would propose a happy compromise, a resolution. We would love for you to arrange a way for us to attend the nuptials in a virtual manner, like this,"—he pointed to the screen—"and then, at your convenience, when you feel you can leave your Bombay Baby for at least a month, we ask that you return to India and reenact your wedding in a traditional Indian ceremony. Then spend a few weeks with us that we might come to know our new daughter better. You will stay in the guest house where you can enjoy your privacy."

Vik's mother lunged toward the screen. "And you will not keep us up all night." She immediately put her hand over her mouth and giggled. We all dissolved in laughter.

♦

A month after we returned from India, Dinesh unlocked the door and escorted us into an expansive space.

"Lease is signed," he said. "The crew will be here tomorrow to begin working on the kitchen. We will be opening Thanksgiving weekend, just in time for the holiday crunch."

"That's great," Vik said. "In ten months, we will have our

second Bombay Baby."

I shared a conspiratorial look with Dinesh. "Not so sure about that."

Vik stared at me. "Seriously. Do the math."

"I have," I said. The corners of my mouth curled into a wicked grin. I took his hand and placed it on my stomach. "Bet this little guy gets here first."

And for the first time in his life, Mr. Vikram Tej Mayur Chatwal was absolutely speechless.

AUTHOR'S NOTE

I'M OFTEN ASKED THE QUESTION: "WHAT INSPIRED YOU TO WRITE *Karma Under Fire*? It all began with a simple idea during a friend's wedding in Delhi, India.

I pondered the question of what would happen if a traditional Indian matchmaker made a match for a modern, opinionated American woman. This sparked a series of questions about her background, life challenges, and relationships. From these questions, the story evolved.

Every character in this book is a product of my wild imagination. From a dashing playboy to the heroine caught between happiness and love, from fashion-forward International "it" girls to meddling family members, they all play their role in this tale.

An essential aspect of *Karma Under Fire* is the culinary journey that takes us from the United State to India. You'll savor descriptions of West and East Indian dishes that might inspire you to explore Indian cuisine further.

This book is a fusion of cultures and emotions, a blend of Southern comfort-style flavor and the glitz of Bollywood glamour. It's a story that may make you laugh and cry. You'll be immersed in a world where love transcends boundaries.

Thank you for choosing *Karma Under Fire* and investing your time in me and in my characters. I love that we can embark on this literary adventure together.

With love,
Love Hudson-Maggio

RECIPES

Vegetable Pakora

This delicious lunchtime snack is similar to vegetable fritters with a South Indian flair. This dish is addictive, aromatic, crunchy, and a perfect snack. Serve them with a cup of tea or coriander and chutney.

Prep Time: 10 minutes
Cook Time: 15 minutes
Total: 25 minutes

Ingredients
1/2 cup besan (gram flour, more if needed)
1/4 cup rice flour
1/2 teaspoon salt
3 green chili peppers chopped or 1/2–1 teaspoon red chili flakes
2 tablespoons mint leaves or coriander leaves or dill leaves chopped
1 teaspoon ginger garlic paste or crushed ginger
1/4–1/2 teaspoon garam masala powder
1/2 teaspoons carom seeds (ajwain)

Oil for deep frying as needed

Mixed Veggies:

1 medium carrot, julienned

1/4 cup capsicum

1 cup cabbage, shredded

1 medium onion, thinly sliced

6 french beans, julienned)

1 cup spinach, chopped

Instructions

1. Wash the veggies and cut two thin 2-inch long strips. Add them to a bowl, along with ginger garlic, green chilies (or chili flakes), slat, garam masala, mint, or other herbs. Mix well and squeeze them gently to release moisture. Keep aside for 10 mins.

2. Add the gram flour, rice flour, along with ajwain. Mix well into a slightly sticky dough. If the dough is too dry, sprinkle a few tablespoons of water and mix. It must be of a sticky dough consistency and not batter consistency.

3. Taste test and add more salt, garam masala, or green chilies.

4. Make the Pakora: Heat oil in a deep pan on a medium heat. Test by dropping a small portion of dough—it must sizzle and come up but not brown. This is the right temperature.

5. Take small portions of dough, and flatten with your fingers to 1 1/2-inch size portions, and gently slide to the hot oil. You won't shape it or drop it in lumps.

6. Regulate the flame to medium. Do not disturb for a minute or 2 until they firm up a bit. Then stir and fry until golden, crisp, and aromatic. Remove the pakoras to a cooling rack or steel colander. To make the next batch, ensure the oil is hot enough but not smoking hot. Fry in batches until you finish all dough.

Baked Jerk Chicken

This traditional favorite is the perfect handheld food for any occasion, especially during the warmer months.

Ingredients

3 lbs. organic chicken wings

2 scotch bonnet peppers, chopped

1 tablespoon onion powder

1 tablespoon garlic powder

2 teaspoons cayenne pepper

2 teaspoons black pepper

2 teaspoons dried thyme

2 teaspoons brown sugar

1 teaspoon ground allspice

1 teaspoon dried parsley

1 teaspoon smoked paprika

1/2 teaspoon red pepper flakes

1/2 teaspoon ground cinnamon

1/2 teaspoon ground nutmeg

1/2 teaspoon ground cloves

1/4 teaspoon cumin powder

2 tablespoons unsalted butter

2 cups BBQ sauce

Broth from baked jerk chicken

2 thyme sprigs

1/2 cup chicken stock

1–2 tablespoons jerk seasoning

1–2 tablespoons cornstarch (mix with 3 tablespoons of water)

Instructions

1. In a large bowl, add your freshly cleaned and rinsed wings, along with the chopped scotch bonnet pepper, onion powder, garlic powder, cayenne pepper, black pepper, thyme, brown sugar, allspice, parsley, smoked paprika, red pepper flakes, cinnamon, nutmeg, cloves, and cumin, mixing everything together until chicken is fully coated. Let it sit for 10–15 minutes. NOTE: For best results, marinate chicken overnight in the refrigerator or for up to 2 days.

2. Preheat the oven to 400 degrees F, and lightly grease a standard 9x13 baking dish or a large foil baking pan. Set aside.

3. Add the chicken to the prepared baking dish, spreading wings out side by side, and tightly cover the top with foil. Bake for 30–35 minutes or until chicken wings are mostly cooked through. Carefully, drain the jerk sauce "liquid (aka jerk broth)" from the chicken into a bowl and set aside. Return wings to the oven and bake for another 5–10 minutes or until they appear more "dry."

4. In a saucepan over medium-high heat, add the butter, and let it melt. Add the BBQ sauce, jerk "liquid" broth, jerk seasoning, and chicken stock, and mix together until combined. Let everything boil for 2–3 minutes. Reduce the heat to medium-low, and add in the cornstarch mixture and thyme sprigs, stirring the sauce until it thickens.

5. Generously brush (or spoon) the BBQ jerk sauce atop chicken wings just until fully coated, and bake (without foil) for another 10–15 minutes until the sauce has "baked into" chicken wings. NOTE: I like to broil the wings for the final 10–15 minutes for the best results. Just be sure to keep an eye on them to avoid burning. Remove from oven. Enjoy!

DISCUSSION QUESTIONS

1. In *Karma Under Fire*, what are the roles of ambition and personal drive? How do ambition and drive differ or how are they similar between male and female characters? Do drive and ambition differ between the age groups?

2. How is ambition showcased as a modern issue versus a traditional issue in regard to jobs, life paths, and family?

3. What role does parental pressure play on the characters? Do you think boundaries are needed in the lives of the characters? Why or why not? How does your answer change in regard to traditions and cultures?

4. How does the hierarchy of social classes function in African American and Indian cultures as described in the book? Contrast and compare the two.

5. Keeping up appearances is a major theme in the book. What roles do fashion and beauty play in the story? Can you relate to similar instances in your life when fashion and beauty were either unimportant or important? Why or why not?

6. How does wealth affect the actions and thoughts of the main characters, Harlow and Vik? How is their success or ideas of success affected by their belief about wealth?

7. How does the combination of wealth and family move along the plot? Have you ever experienced a time in your life when wealth and family positively affected someone you know? How did the experience change their lives?

8. How are Harlow's and Vik's lives shaped and changed by traditions and customs? Are there parallels to the pressures they feel?

9. What traditions and customs do they enjoy versus tolerate? In your own life, what traditions and customs do you still enjoy? What traditions and customs have you changed based on your evolving personal preferences?

10. What issues and situations in the book shed light on information, customs, and traditions you didn't previously know? What did you enjoy learning about the most?

11. If given a paid-in-full plane ticket to India during wedding season, would you go? Why or why not? Do you prefer to book travel or travel in person?

12. Food, community, and family recipes are important aspects of this story. Which character in the book would you most like to have lunch with? Where would you want to go and what would most like to order as your meal?

ABOUT THE AUTHOR

LOVE HUDSON-MAGGIO STARTED writing at the tender age of five, and has lived a creative life full of writing songs, poetry, and screenplays, pursuing her MBA, and even being a member of an R&B duo that was selected to sing backup for Mary J. Blige. She writes southern women's fiction with a travel flair about smart people with a lot to learn about life and love. Love's passion for travel is reflected in her books as she transports readers between the southern sweetness of Georgia to other picturesque locations around the world. She believes that the love you give away will find it's way back you. Her books reflect this truth. Love current resides in Atlanta, Georgia with her husband, their two sons, and pet Morkie.

Connect with Love at lovehudsonmaggio.com
Instagram: @love.hudsonmaggio
Facebook: @love.hudsonmaggio
BookBub: @lovelhudson
Linkedin: @lovehudsonmaggio

Printed in the USA
CPSIA information can be obtained
at www.ICGtesting.com
LVHW011310020124
767880LV00004B/247

9 798886 806854